Famous in a Small Town

Also by Viola Shipman

THE WISHING BRIDGE
FAMOUS IN A SMALL TOWN
A WISH FOR WINTER
THE EDGE OF SUMMER
THE SECRET OF SNOW
THE CLOVER GIRLS
THE HEIRLOOM GARDEN
THE SUMMER COTTAGE

For a full list of books by Viola Shipman,
visit violashipman.com.

VIOLA SHIPMAN

Famous in a Small Town

GRAYDON
HOUSE

GRAYDON HOUSE®

Recycling programs
for this product may
not exist in your area.

ISBN-13: 978-1-525-80507-3

Famous in a Small Town

Graydon House
22 Adelaide St. West, 41st Floor
Toronto, Ontario M5H 4E3, Canada
www.GraydonHouseBooks.com
www.BookClubbish.com

Printed in U.S.A.

To my grandmothers, who were my best friends growing up. There should never be an age limit on friendship, new adventures or restarting your life. Be the legend you were meant to be.

Famous in a Small Town

THE LAKE EFFECT EXPRESS

August 1958

"Good News from Good Hart!"
by Shirley Ann Potter

It was the spit heard 'round the world!

Our town is still atwitter over the news that the daughter of Mr. Peter Jackson was crowned the 35th Annual Cherry Pit Spittin' Champion of Leelanau and Emmet County last Saturday. Fifteen-year-old Mary Jackson, an Emmet County high-school sophomore, was not only the first woman—uh, girl—to win the contest, but her stone flew a *Guinness Book of World Records*–breaking distance of ninety-three feet six-and-a-half inches, shattering the previous record set by "Too Tall" Fred Jones in 1898 at the state's very first Cherry Championship right here in Good Hart.

News of her accomplishment has flown farther than her cherry pit, with reporters from as far away as New York and London anointing our town sprite with the moniker "Cherry Mary."

I caught up with Mary at the Very Cherry General Store—our beloved post office/grocery store/sandwich-and-soda-shop run by Mary's mother and grandmother—to see how she managed such a Herculean feat.

"My mom taught me to whistle when I was a kid (*"A kid!" Don't you just love that, readers?*), and I had to be loud enough for her to hear me when she was down at the lake. I think that made my lips strong," Mary says. "And I started eating sunflower seeds when I was fishing on the boat with my grandma. She taught me how to spit them without having the wind blow them back in the boat."

Mary says she practiced for the contest by standing in the middle of M-119—the road that houses our beautiful Tunnel of Trees—and spitting stones into the wind when a storm was brewing on Lake Michigan.

"I knew if I could make it a far piece into the wind, I could do it when it was still."

While her grandmother was "over the moon" for Mary's feat, saying, "It's about time," Mr. Jackson says of his daughter's accomplishment, "It's certainly unusual for a girl, but Mary isn't your average girl. Maybe all this got it out of her system, so to speak. I hope so for her sake."

The plucky teenager seems nonplussed by the attention, despite seeing her face all over northern Michigan in the papers and the T-shirts featuring her face—cheeks puffed, stone leaving her mouth—and the words *Cherry Mary* in bright red over the image.

"A girl can do anything a man can," Mary says in between retrieving mail, spreading mayonnaise on a tomato sandwich and twirling a cherry around in her mouth, before perfectly depositing the stone in a trash can across the room. "You just gotta believe you can. That's the hard part. Harder than spitting any old pit."

Mary seems ready to conquer the world, readers. Cheers, Cherry Mary! Our hometown heroine!

PART ONE

"You can't pick cherries with your back to the tree."

—J.P. Morgan

BECKY

June 2023

"Okay, Benjie, would you like it if Ashley did this to you?"

He scrunches up his face to stave off tears and shakes his head. "No."

"Well, it's not a nice thing to do."

I study Ashley's hair, then take her face in my hands. "It's going to be okay. Trust me?"

The little girl nods her head. I give her a hug.

I walk over to my desk and open the bottom drawer . There is a large jar of creamy peanut butter sitting next to a bag of mini Snickers. The peanut butter is for emergencies like this: removing gum from a little girls' hair. The Snickers are for me after I'm finished with this life lesson.

"Well, I'm just glad neither of you are allergic to peanuts," I say. "Allows me to do this."

I cover the gum stuck in the back of Ashley's pretty, long, blond hair and then look at her.

"I promise this works," I say. "I've performed a lot of gum surgery."

She nods. Her eyes are red from crying, her cheeks blotchy.

"Why did you do this, Benjie?" I ask the little boy seated in the chair before my desk.

He ducks his head sheepishly, his brown bangs falling into his eyes, and murmurs something into his chest.

"I didn't catch that," I say. "What did you say? Remember it's okay to express your emotions."

He looks at me, freckles twitching on his cheeks. "I can't say," he whispers.

"Yes, you can," I say. "Don't make this any worse than it already is."

Benjie glances toward the door to ensure that it is closed. "Tyler Evans told me to do it or he'd punch me on the way home."

Being a grade-school administrator is akin to being a detective: you have to work the perp to get the truth. Eventually— no matter the age—they break, especially when a verdict on punishment is waiting in the balance.

It's the last day of school. Benjie does not want his summer to be ruined.

I lean down and slide the gum out of Ashley's hair. I go to my sink, dampen a cloth and put some dish soap on it, return and clean the rest of the peanut butter off her locks. I move to a tall filing cabinet and retrieve a clean brush. The filing cabinet is filled with bags of sealed brushes and combs, toothbrushes and EpiPens, certificates and old laptops. I run the brush through her hair. I hold up a mirror for her to see the back of her head.

"See, good as new."

"What do you say to Ashley, Benjie?"

"I'm sorry."

"Do you accept his apology?"

Ashley shakes her head no. "You ruined the last day of school. You're a big ol' meanie."

"Ashley," I say, my tone sweet but authoritarian.

"I accept your apology," she says.

"You're free to go," I say to her.

"But you're still a big ol' poop head," she says, racing out of my office, bubblegum-free hair bouncing.

I actually have to clench my hands very hard to stifle a laugh.

Big ol' poop head.

How many times a day would I—would any adult—like to scream that at someone?

"Are you telling my parents?" Benjie asks.

"I have to," I say, "but I'll tell them *why* you did it, and then I'll have a talk with Tyler."

"No!"

"I have to do that, too," I explain. "And I'll talk to his parents as well."

He looks at me, his chin quivering.

"We have a zero-tolerance policy here for bullying," I say. "Trust me, Tyler won't do it again. You have to stand up to bullies. You have to show them the right way to do things. Otherwise, they never change."

In addition to being a detective, an assistant principal is also akin to being the vice-president of the United States. Everyone knows your name, everyone knows you've achieved some level of status, but nobody really understands what the hell you do all day.

"I promise it will be okay," I say. "Just promise me you won't do it again. You're a nice boy, Benjie. That's a wonderful thing. Always remember that."

"I promise." He looks at me. "Can I go now?"

"One more thing. You know you aren't supposed to bring gum to school."

"I know. But one of the moms was handing it out before school."

Mrs. Yates, I instantly know. She wants to be the cool mom. She's Room Mom for 2A, and, Mrs. Trimbley, the Room Mom for 2B, told me that competing with her this year was like being a contestant in *Squid Game*.

Benjie continues. "It's Bubble Yum. My favorite. My mom won't let me have it because it's bad for my teeth."

Benjie opens his mouth and smiles. He resembles a jack-o'-lantern. He's missing teeth here and there, willy-nilly, black holes where baby teeth once lived and adult teeth will soon reside.

Too late, I want to say to Benjie, but he won't get my humor. Only my best friend, Q, understands it, and my grandparents who made me this way.

I think of how much I loved chewing gum as a kid.

"Do you have any more?"

"Am I going to get in trouble again?"

"No," I say with a laugh.

He reaches into the pocket of his little jeans and hands me a piece of grape Bubble Yum.

My favorite.

"Do you know what my teacher used to say when I'd sneak gum into class?"

"You snuck gum into class?"

He stares at me with more admiration than if Albert Pujols from the St. Louis Cardinals suddenly appeared with an autographed baseball.

"I did," I say. "It was about the only bad thing I ever did. My teacher used to hold out her hand in front of my desk and ask, 'Did you bring enough gum to share with the whole class?'"

"Did you?" Benjie asks, wild-eyed.

"No," I say. "That was the whole point. She wanted to embarrass me. And it always worked. Teachers just liked to say that."

I take the gum from Benjie. "This is just between us, okay?"

He giggles and nods.

I pop the gum into my mouth. It's even more insanely sweet and sugary and tastes even better than I remember. My taste buds explode. I chew, Benjie watching me with grand amusement, and then—looking out my window to make sure the coast is clear—blow a big bubble. A massive bubble, in fact. It expands until it's the size of a small balloon. Benjie continues to watch me in silence as a child today might do today trying to figure out how to use a rotary phone. After a few moments, the flavor subsides.

"Want to learn a trick?" I ask.

"Yeah!"

"If you ever get caught chewing gum, don't stick it in a nice girl's hair or swallow it. Learn to do this." I narrow my lips as if I'm going to whistle, puff my cheeks and spit my gum into the air as if Michael Jordan were draining a game-winning three-pointer as time expired. The purple gum arcs into the air and deposits directly into a trash can next to a low-slung sofa ten feet across my office.

Benjie pumps his fist and lifts his hand to high-five me.

"Where did you learn to do that?" he asks.

"Sunday school," I wink. "My grandma taught me."

I stand, and he follows suit. I look him square in his big brown eyes.

"I'm telling you all of this because you're a good kid, Benjie. I just want you to know sometimes you have to stand up for yourself against boys who might not treat you so nicely. Don't take their anger—and your anger—out on other people. Kindness is like a wave on the Mississippi River. It ripples out." I pause. "I didn't stand up enough for myself growing up. I wasn't proud of who I was."

Benjie looks up at me. "Tyler says I read too much. He says only weirdos like books."

"Listen to me. He's wrong. Only the best people like books. Be proud of yourself, Benjie. There's no one else in the world like you."

He throws his arms open, and I hug him. In a world—and school system—where hugs are not often allowed anymore, I still hug. I know sometimes that can make a huge difference in the life of a child who may not get enough of them.

"Have a good summer, and be a good boy. Promise?"

"I promise, Mrs. Thatcher."

He ambles out of my office, half skipping, despite knowing he's going to get in trouble.

Mrs. Thatcher.

I glance down at the nameplate sitting on my desk.

Ms. Thatcher.

Ms.

Not Mrs.

My heart hiccups.

"Ms. Thatcher to the playground immediately. Ms. Thatcher to the playground."

I jump at the intercom booming in the hall.

Will this school year never end? How can the last day feel as interminable as a documentary on fruit flies?

I hurry out of my office and down the too-slick hall, skidding around the corners. I beeline through the cafeteria and out the double doors into the adorable little playground set squarely in the midst of a city neighborhood.

I look around.

Everything looks normal. Kids are screaming and playing, celebrating their last day before summer begins.

"What's going on?" I ask Mrs. Price, the beloved third-grade teacher who, I believe, is made of spun sugar and pumpkin spice and glitter.

She shrugs innocently, but as she does, kids from across the playground come running to form a circle around me. Teachers follow them.

"Happy birthday!" they yell.

"Thank you so much! I can't believe you all remembered, especially on the last day of school."

I notice Janice Mott, our principal and my boss, smiling at me. Or, at least, she's trying to smile at me. Mrs. Mott has one of those upside-down mouths that makes it look as if she's frowning even if she's smiling. And she's not a particularly sunny person by nature, either. Every cloudy day to Janice holds the potential of a lightning strike. Every jump rope is a tripping hazard. Every cafeteria French fry is a choking hazard. I guess when you go to a grocery store or out to a restaurant for thirty years and children run in the other direction, it takes a toll on your soul.

"Well, we certainly couldn't let the big four-oh go unnoticed, could we, Becky?"

It comes out as *farh-oh* in Janice's pronounced St. Louis accent. I was slightly immune to the accent having grown up in Hannibal, Missouri, before moving to St. Louis the summer I was seven, the age of many of my students right now. But it's creeped in over time, and I say *fahrty*, too.

Oh, by the way, you heard right. My name is Becky Thatcher from Hannibal, Missouri. And I can imagine what you're thinking already. *Just how cruel or clueless were my parents?*

But you haven't met my parents.

But I have never been the leading lady in a Mark Twain novel much less an unattainable aristocratic lady. My father worked at the brewery. My mother was a stay-at-home mom. Although I was an only child, when kids started to pick on me about my name I asked my parents why they didn't have another daughter and name her Margaret just to ease my burden.

They never laughed at my humor, either. They always played by the rules. My life was defined by rules.

"Don't upset the apple cart, Becky," my dad would say.

"Slow and steady wins the race," my mom would tell me.

"Becky," Janice is saying. I blink and look at her, returning from my thoughts. "Happy Birthday."

"Thank you so much," I say. "This is such a…"

As the words leave my mouth, the children scream, "Surprise!" and reveal a birthday cake with a giant candle shaped like a *40* burning brightly on top of it sitting on a brightly colored kids' picnic table. They begin to sing, their little voices serenading me with "Happy Birthday." My kids have turned into sweet songbirds.

I applaud wildly when they finish.

"Blow out the candle!" a child yells when everyone is done.

I walk toward the cake.

"Make a wish! Make a wish!" the kids begin to chant.

I look at the cake and then into the candle. I know exactly what I want this year.

I shut my eyes and blow. When I open them, the children part, and I yelp.

My boyfriend Matt is standing before me, holding a velvet box in his outstretched hand.

My wish came true! It's finally coming true!

"Matt? What are you doing here? What's going on?"

"It's a big day for you," he says. "Fortieth birthday. Last day of school. It just seemed like the right time for…well, this."

He hands me the box. I open it, the world now in slow motion.

Will it be his great-grandmother's heirloom-inspired solitaire, the beautifully balanced ring his mother has talked about and pulled out of the safe endlessly for years?

Will it be the oval peach sapphire ring I adore, the one adorned with a diamond on either side of the center stone, set in a solid rose-gold band?

Or will it be the traditional diamond cut with no-frills design that Catholic Matt—St. Matthew as his friends call him—so loved?

My heart literally stops as I open the box.

I blink, hard, not understanding, and look into Matt's blue eyes.

"A key?"

Matt beams. "It's symbolic," he says, his voice rising in excitement, or as much as it can for such a buttoned-down guy.

"It not only represents the key you have to my heart but also for the key you always dreamed of having."

I continue to stare, confused.

"The key to a vacation home in northern Michigan!" he finishes.

My head is reeling.

He didn't ask me to marry him—although we've been living together now for a decade, a virtual shamefest for not only our Catholic families but also the very Catholic city of St. Louis—but he bought us a vacation home?

I blurt out my thoughts. "You bought us a vacation home in Michigan? Matt, this is so unlike you. What's going on? I don't understand."

He shakes his head and laughs. "Let's sit, Becky," he says.

I follow his lead. I sit on a red bench, and Matt sits on a yellow bench, and it's then I realize there's folder on the purple table before us, right next to the birthday cake.

I look around at the kids and teachers waiting patiently for me to cut the cake. Nothing brings a school together more than free pizza or birthday cake.

"I'm forty. You're forty. We need to start acting like it." Matt opens the folder. It's filled with documents littered with yellow stickers shaped like arrows that read *Sign Here*. "I didn't buy us a vacation home. That wouldn't be financially prudent at all. But we *can* start saving for one. Now. Together. And what better time to mark this new beginning than by starting a vacation-home fund."

He rotates the papers toward me.

"If we each invest five percent of our total annual income over the next twenty-five years, then we could be in a very good position to purchase a home by the time we're sixty-five." Matt looks at me and nods convincingly. "Without taking a loan!"

What?

"I already max out my retirement at work," I mutter. "And

my salary isn't as big as yours. I just finished paying off student loans."

"But it must be equal," he says. "That's only fair."

I can only stare at him.

"Equal?" I ask. "But I already own the house in Brentwood."

"Own?" he says. "No, Becky, you have a mortgage."

"Exactly," I say. "*I* have a mortgage. *You* live with me. How is *that* equitable?"

Somehow, the math is lost on the financial planner. Instead, he begins to run numbers, calculate how much I would have to save and how much I would have to cut back every year on so-called luxuries like eating out, my yoga membership and travel. He calculates the soaring costs of vacation homes on the lakeshore in northern Michigan and what they might cost when I'm sixty-five. He calculates how much my salary might increase over the years, especially if Janice, who's about my age, never retires, and I remain here for life.

Life?

Life!

And then I begin to calculate how many years I have left in my life's bank. If the average life expectancy for a woman in the United States is seventy-nine, then my life is more than half over, starting tomorrow. I only have four hundred and sixty-eight months left to live.

Four hundred and sixty-eight!

There is a church down the street that towers over the playground. An ornate angel hovers near the top of the church, wings fluttering, eyes closed, and I've always wondered if it were soaring toward heaven or being sent back to earth.

Growing up Catholic, we had to learn our saints just as we had to learn the Stations of the Cross.

Matt has turned his attention back to the papers and is gleefully signing away. St. Matthew. His symbol is an angel. He is the patron saint of tax collectors and accountants.

I look at Matt, the angel, the steeple, the heavens, and I begin to laugh.

He glances up. "What's so funny?"

"I thought you were going to ask me to marry you just now," I say, my voice barely audible over the screams of happy children carried on the breeze. "I thought the velvet box was a ring. Maybe your great-grandma's, or the ones we've looked at every time we walk through the mall."

"Oh, Becky, we have such a good thing going," he says. "Why ruin it? Just let it ride."

He holds out his hand to take mine. I react as if his fingers are snakes and pull my hand away.

"Just let it ride? What am I, a slot machine?"

Teachers herd kids toward the playground, knowing the cake may be forever delayed and uncertain as to what I may say next.

"It's just that you always said your parents were too traditional," Matt says. "You said you wanted to do things differently."

"They were, and I do!" I say, my voice rising.

I look around. Teachers are staring. I lower my voice.

"But that doesn't mean I didn't want some of those traditional things, too. I wanted to get married. I wanted kids. I told you all that. But I wanted our marriage to be different. I wanted it to be filled with more risks and excitement. I wanted to raise our children to believe that anything was possible, every day was a miracle, that they could be anything they dreamed."

He just stares at me.

"Do you *ever* want to get married?" I ask.

"I don't know," he says, turning his eyes toward the papers before him.

"You don't *know*?" I ask. "We're Catholic. We're supposed to get married and have children. Lots of them. What are you so unsure of? We've known each other since college."

His blue eyes search the papers, then the cake, then my own.

"I don't know," he repeats. "I've played by the rules my whole life, too. And it's been fine. I just feel—I don't know—comfortable with you."

"It's been *fine*? You feel *comfortable* with me? What, am I, your favorite sweatshirt? That kind of comfortable?"

"Becky." His voice is steady, like he's talking to a client after a dismal day on the stock market. "I don't want to do this right now."

"But?" I prompt him. "A line like that always comes followed by a *but*."

"But I don't want to get married, either."

I blink. It's a hard blink, like slamming a car door.

"Do you ever want to get married?"

He shrugs.

"To me?"

Matt shakes his head. "I guess… I don't think so."

I feel a tear run down my face. I didn't even feel it start.

Somewhere, deep inside, I've always known this. I've always, like my mom and dad, buried my head from what was really happening in the world around me. It was easier that way. Safer.

Before Matt moved in with me, he broke up with me—running a span from college into his late twenties—a half-dozen times to date other women.

Why did I take him back so readily so many times?

Because I believed I couldn't do any better.

Because I was comfortable, too.

Because I was play-it-by-the-rules-don't-upset-the-apple-cart-slow-and-steady-wins-the-race-Becky.

We talked about getting married hundreds of times. The same with having children. And it was just talk. I knew it was just talk, and I was okay with that all these years.

I stare at the *40*-shaped candle.

Somewhere, deep inside, I knew it would never happen with Matt, and yet the years slipped away.

Matt lifts a finger toward the cake. I know him so well. He wants that icing.

Why did *he* come back so many times?

I think of what he just said. *It must be equal. That's only fair. But it's never been equal.*

Matt moved into *my* apartment our senior year of college and then into my bungalow in Brentwood and has never paid a cent toward the mortgage. I worked two full-time jobs—as a teacher and then as a tutor in the summer—while earning my master's degree in education, but Matt lived with me while going to MBA school full-time without a job. Vacations—which I planned—were always paid largely by me.

"Becky," Matt finally says, "we make such a good team on paper."

As a kid, as a student, as a human and as an administrator, my whole life has been *good on paper*.

I wrote every goal in a marble notebook and color-coded timelines for my future accomplishments.

Even my personal life.

I wanted to be a principal by thirty.

I wanted my first child at thirty-two, my second at thirty-four, so they were perfectly spaced in life and career.

Then I would be a superintendent at forty-five.

My mother pushed me to have children, and so I pushed Matt. But now...

Matt finally sticks his finger into the icing and licks it clean. He nudges the papers toward me again. The patron saint of tax collectors is still running numbers in his head.

They just don't add up for me any longer.

Matt sounds like such a schlump, but I realize he made me feel safe. He never raised his voice, he relished routine, he attended Mass, he loved my parents, he was all I believed I should have.

I may never have felt special or wanted, but at least I felt safe. And that's all I believed I needed.

Until this very moment.

My life has been a mirage.

The world spins around me, just like the miniature merry-go-round kids are playing on right now.

I remember seeing a Maya Angelou interview with Oprah from the 1980s.

"When someone shows you who they are," she said, "believe them."

It's not Matt's fault this is happening. He's always been the same person. He showed me.

It's my fault. It's always been my fault.

Did I even want to marry Matt? No.

Did I even want children with Matt? No.

And yet I stayed, knowing there was no great passion—for me or life. I stayed because I was as complacent and comfortable as Matt was. I never truly, madly, deeply loved him, and he was never crazy in love with me. We were simply marble notebooks filled with accomplishments, timelines and pretty color-coded writing and shiny stickers but zero emotion.

"I am such an idiot," I finally say. "I teach children every day not to be dumb. I teach them to reach for their dreams. I've never taken the time to remove the gum out of my own hair."

"Becky," Matt says, looking around to see if anyone is watching.

Never-make-a-spectacle-Becky.

"It's not you, Matt," I say. "I blame myself. I took the easy route just like my parents did. But it's never been the path I wanted. I want more, Matt. I want someone to love me, not on paper but so deeply in his heart that the heavens weep and our souls crack when we're not together. I want adventure. I want to be like my grandma. I don't want to look back after another forty years have passed and be filled with regret for being too scared to live."

"You will never feel this safe again, Becky."

As if on cue, the school bell rings.

"Good."

I stand and head back toward the school, the mouths of some teachers wide open, heads turning as I go.

As I pass little Ashley, she asks, "No wedding?"

I stop. Another surprise tear. "No, sweetheart. No wedding."

"Boo!" she says. "Big ol' poop head."

I smile, which turns into a laugh. The honesty of children.

When did I lose my own integrity?

"Yeah, you're right," I say to her. "Boo!"

I turn around and walk back to where Matt is still sitting.

I grab the papers from the table and throw them into the air.

He stands and looks at me, eyes wide.

"Becky," he starts.

"Boo!" I yell. "Boo to both of us!"

Some of the kids start booing, too.

"We both deserve that," I say to Matt. "We've never played to win. We've never even fought to the end and lost. We settled for a tie. And that deserves to be booed."

I start to turn away but stop. I grab my birthday cake and begin to walk away again. The cake is from Schneider's Bakery with the real butter-cream frosting.

"Hey!" Matt cries indignantly.

Of course he would be angrier at losing the cake than me.

"My birthday! My cake!" I yell. "My life!"

I stick my hand in it and take a big bite. "Sooo good!"

And it is. Sweet, decadent, delicious.

Just like life should be.

I look at the top of the cake, where my hand has swiped through the icing, erasing the word *Birthday*. The new message simply reads *Happy Becky!*

I walk toward the school.

I want my cake and to eat it, too.

MARY

June 2023

"Oh, my gawd! Look, Brant! A tomato sandwich. What even is that?"

I spin a Montmorency cherry around in my mouth, removing all its juicy tart-sweet goodness, and then turn and spit the pit into a tin pail about five feet away in the Very Cherry General Store.

Ping!

A young woman, maybe early twenties, dressed all in hippie chic that's all the rage, the exact same outfits I used to wear as a young woman—floppy hats, colored sunglasses, bell-bottom jeans, crop tops, buffalo sandals—is pointing at the chalkboard menu over the lunch counter. Her beaded bracelets slide down her arm.

"A tomato sandwich is sliced tomato on bread," I say.

Pretty self-explanatory, I don't say.

"Brant!" she calls.

A blandly handsome young man is staring into a glass domed stand in which we display our homemade cookies. A handwritten sign done by yours truly reads *Michigan Maple Snickerdoodle*. He is so close that his breath is steaming the glass.

"Can you imagine the carb and sugar content in those?" he

marvels. "And look at this." He picks up a packaged loaf of our glazed cherry sweet bread. "This is, like, poison."

"Brant, come *here!*" the woman calls. "I have to go live on Insta. My followers will eat this up. Hold my phone."

She pulls some gloss from her bag and refreshes her already shiny lips, fluffs her thick blond hair with a free hand and tosses it over her shoulders, extends a leg and puffs out her chest. She nods at Brant.

"Hi, everyone, it's Candy!" She blows a kiss to the camera. "I'm here to bring you another one of Candy's Sweet Spots. Today, I'm in Good Hart, Michigan." She holds up her hand toward the camera. "If you're from Michigan, like me, the shape of your hand serves as your map. Today we're here." She points toward the top of her middle finger. "This tiny town located in northern Michigan's Tunnel of Trees, which I'll be showing you next as we drive—top down! Woo-hoo!—is home to the Very Cherry General Store." She gestures for Brant to follow as she makes her away around my store.

"I mean, what is any of this stuff? It's like being in an antique mall!"

Candy begins to point to the original features in the space and gesture with her hands, palms up, as if to say *What is this? Who knows?*

She walks to the side of the tiny store where the post office still resides and points to an antique brass mailbox door, with the post office number on the little window.

"Um, you tell me?" she says to the camera.

Then she drifts over to the glass-front counter bins—filled with coffee beans—where the original 1901 National Cash Register still resides and then over to the carved-oak cooling case, which I'm sure she doesn't realize was just that in its day, a cooling case before electric refrigeration was available in the area.

Candy gestures again.

"The magical mystery tour continues," she says. "I feel like I'm in an old black-and-white movie. I need a parasol!"

She moves toward the other side of the general store whose warped wooden shelves are stacked with the staples that locals, vacationers and road-trippers alike all need, from bread and Hamburger Helper to chips and cereal.

"What do you want me to make tonight?" she asks with a giggle. "Put it in the Comments!"

Finally, Candy circles back to where I'm stationed before a minuscule kitchen where I can bake any cookie in the world, make any sandwich you dream—from liverwurst to pastrami— or dish up one of our homemade potpies.

This general store is just like its owner: a throwback. A relic.

And yet this old gal can do anything you ask her to do.

Candy stops and points. Brant follows her finger and trains the camera on an old framed photo behind me. It is a faded newspaper article featuring a picture of a young girl spitting a cherry pit, lips puffed and blowing like an angel with a trumpet, the seed flying from her rounded lips.

"Was that you?" she says, looking incredulous, from the photo to me and back again, wondering—as young people do—if an old person could possibly have once been like them.

I nod. *Still is me.*

I turn and stare at the memory, faded behind wavy glass, just like me. I can remember that moment as if it were yesterday. So much time has passed, and still I wait.

For the next me. For the heir apparent.

Candy sure isn't it.

"Well," she finally says to the camera, "this place is insane! You have to see it to believe it! Everything is so old. It's like I stepped back in time."

"*Everything* is old?" I ask.

The color flushes from her youthful cheeks—as red as the

cherries I'm eating straight from the little cardboard crate on the counter—and she stutters a hurried goodbye to her followers.

"Ummm…so… I think that's all the time I have. Until I see you again at my next travel sweet spot, this is Candy. Love ya!"

Candy looks at me. She blinks her heavily mascaraed eyelashes.

"I was just teasing," I say. "I *am* old. And that's a blessing, not a curse. Remember that."

Blink.

Blink, blink.

Poor thing doesn't know what to say.

"Now, what I can I do you for?" I continue.

"Well," she says, scanning the chalkboard menu over her head. "Brant doesn't eat white bread or meat. There's no way he would ever eat a potpie." Candy turns and looks around the store again. "Brant won't let me eat sugar. I have to follow his diet plan all the time."

"I try to be as healthy as I can, too."

"He says I'll lose all my followers if I gain any weight," she says. Then she whispers, "He says he'll leave me if I gain any weight."

My heart shatters for this child.

I lean toward her. "But you gotta have a little fun in life, too." I reach under the counter and surreptitiously hand her a few chocolate-covered cherries, true heaven on earth. "Candy for Candy."

She turns to look for Brant, who has his face pressed against one of the mailbox windows, trying to see inside. She pops a cherry into her mouth. Hey eyes widen, and she giggles like a girl.

"Just one more," she whispers.

"Attagirl," I say with a wink.

"So anything in here that's healthy?" Brant asks, shoulders back, bro-walking toward us. "All your food is a death trap."

"Life causes death, Brant," I say.

He stares at me, not understanding the irony of my turn of phrase.

"May I suggest a basket of fresh cherries and fresh strawberries," I continue. "And we have bottled water right over there, from coconut to ionized."

"Now you're talking!" Brant says. "Get all that stuff, babe, I'm going to take some shirtless selfies outside."

He swats Candy on the tush and says, "You need to do more squats, babe," before jogging out of the general store. Candy pulls a credit card from her purse.

"Where are you two headed?" I ask.

"Back down to Charlevoix," she says. "Brant's family has a place there. Weekend trip. This area is just so beautiful and peaceful."

"That's why I love it," I say.

"Were you born and raised here?" she asks.

I nod.

She hands me her card, then looks around the store and back at me. Candy doesn't say *You're a relic*, but her face does.

"Everything comes back in style," I say to her, reading her mind. "Except for bad men. They never go away."

I hand her the receipt.

"You can do better than Brant."

Her face freezes. Her hand trembles just a little as she takes the receipt. I place her waters and fruit in a paper bag, and she walks away toward the exit as if in a trance.

The bell on the screened door jangles as she leaves. I watch Brant again smack her on the behind, pull his shirt back on and jump into his bright yellow convertible, leaving Candy to juggle the bag and the door. I step from behind the counter and walk toward the door. Brant peels out in the gravel parking lot, and the last thing I see is Candy turning toward me.

And then they are gone. Only dust remains.

A mirage.

I walk outside, the dust settles, and the world comes back into focus.

I stand at the edge of M-119 and look back at the Very Cherry General Store. Today, travelers from all over the world descend upon this tiny burg—barely a dot on the map—to drive through our breathtaking canopy of hardwoods and evergreens known as the Tunnel of Trees. The dense growth covers the road and drowns out the sky. Tourists drive north into Michigan to escape the world and head back in time. They can't help but notice my quaint store—its sign proclaiming *U.S. Post Office & General Store*—situated steps from the scenic roadway. This clapboard building was built in 1874, and it's always been painted bright red, with cheery American bunting, red-and-white-striped awnings and hand-painted signs in the windows reading *Fresh Michigan Cherries! Homemade Cookies, Sandwiches & Potpies! Stop for a Pop & Pictures!*

It's Mayberry, a Currier and Ives print come to life.

The Very Cherry General Store epitomizes what we all want and desire in our lives again: nostalgia. Escape. A return to the simplicity of small-town life. Life as it should be, on our own terms, not as it really is.

Four cars, one right after another, pull into the parking lot, and the dust flies.

A big wind scoots off the lake, carrying the dust away and rustling the dense canopy of green hugging the road.

The trees talk to me.

I look right, then left, and step right into the middle of M-119. I pull a cherry from the pocket of my apron, swirl it around in my mouth savoring every juicy morsel. I wait until I can see another gust of wind approaching, going tree by tree, as if playing a childhood game of telephone. Just as it arrives, I inhale with all my might, puff my lips and blow the pit. It sails into the air, down the Tunnel of Trees and lands in the middle of the road, bouncing this way and that, before taking a giant leap at the last minute, somersaulting toward a car driving much too fast.

I scoot to the edge of the road.

A canary-colored convertible blows by me.

At the last minute, I realize it's Candy.

She lifts her arm out of the convertible and waves at me. Then she corkscrews her body around in her seat and blows me a kiss that drifts my way on the breeze.

Did my advice sink in already?

And will she have the strength to believe in herself and move on?

Sun blinks through the dense branches of the trees, and my life flashes before my eyes.

Women must always be the strongest to survive.

I head back into the general store and greet my customers with as much sweetness as Aunt Bea from *Andy Griffith*.

"Is that you?" a young boy asks, pointing at the news article behind me.

"Sure is," I say.

"Wow!" he says. "Mom, Dad! Look!"

As I make their sandwiches, I turn and squint at the old newspaper article, which is framed alongside the first dollar my grandma ever earned running this place and the deed of trust to the store.

History makes my heart hiccup.

I stop for a moment, reading the faded text from the newspaper article.

"You just gotta believe you can. That's the hard part. Harder than spitting any old pit."

"It's always been hard," I whisper to myself. "But you still gotta believe, Mary. And be patient."

"Sorry, did you say something?" the mother asks.

"Yes. Mayonnaise or mustard?"

BECKY

July

"I'm melting!"

I turn and stare at Q, along with the winding line of St. Louisans waiting in the early-summer heat for Ted Drewes ice cream to cool them down. Sweat runs off my neck and down my back.

It is not just steamy in the city, it is a virtual rain forest.

Q begins to mimic the Wicked Witch from *The Wizard of Oz* after she sets the Scarecrow on fire and Dorothy accidentally tosses water on her.

"I'm melting, melting!" Q cries, slowly collapsing onto the sidewalk. "Oh, what a world, what a world!"

"Stop it!" I say, my face now flushed from embarrassment along with the heat. "Get up!"

Q bounds to her feet and—though no one is applauding—takes a bow.

"I actually played the Wicked Witch off-Broadway," she calls to the crowd.

"No one is asking," I say, looking around.

"In fact, it was way off-Broadway," Q says to me in a theatrical whisper. "Kearney, Nebraska."

I laugh.

"Gotta love a St. Louis summer," Q continues, now chatting with an older woman behind her. "You from around here?"

The woman shakes her head no.

"Well, we call it *the screened door to hell*. Devil comes here to vacation."

The woman looks at me, and I shrug.

My best friend has always been theatrical. The hot summer day that my family moved from Hannibal, Missouri, to St. Louis, Q was stationed at the corner of Lawn Avenue selling lemonade and belting out numbers from *Hello, Dolly*.

She was seven.

My first year at Brentwood Elementary was third grade. Our teacher, Mrs. Krause—who looked exactly like Angela Lansbury from my dad's favorite TV show, *Murder, She Wrote*—was intent on teaching us cursive.

Mrs. Krause did not like the way Monique drew her capital Qs. Monique, fittingly, would stalk to the blackboard, pick up the chalk and—between the carefully drawn lines—write a curling, frilly Q fit for a queen. It was not, however, the old-school Q—an elusive, looping letter which resembled the number *2*—that Mrs. Krause preferred.

"Do it again," she would admonish. "Another *Q*."

And so it began.

Q was born.

I look at her tangle of red curls blowing about in the muggy wind. Her skin is alabaster. She burns under a forty-watt bulb, and yet she loves the sun and summer. On the other hand, I am the quintessential St. Louis Catholic girl: blonde, blue eyes, wine in the communion cup and also perhaps with every dinner? Yes, please.

Q looks up at me—knowing I'm staring—and winks.

She made her dreams come true. Q is now head of the Muny, America's oldest and largest outdoor musical theater nestled in beautiful Forest Park, site of the 1904 World's Fair. For over one hundred years, St. Louis's cultural treasure has brought Broad-way-style theater to the city. Q makes it all happen, working with Broadway stars, child actors, producers, directors, a wealthy board of directors and lots of mosquitoes.

I look up. The line, like my life, has not moved much.

I still live in the same neighborhood where I grew up. I still walk the same sidewalk to Brentwood Elementary. I still come to Ted Drewes. And my world—from misbehaving second grad-ers who like to leave worms on their teachers' seats to my child-ish, now-ex, boyfriend—has revolved around miscreant boys.

I have not exactly made all my dreams come true.

"Are you okay, Becky?" Q asks. "You have that look on your face. The one that looks like you ate a bad hot dog in the school cafeteria." She stops. "It's kind of become your look lately."

"You think?" I ask. The world falls away before my eyes. "Good ol' Becky playin' by the rules. That's really turned out well for me, hasn't it? I mean, what chance did I ever have? How clueless—or cruel—were my parents to name me Becky if my last name was Thatcher? Especially being born in Hannibal. I'm cursed. My life is as outdated as a Mark Twain novel."

Now the line turns to stare at me.

"Come back to me," Q says very softly. "You're gone. Come back."

I smile. That's what she always says to me when I lose it.

"I'm back," I say, teeth gritted.

"Looks like it," Q says with a laugh.

"Do you own the *Becky Thatcher* riverboat?" a man in line asks, referring to the nineteenth-century replica steamboat, along with the *Tom Sawyer*, that cruises the Mighty Mississippi River. "My family just loves that."

"They do," Q says, voice low. "She just prefers not to discuss it. I'm sure you understand."

The man nods. "I do," he says. "I bet you live on it."

"Oh, my life is a paddle wheel, all right," I say. "Everything is very muddy."

"She's not a writer," Q says to the man. "But she's starting a new chapter." Q waits a beat. "See what I did there?"

Q puts her arm around my back and continues. "Come to mama," she says, drawing me close. "Ice cream's gonna make it all okay."

I laugh.

Ice cream has always made it better.

Q releases me, and our skin sticks together in the heat.

"Ewww," she says with a laugh. Her cell trills. "Sorry. Hold on. Actor drama."

I stand and watch her scrolling through her texts, humming the Backstreet Boys to calm her. This was our jam when we worked at Ted Drewes in high school.

Our world was ice cream, the Backstreet Boys and, well, boys. *And each other.*

Q and I worked here every summer in high school and during winter break when the parking lot turned into a Christmas-tree farm, and it's been the place where we've gone to share every monumental piece of news in our lives.

Nothing has changed.

Some women might go shopping, some might head to the bars, but ice cream has always been our go-to. Blood may be thicker than water, but Ted Drewes concretes are thicker than anything.

Ted Drewes is iconic in St. Louis, famed for its concrete, which was created in 1959, a malt or shake so thick that it's served upside down.

How do I know?

Every time a customer was served a concrete—be it a Fox Treat, which is made with hot fudge, raspberries and macadamia nuts, or a Dutchman with chocolate, butterscotch and pecans—Q and I had to turn it upside down and serve it like that to the customer.

You would think it would be a challenge in the St. Louis summer heat like today, but Ted Drewes ice cream is so thick, so rich, so deeply vanilla, that it is as thick as concrete.

There are only a couple of locations in south St. Louis. This one resembles a white ranch house, its gables lined with lights that resemble icicles, dotted with service windows that open and shut constantly like the *Laugh-In* set.

When we finally reach the front of the line, we order our favorites—what we get every single time, never even considering a different menu item—saying it immediately with gusto and excitement as if we can no longer contain it.

"Cardinal Sin!" I say, ordering a concrete with tart cherries and fudge.

"Caramel apple concrete!" Q calls.

We laugh, and the young girl in the window looks at us the same way we used to when middle-aged women would order their favorite sundae. She slams the window down, and my reflection stares back at me.

Inside, I am the same girl I used to be. But my face tells a different story these days. I'm not old, but I look—and feel—a bit worn, much like the ancient caramel-brown carpet my mother has refused to replace for the past twenty years. I think I just got used to things as they were, no matter how tired and worn they'd become. Change is hard. The same is so much easier.

My mother's carpet has a well-worn footpath running through the entire house—and yet she can't find the willpower to change it. Every couple of years, she will bring home new carpet samples—most of which look exactly the same—but will always say "I think this can go a little bit longer."

I look at myself again in the glass.

I've been exactly the same.

I'd thought about leaving Matt before. I'd thought about leaving my job, either for a promotion at a new school or leaving teaching entirely and doing something new. Teaching has become, I'm sad to say, more of a slog than a joy, between the constant worry about our students' safety, new teaching standards, overbearing parents who bully teachers and administrators, modeling that bad behavior for their own children. I'd even thought about leaving St. Louis and starting over somewhere else.

But here I remain.

"Muddy Mississippi!" an employee a few windows down yells, holding a concrete upside down.

I've become stuck in the mud.

Our window pops up suddenly, and before the girl can even do it, Q yells, "Do it! Turn it upside down!"

The girl tries hard not to roll her eyes and then turns the bright yellow cups with the Ted Drewes logo on them on their heads.

"We used to work here," Q explains.

"We're hiring," the girl says.

She says it with just enough sweetness not to be rude, but I see Q's eyes widen. She opens her mouth to say something, and the girl yells, "Next!"

As we walk away, Q mumbles, "These teenagers need to stop watching *Euphoria*," she says, referencing the popular cable drama about troubled, smart-mouthed teens.

"Think teenagers are bad?" I ask. "You should run into a middle-school girl on a bad day."

We take our concretes and do what we always do: nab a picnic table and sit directly on top of it, our feet on the bench.

I take a bite of my concrete and shut my eyes.

Nothing has changed.

Everything has changed.

"Okay, let's get real," Q says, "before I have to get back to work. I'm sorry about Matt."

I look at her, cocking my head dramatically.

"Okay, I'm not sorry. I never liked him. You know that. He was just so…placid. They say still waters run deep, but he wasn't deep at all. More like a wading pool. A cheap one you get at Target and blow up in the backyard…"

"I get it," I say.

"My heart goes out to you," Q says. "It really does. I know you're hurting, I know it's a big life change, and I know it's going to take you a while to recover, but the man you've devoted your entire life to for the last two decades gifted you a key to a make-believe vacation home that required you to contribute five percent of your monthly income while he's been living in your home mortgage-free his entire adult life. Am I getting that right? What am I missing?"

I take a bite of ice cream. It's the only thing I can do right now.

Q continues. "And that's the way it's always been, Becky. How many times did I beg you to leave him? How many times did I tell you that you deserved better? It just made you become more defiant and entrenched, so I stopped pushing. I know I sound harsh, but I cannot tell a lie."

My friend's brutal honesty is one of the things I love—and hate—most about her. She never lies to me.

"You sound like George Washington."

My mind flits back to when I was a teacher and taught students about the enduring legend of the first president, a story I shared more about the importance of being honest than the history of the U.S. The story goes, when Washington was six years old, he received a hatchet as a gift and damaged his father's beloved cherry tree. When his angry father found out, he confronted young Washington, and the boy bravely admitted to doing so, confessing, "I cannot tell a lie." Washington's father embraced his son, telling him that his honesty was worth more than a thousand trees.

I share this with Q, and she nods.

"Your relationship has been history as long as that story," she says. "I mean, he didn't even buy you a cherry tree, and you love cherries more than anything in this world. Besides that, Mrs. Lincoln, how was the play?" Q stops. "Sorry, I had to. I mean, I staged *Hamilton* last year. Presidential humor."

I hold up my ice-cream container and cheers her with it.

"You deserve more than him, Becky. You deserve unconditional love. You deserve to have your heart flutter when a man touches you. You deserve everything your grandparents had."

To keep myself from blubbering, I shove a mammoth spoonful of ice cream into my mouth.

Brain freeze.

My head begins to throb. I set my ice cream down and rub my temples. As my brain strobes, I see my Memaw and Pops in flashes: taking me to Cardinals games, feeding the animals at Grant's Farm, riding the roller-coaster at Six Flags, jumping into Lake Michigan, holding hands, kissing in public like teenagers.

"I do," I say.

Q grabs my hand and gives it a squeeze.

"But they took chances. They had fun. They knew how short life was and how to enjoy every moment."

I think of the scrapbook my grandparents gave me on my eighteenth birthday. I thought it was a sweet gift but very old-fashioned. But now, it seems as precious as gold.

"We should view our lives as tourists do," I mumble to myself. "Live every day like you're on vacation, even when you're not."

I forgot that. I forgot all of that.

Matt wasn't a bad man. He just didn't love me. Instead of igniting a fire in life every day, he sucked the oxygen out of the room until I couldn't breathe any longer, until I no longer had the energy to stand up and move on by myself.

"That's why I love the theater," Q says. "Every day is a new adventure. Every day is a fantasy."

Her cell trills again.

"Every day is a royal pain," she deadpans. "When I say *Break a leg* to this particular actor, I actually mean it."

She takes a bite of ice cream, and I follow her lead.

All of a sudden, she gasps.

"Brain freeze?" I ask.

"No!" she exclaims. "I have a brilliant idea!"

She grabs her cell and begins to text more quickly than an animated GIF.

"What?" I ask. "What is going on?"

She briefly stops texting and mutters, "Presidents. Actors. Cherries. Hold on."

"Is there tequila in your concrete?"

"Not a bad idea," she says. "Just…give…me…one…more… second…and… There! I'm done!"

"Done with what?"

"Girls' weekend!" she yells.

I look at her. "What? Where? When?"

"Are you training to be a journalist?" Q asks. "Northern Michigan."

My heart pings. My happy place. The place of happy childhood memories with my grandparents. The cherry capital.

The impossible.

"You're sweet," I say, "but delusional. This isn't theater. We can't just build a set and pretend we're there. We can't rent a place this late. Every hotel, inn and Vrbo sells out years in advance now." I take a breath and a bite of ice cream and continue. "And you have two more shows in the next month at the Muny."

Her cell trills.

"Already done."

"How?"

"I called in a favor."

"Who?"

"See, you do want to be a journalist."

"Stop with the vaudeville banter," I say.

"Do you know the actor Jeff Daniels?" she asks.

I nod. "Of course. *Terms of Endearment, The Purple Rose of Cairo, Dumb and Dumber.*"

"Well, he starred in *To Kill A Mockingbird* and *Frost/Nixon* with me at the Muny, and he fell in love with St. Louis's famed toasted ravioli."

"And?"

"And I still send it to him every year," she continues. "All of our presidential talk, my actor texts and thoughts about cherries reminded me that he lives in Michigan, might know someone and might feel compelled to repay me for my ravioli kindness," Q says. "Well, he does. Turns out he has a dear friend who has an old log cabin in northern Michigan in a tiny town north of Charlevoix." She waits for me to look at her. When I do, she says, "On! The! Lake!"

"I know where it is!" I say. "That's the area I used to go with my grandparents."

"Jeff says his friend is going to be out of the country in August shooting a movie in Nova Scotia. It's ours if we want. For free!" She stands up on the picnic bench and exclaims, "Let's do your fortieth up right. Just the two of us. Mark a new beginning in your life and our friendship. Make new adventures."

"But you're busy," I say. "You have a busy slate of shows, and I have in-service meetings starting the third week of the month."

"My shows end the first week of August due to the heat, and have you ever heard of Zoom?" Q asks. "The world got used to it the last few years. Believe me, Becky, they don't need you there in person, and you could open that school back up in your sleep. Moreover, you don't need to be wearing pants in St. Louis in August anyway." Q looks down at me. "And, to be completely honest… "

"Again?" I ask.

"Brentwood probably would've put you on leave if it hadn't been the last day of school," she says. "Just play the sympathy

card. Tell them you need a little more time to recover so you
can be your best self when you return. They'll understand. And
probably be a bit relieved. Let's play hooky from life. Remember
what that was like? Just like *Ferris Bueller's Day Off*."

I smile.

Oh, the fun we used to have when Q would challenge my
by-the-book ways. We'd sneak off to the mall or the riverfront
or head to a Cardinals game, sit in the bleachers and pay strangers to buy us beer. We'd head to the Manchester pool and wear
big hats to cover our faces so no one would rat on us.

"Okay," I say. "Girls' weekend!" I stop. "*If*—do you hear
me?—if everything works out on my end."

Q nods.

"Don't leave me hanging up here, girlfriend!" she says. "Take
a risk, Becky Thatcher, for once in your life! Become a legend!"

I stand. Q grabs her cell and starts playing "Everybody (Backstreet's Back)." We dance like schoolgirls. I dance, for once, like
no one is watching.

"Are you really Becky Thatcher?"

I look down at an older woman before me.

I nod.

"I overheard you say in line that you own the riverboat named
after you. I just love riding on that thing when we visit."

"That's nice," I say.

I look at Q and shake my head and then take a big bit of my
concrete.

"Smile!"

I look down again, and the woman is snapping photos of me.

"That's a keeper!" she says. "See?"

She swivels her cell my way, and I lean down to see an image
of me, mouth full of ice cream, face contorted, chin doubled.
The woman toddles away.

"Wait!" I say. "That's a terrible picture."

"I actually think it captures your essence," Q says.

MARY

July

"How's it goin', Taffy?"

"Back's out, mind's worse, but money's good."

I laugh and raise my cup of coffee to him from the beach. It is dawn, and while the vacationers sleep, the locals are already up and working.

So much for living in a resort town.

Taffy runs a board through his table saw—the sound echoing over the lake—and then stops to take a sip of coffee from his insulated mug. Taffy is already sweating, the bandanna around his head as dark blue as the deep water. It's a warm early morning, and the trees hang on the bluff, limbs still, as if they've yet to have their cup of joe. I take a sip of my Cherry Republic Chocolate Cherry Boom coffee—which tastes as if you melted chocolate-covered cherries into a dark roast coffee—and consider the scene before me.

Everything has changed.

And yet, nothing has changed.

"Think they're up yet?" Taffy asks, nodding up at the house.

"Is it noon yet?" I ask. "They're still on California time."

Taffy laughs and runs another board through the saw. "They're in their own world." He turns and calls, "If the saw won't wake them, this will."

He walks over and cranks up his radio. Jimmy Buffett begins to sing "Son of a Son of a Sailor."

Taffy lifts his cup to me, and I silently salute him again.

First, you might want to know why a long-haired, rough-and-tumble contractor with a penchant for beer and a love of Jimmy Buffett is known as Taffy. It's simple: I nicknamed him that, and it stuck like, well, taffy. As a boy, Vance Vanderloo used to wander into the general store and try to steal candy from the glass containers. Kids didn't know that—in the days before cameras—mirrors were placed just so to keep an eye on folks. Vance always went for the saltwater taffy, particularly the newfangled flavors like granny's apple pie, lemon meringue, birthday cake, red velvet batter, cookie dough, cinnamon bun, banana dream pie—and, boy oh boy, did that kid have sticky fingers and holey pockets. You could literally track his theft as if he'd left a trail of bread crumbs.

Taffy's dad didn't do much except complain, but his mother was a hard worker, cleaning vacation houses during the summer months and a nearby hotel in the winter. I talked to her, and we put him to work in the general store mopping floors, helping with deliveries, putting up the mail to pay off his taffy debt. Slowly, he began to do repairs to the place and was pretty darn good at it. He said I saved his life. But he's wrong. Every rescue rescues us in some way, eventually.

When my mother died and when my son sailed off to the big city, Taffy was there.

He's still here.

Still trying to save me from all of life's inevitable changes.

Three well-worn paths lead from the beach through the dunes grass and up the bluff to three homes nestled in the trees overlooking the lake. For decades, locals referred to the homes on the bluff as Widows' Peak.

Francine Mosley, Myrtle Tamm and I owned these old cottages for decades, long before anyone had ever heard of the wonders of northern Michigan, the Tunnel of Trees, much less Good Hart. Myrtle and I had lost our husbands long ago, and even though Francine was married, he was rarely here, save for special occasions, and the locals saw us the same. Thus, the local moniker stuck, and there was nothing we could do to change it.

And then widowhood became reality for Francine.

Turtle Myrtle came here first after she'd been widowed. Myrtle moved as slowly as her nickname, never rushed, never panicked, ducking her head into a book whenever the world got to be too much. She bought an old farmhouse—updating its electrical and plumbing—but keeping most of it exactly the way it was.

Francine came from Indianapolis with her husband and bought an A-frame that required a lot of love, which Francine provided. At night, when we'd have a glass of wine and look back at that cottage, it seemed to wink at Francine as if to thank her for saving it.

Our beaches were filled with Adirondack chairs in our three favorite colors: red for Cherry Mary, brown for Turtle Myrtle and purple, Francine's favorite color.

Myrtle died a few years ago, followed by Francine's husband, Bill. Francine had closed up her house for two years while she cared for Bill, and her kids never come to Good Hart anymore. She said she plans to return in mid-July, but I'm not counting my chickens. Once a place leaves your heart, the memories fade like that poster of me in the general store. Not only have I lost my two friends, but Myrtle and Francine also left me to contend with new neighbors. Myrtle's home sold to a young couple who both work in technology. They work from home, a new concept to me, and I rarely see them save for when they want or need something. They tore down Myrtle's old farmhouse and replaced it with a new farmhouse—white with black windows like every other house being built in this world, a farmhouse that wouldn't recognize a farm if a cow knocked on the front door and asked to borrow a gallon of milk. The couple, Geoffrey and Moira—you have to say her name as if you're visiting the doctor, sticking your tongue out and saying "aaahhh," or she will correct you on the spot—walk around in caftans and have friends visiting all summer who do not like the sun or the water. They have unlimited ideas and budget. Taffy has worked on their home nonstop for years, pleading and cajoling with them and their architect to respect the environment and the original cottages that surround it. He's had some success swaying them: Taffy showed me photos of the interior—I've never been invited inside—which utilizes local timber and stones, and the infinity pool they are now building will have a terraced deck filled with native Michigan flowers, dunes grass and plants to make it disappear into the bluff.

"We have a big pool right here," I call to Taffy, sticking my foot in the water. "It's called a lake."

"Ain't fancy enough water I guess," he says with a laugh. He then puts a finger over his mouth as if to shush himself.

And now I've heard through the grapevine that this couple has been snooping around Francine's beautiful A-frame and asking lots of questions. Taffy told me that Virgie Daniels, the big realtor in town and my former childhood BFF, said Geoffrey and Moira have friends interested not only in the lot but also in tearing it down to build a look-at-me mini mansion much too big for the lot. They've even talked to Taffy, who told them Francine won't sell but also begged them to rework the original structure in the event she does. But they, like so many now, buy it for the land value and not the value of the history.

History doesn't seem to carry much weight anymore.

My cottage, which my mother inherited from her mom, is all knotty pine with soaring, angled white ceilings, a tiny kitchen with retro turquoise appliances and overlooks the water and has a loft bedroom with breathtaking views of the lake. It's like living in a grown-up treehouse.

I know my son, Jonah, will likely not want this cottage in the middle of nowhere. He's a real-estate developer who loves high-rises and new condos with all the amenities and will likely use the cash to build something even newer in the city or tear this down just like all the rest.

I call him all the time, or he calls me, but—ironically—we never really talk.

I hear a mother calling for her son. I turn, and her little boy flies down the beach, arms outstretched like a seagull.

Did I push my own son away because of a legend—and destiny—I've long believed, or did I simply allow him to fly?

A mother's dilemma.

I glance at my beautiful cottage and hope it will not be destroyed by a wrecking ball and earthmover, a lifetime of memories erased in just a matter of hours.

I watch the boy running along the shore, and I now think of my grandson, Oliver—Ollie—and how much he loved his childhood summers here running the beach, playing in the lake, working alongside me. I thought he might be the heir apparent, that perhaps I've been misguided in my belief in the legend of the fourth woman in which I've long believed, but he seems to have followed in the footsteps of Jonah.

And so I wait.

Or will die waiting.

Why does today's generation seem to turn its collective nose at anything that's not new, fancy, the hippest or the latest? There seems to a be a lack of appreciation for those things—and people—that have a history, that tell a story, that have lived a long life.

So many estate companies and antique malls filled with heirlooms and family history.

All to be forgotten.

The boy races down the beach. The waves erase his footprints.

All of my memories of family are here. I don't want them to just be washed away.

"How's your summer been?" Taffy asks, knocking me from my thoughts.

"Can't find a soul to hire," I say. "Ones I do can't keep up with the pace. I'm actually looking for a kid to come into the store and steal from me."

Taffy laughs. "I can't either, Mary. Harder to find someone to work than it is to find salt in Lake Michigan. You never stopped working."

"Neither did you!"

"Here's to hard work."

Taffy raises his mug again.

"You sure you just have coffee in that?" I ask. "You're drinking it fast."

"For now!" he calls. "I'll pop in for a liverwurst sandwich later, Mary. Bye."

I head down the beach a ways and take a seat on the sand with my coffee. After a long, exhausting weekend at the store, I take an extra half hour for myself on Monday mornings. The beach is still a bit cool, but the coffee and the sun instantly warm me.

The lake, like the trees and new neighbors, has yet to wake. It is just me and the water. The waves try to lap at the shore but seem to lose energy and fall asleep on their journey.

My entire life has been spent on this same shoreline, and yet no day is ever the same.

Right now the sky is gold, as if heaven is melting into the water, and the sun sparkles on the surface of the lake. Tomorrow, the sky might be as red as my store or as purple as Francine's favorite tops.

I take a sip of my coffee and then set my mug into the sand. I stand and wade—I'm always barefoot on the beach in the summer, just as I was as a girl—into the lake.

What people don't realize until they see it in person is that the water in northern Michigan is as beautiful as any ocean or any lake in Italy. It is so breathtakingly blue, so crystal clear, that you feel as if you're standing in a glass-bottomed boat. This morning, I can see every sandy striation underneath the water's surface. In many ways, it matches the creped skin on my legs, although it's much more attractive.

When you stand here and look out onto the lake, with the water this still, it looks as if God has finger-painted the entire world in blue and gold stripes and then illuminated it as if the lake were a vintage Helmscene lighted picture, just like the ones I have on my screened porch.

"What'cha doin'?"

I jump.

A little girl—no more than seven, already dressed in an adorable pink swimsuit—is standing beside me.

"Thinking," I say.

Her mother is standing on the beach. "Sorry we startled you. She likes to get down here early every day of vacation."

"What are you thinking about?" the little girl asks.

"Life," I say.

"I don't like to think about life," the girl says. "I just like to do life."

She leans down and splashes herself with water, eliciting a big scream of joy.

"Good advice," I say.

I lean down and splash myself with water, and the girl giggles and then tosses a bit of water on my legs. I return the favor. She holds out her hand, and I take it. She leads me back to shore.

"Thank you," I say to her.

"You're welcome!"

"She's so thoughtful," I say to her mother.

"She's so headstrong," her mom says with a laugh.

"It takes a girl to do things right!"

The child says this with such emphatic pride and belief that I can feel my legs melt right into the warming sand.

Summer 1953

"Are you in or not?"

"Not!"

"Scaredy-cat!"

"You'll never know, then. See ya later!"

My best friends, Virgie and Sally, take off down the beach. I stand in the sand, paralyzed. The sun is setting. It stays daylight forever in the summer in northern Michigan, and there is last light in the sky until well after ten o'clock. But I know it will go from light to dark in a matter of moments.

I watch them walk away, their bodies becoming shadows.

What will I tell my mom? I'd already said I was spending the night at Virgie's parents', who were gone for the weekend. *What if they call them?*

I take off running, the fear of the known scarier than the unknown.

"I knew you'd come!" Virgie yells when I catch up with them.

We are a tough group of girls. Our fathers are laborers. Hard drinkers, hard as the winters here. We are raised like boys but expected to be girls.

Life, even at this young age, is filled with contradictions and myths.

Hairpin turns.

"There!"

I follow Sally's finger. A tiny path winds from the beach along the bluff and to the road. Dusk begins to call. My body shivers slightly despite the summer warmth. I wrap my arms around my body, and we begin our hike uphill.

When the path finally spits us out on the road, the trees are blue.

There is a time of day in Michigan known as the Blue Hour—

just after sunset and just before sunrise—when the sun sits below the horizon and the remaining light takes on a blue glow. Objects are still distinct and yet softening, ethereal, and the world feels mysterious, beautiful, as if anything is possible.

The three of us walk along the edge of the road, hidden by the trunks and tall grasses, blurred by the blue. The canopy of hardwoods and evergreens, known in these parts as the Tunnel of Trees, creates a breathtaking canopy over the road. Tonight, it resembles a blue shag carpet. The breeze off Lake Michigan, cool at dusk, occasionally rustles the branches, and we stop on a dime, midmotion, and listen.

I squint and scan the distance, searching for the sign.

The Blue Hour, I know, doesn't even last an hour. It is a half hour at best, just enough time to be unseen and yet to see—and hear—things clearly.

And then we see it.

Just down the road a bit from Good Hart sits a hairpin turn on Lakeshore Drive locals call Devil's Elbow. There's even an old sign, the vintage, hand-lettered kind that you might come across in a Cinderella movie or a Brothers Grimm fairy tale. It hangs from a wooden post and reads

A Flowing Spring In This Ravine Was Believed By Indian Tribes To Be The Home Of An Evil Spirit Who Haunted The Locality During The Hours of Darkness

Everyone in town knows the legend. Everything in this town seems to be legend. This spot marks the location where the devil scooped out a giant hollow after Native Americans suffered a devastating plague. The local legend was that former residents could hear voices and sounds coming from the ravine after dark.

Parents in town told their kids to avoid the site, but, of course—kids being kids—we just had to sneak to see if the legend were real.

The three of us touch the sign and then giggle nervously as if ghosts and goblins will suddenly appear.

Virgie grabs Sally's hand and then mine, yanking us off the road and into the woods. The trunks, the leaves, the limbs, the air glow blue.

Sally giggles nervously again, and Virgie shushes her.

We stand in silence, hand in hand, waiting to hear a voice, waiting to hear a sound, waiting for anything, for what seems like eternity.

The blue begins to fade.

"I knew it," Virgie says. "Just a legend."

In the near distance, a branch cracks.

"Squirrel," Sally reasons.

Another branch, closer.

"Rabbit," Virgie says.

And then what sounds like footsteps.

I squint into the blue-black. Slowly, one tree becomes two, as if separating.

It is a figure, shadowy, moving toward us.

"Ghost!" Virgie yells. "It's haunted! It's real!"

Virgie runs, lickety-split, like a deer at the sound of leaves crunching. Sally follows, hightailing it out of there, with a bellowing scream that keeps going, a human locomotive fading the farther it goes.

I remain paralyzed, as I had been on the beach.

"Hello?" I call in a warbling voice.

A woman appears. She is old and carrying a walking stick.

"Are you a ghost?" I ask.

A laugh.

"Not yet."

"What are you doing out here?" I ask.

"I could ask you the same thing." Silence. "Evening walk."

She comes closer. I remain as rooted in the ground as the centuries-old trees.

"You're the Jackson girl, aren't you?" She bends down until her eyes are in the last light. I recognize her from town. "Your mom and grandma run the general store and post office."

I nod.

"Good women," she says. "Hardworking."

One step closer.

"You here to find out if the legend is real?"

I nod again.

"Follow me."

My heart leaps into my throat.

I follow—her walking stick thumping the ground before us. I can feel the reverberations in the earth. I don't know why, but I trust her. I feel in my heart she is leading me somewhere I need to go, someplace I need to see.

We walk in silence. The only words she utters are "Girls are braver than boys. Always have been. Always will be."

About a quarter mile deeper into the woods, we come to a log cabin.

"That's my house," she says. "Where I make quill boxes."

"My grandma has one at the general store," I say. "I didn't know you made it."

The woman turns and looks at me. "I make them from birch bark, sweet grass and porcupine quills. My ancestors used birch bark to store food because it has natural antibacterial properties. Quills were harvested from animals we hunted for food. When moistened, the quills become pliable and easy to use and dye. Now I make the boxes as art for tourists."

She takes a beat to consider me and continues walking. "That is what's happening to our land. Our history is being forgotten. Our world is transient. Our importance is being overlooked."

We stop at a log stool and a little bench in front of the house. She picks up a box and hands it to me. It is beautiful, intricate. There is a star pattern on the top, and it is trimmed with sweet grass.

"This is my legacy," she says. "And the general store is yours."

Goose bumps.

I open the box. It is empty inside. I place the lid back on top.

"How do you know that?" I ask. "It's just a dumb little store."

She walks past her cabin and to the edge of the bluff. She points into the distance.

"Look there, on the horizon," she says. "What do you see?"

At first, I see nothing. Then, on the horizon, barely visible as the Blue Hour begins to fade to dark, I see a figure walking on the water.

Directly toward us.

I shake my head, shut my eyes, blink hard and look again. This time, there are three women—blue, misty, but so very real—walking my way across the water.

"Three women," I finally say. "Are they my friends?"

"Look again."

A fourth woman has joined them.

"You came to the woods for a reason," she says. "You stayed for a reason. To learn your fate. This is it."

My heart is racing.

"I don't understand."

"Fata Morgana," the woman says.

"I still don't understand."

"It's an Italian term that translates the name of the Arthurian sorceress, Morgan le Fay, or Morgan the Fairy," the woman says. "In the legend, she was a powerful sorceress and adversary of King Arthur. People used to believe that she conjured up mirages—like fairy castles in the air or false land—in order to lure sailors to their deaths."

Goose pimples again cover my arms and legs. I clutch the box harder between my hands.

"These were legends created by man, I believe, to diminish the power of women who not only spoke their minds but had visions," the woman says. "Women like your mom and grandma.

Men feared that women like this were trying to harm them or others, but they were misguided. Morgan le Fay simply wanted to empower women to take control of their lives and the world. She knew men were easily led astray. Women remain loyal to their families, their histories, their past."

She turns to look at me and continues. "You will become such a woman. Strong. Brave. Powerful. Men will want to take over this area one day. They will want to take over your life, too. Outsiders will want to tear down what is ours. It's already happening."

"You're scaring me."

"Don't be scared. Be strong," she says. "Look!"

I follow her finger.

The four women have reached the middle of the lake.

"Who are they?" I ask. "What do they mean?"

"Their meaning is up to you," she says. "Their meaning is inside of you."

"Help me understand," I beg.

"I am helping you."

I stare into the lake.

"They are my family," I finally reason. "Me, my mom and my grandma. The fourth will be my daughter. It's our family destiny that the women have only girls."

The woman smiles.

"But you will have a boy," she says, "who will have a boy."

"No," I say.

"Just know there will be another woman who will join you, just like there will be another who will join me. It may take a lifetime. Be patient. Your life will be filled with people who misread your power. It will also be filled with those who embrace it. Choose to believe no matter how long it takes."

"But how will I know? When will I know?"

"You will simply know. It will all make sense one day, these four women. Time. It will take a lot of time for this to make sense. Just remember that time isn't a clock or a calendar. Time is a wave like those right now on the lake. Time may seem finite, but it's not. The story of us can last for infinity, like those waves you see. Our time will end, but our legend will wash up, over and over again, a wave to the shore, if our time here is filled with goodness, connection, friendship, meaning. That is the ripple effect of kindness."

I look toward the lake, and in an instant—as the Blue Hour ends and darkness begins to choke out the day—the women disappear.

In the distance, I hear the sound of a drum.

"According to my people, the drum is heard each time a life is lost in the waters of northern Lake Michigan," she says. "I believe the fourth woman we saw is a future soul that could be lost, or saved. It's up to you to decide."

"Decide what?"

The woman takes her box from my hands and opens it. She presents it to me.

It is filled with fresh cherries.

"Decide whether what you believe in your heart is true or not," she says. "Decide whether what you see on the horizon is real or simply a mirage. Legend lives within us. Only we can make it real."

I stare at the horizon.

The sound of the drum picks up, a haunting beat that echoes over the water. And then, just like the women on the lake, the drumming fades.

When I turn, the old woman is gone.

I run toward the road, disappearing like a mirage into the blue.

BECKY

Present day

I've been set up.

My parents' ranch house is actually a trap, and Betty and Darryl Thatcher are spies.

I was cornered after Mass and summoned for an impromptu summer barbecue at my parents' house, just a few blocks from our church and my house.

My parents are not spontaneous. Impromptu for them means a year of considering something, six months of planning it and then two weeks to cancel because they just weren't ready.

When I arrive, my father is seated in his beloved brown recliner watching the Cardinals game. He keeps the TV angled toward the kitchen, so he can call to my mom to bring him a beer whenever she passes.

My mother has pulled out carpet samples that I got with her well over two years ago.

"Which do you think?" she asks. "They're all so different and such a big change for me."

The samples are all the same shade of brown that she already has, and I can barely discern them from the worn carpet on which she has placed them.

"Are we grilling this shag carpet today for Sunday dinner?" I ask.

My mom and dad look at each other.

"You can stop the shenanigans already," I continue. "I already know what's going on. This tiny neighborhood has a big mouth, especially when you've lived here forever."

They look at me.

"Yes, I broke up with Matt. And, yes, you already know that."

My mother gasps and throws a hand over her mouth, as if she's starring in a soap opera. My mother gasps at everything: when someone walks into a room, when the laundry machine buzzes, when the telephone rings. I think it's a prime reason I've been able to work in an elementary school so long—nothing surprises me after living with her.

"You should have told us," my father scolds.

"Yes, you're right. I should have. I'm sorry. I just needed a little time to process everything."

"Has he moved out already?"

I nod. "He rented an apartment in Chesterfield," I say.

"That poor..."

"Don't you dare finish that thought, Mother," I say. "He's not poor. He's not helpless. He's—" I stop, the emotions of the last couple of weeks overwhelming me "—he never truly loved me."

My parents look at one another again.

"So which carpet sample do you prefer?" my mom asks.

Vintage Betty. She may not ever be able to get new carpet, but she can sweep anything under the rug.

"Mom," I say, "I know you liked Matt. I know he's been a part of our lives for a very long time. But he wasn't the one. He was never the one. And I'm glad I figured that out now while I'm still young."

My father coughs.

"Not funny, Dad," I say.

"Don't you want to be married?" my mom asks. "To a nice

Catholic boy? Don't you want children? I thought you wanted children. You had all those notebooks filled with all those wishes growing up."

My dad swivels in his chair. "Don't you want to be happy?" he asks.

This is how my parents console me. They shower me with doubt.

"I do. And I am," I say. "But I wasn't going to be happy with Matt. I don't think he was even ever going to ask me to marry him. I was…" I search for just the right word "…comfortable."

"Comfortable's okay, honey," my dad calls over the TV. "This recliner's comfortable. My robe is comfortable. Your mother and I are comfortable." He takes a sip of his beer and glances toward the game. "This game's not as comfortable as it should be, but life should be comfortable."

"But I can't be safe anymore," I say. "How far has that gotten me?"

"You have a good job, and you have a good boyfriend." My mom stops herself and then mumbles, "*Had* a good boyfriend."

The air-conditioning begins to run, and over its low hum I hear lawnmowers running outside, kids yelling, the thwack-thwack-thwack of sprinklers. Through the window, I can see Mrs. Babcock watering her flowers, just as she always has. She is chatting with Mr. Lawrence, who has been pulling the same weeds from the same cracks in his sidewalk just like the first day we arrived. I take a step toward the dining-room window and look out at my mother's front porch. The puny boxwoods my mother has always hated have never grown much or been replaced. The front doormat's seasonal insert has, as usual, immediately been switched from the Fourth of July to colorful summer flip-flops, even though my mother wouldn't be caught dead in flip-flops.

The neighborhood—*my* neighborhood—sounds just as it did when I was a kid. I still feel like a child in my childhood home.

And please don't get me wrong: that is sublimely comforting.

I have led a comfortable life, and that is a rare blessing. I've had opportunities, love and safety, a life so many others only dream of. And now I lead a comfortable life.

I turn and watch my father watching the Cardinals game.

He taught me the Thatcher Rules. A two percent raise is fine. A four percent return on your investment is grand. A promotion every decade is well-earned. A thirty-year mortgage under five percent is wonderful. A year-end bonus of a thousand dollars is gravy. An in-state vacation every five years is marvelous.

My eyes wander to a photo of my grandparents at Six Flags. It's one of those pictures theme parks take when you're about to plunge to your doom. Pops and Memaw aren't screaming. Their eyes aren't shut. They're looking at one another, holding hands which are flung over their heads, and they don't look old. They look like kids. They look as if life is still fun and exciting, as if new adventures are waiting at every twist and turn, not worrying about the horrifying plunge that awaits.

With great blessing, shouldn't there be great responsibility? A responsibility to do more with one's life? Or, at least, to take a thrilling ride before it's all too late?

With great ease can come complacency.

Mrs. Babcock waters, Mr. Lawrence weeds, my dad watches, and my mother contemplates the carpet that—unlike the seasonal switch mat for her front door—will never change.

Just feet away, a red convertible sits in my parents' garage. My grandparents purchased it late in life.

When they drove to our home, top down, one glorious early-summer day—my grampa in a Cards cap, my grandma's head wrapped in a billowy scarf like a '50s starlet—my dad raced out and exclaimed, "How much did this cost? Have you lost your minds?"

"Everyone needs a red convertible once in their lives," my grandfather said. "Especially you, Darryl."

One of my father's favorite TV programs of all time was a detective show called *Hart to Hart*. It starred Robert Wagner and Stefanie Powers as a rich, married, jet-setting couple who always seem to be stumbling into murders and solving them. My father loved whodunits, as he called them, but *Hart to Hart* also indulged his passion for cars. The Harts tooled around SoCal in expensive convertibles, including a yellow Mercedes.

"Now, that's a beautiful car," my dad would say, his eyes wide with admiration as he downed a beer. "V-8, top down, hair in the wind…" Then he would sigh and say, "Someday. Someday."

That day never came until my grandparents died. The car was left to my parents. Inside the glove box was a note from Pops to my dad that read *Life—like money—is often too short, but sometimes, you have to put the top down and just enjoy the ride.*

That ride—like the carpet—has never come. The convertible sits idle in the garage, never driven, the odometer forever remaining at 3208. My dad cannot let himself enjoy the moment, and so the car sits before him—a gift and a curse—every time he passes it to get into his Toyota Corolla.

"I don't want to be comfortable any longer," I say. "I don't want good. I want great. I don't want two percent. I want amazing. I want cuckoo for Cocoa Puffs!"

My mother looks up and my father looks back.

Silence.

Finally, Dad takes a sip of beer and says, "I think you're already there."

He taps on his empty beer can, and my mother pops up like there's a spring underneath her and heads to the fridge.

She hands a Bud Lite to my father and then zips back into the kitchen and returns with a glass filled with ice, a diet soda still fizzing and frothing. The glass is one of my favorites from when I was a girl featuring a unicorn with my name *Becky* in script. She hands me a straw still encased in paper and gives me her *There, there* eyes.

My mother has been performing this soda-straw ritual since I was thirteen and had to have my wisdom teeth removed at too early an age because my mouth was too small for them to grow into proper position.

She thinks it will not only make me feel better and solve all of my—and the world's—problems but also because she believes I can't simply drink out of an adult glass without a straw.

"Why don't you just call Matt and work it out?" my mother asks, patting me on the shoulder. "Now, what should we have on the grill? Pork steaks or chicken?"

"Pork steaks!" my dad yells. "I'm grilling. I get to decide."

I know that my mother will never change her carpet. I know my dad will always pick pork steaks. And that's all good.

But maybe it's not what I want.

"Do you want me to invite Matt over?" my mom asks. "It's just not the same without him."

"Good idea," my dad says. "Miss having someone to watch the game with."

I tear the top of paper off the straw and then inhale deeply, purse my lips and blow the paper. It flies like a jet fighter directly toward my father, striking him in the back of the head.

He grabs the paper and pivots to look at me.

I smile innocently, place the straw into my unicorn glass and take a big sip.

"I'm thinking of heading to northern Michigan for a month to vacation with Q," I say, knowing this will implode their world. "And I may ask the school for an extended leave of absence."

Silence. Utter and complete silence.

I'm still not done.

"And please don't ever ask me about Matt or say his name in front of me again. I'm your daughter. He's no longer part of the family. Got it?"

My parents look at each other. I take another sip from my unicorn glass.

"That girl has always been a bad influence on you," my mother says.

"And you've always been full of hot air," my dad says, shaking the paper wrapper at me.

"Speaking of hot," I say, "I'm starting the grill so I can eat and leave before I explode into flames."

I head toward the kitchen.

"And I'm having a beer, too!" I call. "No straw!"

I have decided—on this beautiful Monday morning—to become a *flâneur*.

Fittingly, since St. Louis is a decidedly French city founded—which I know as a teacher and lifelong resident—by French fur traders in 1764 who named it for Louis IX of France. Our neighborhoods and streets are named Laclede, Chouteau and Soulard, and yet so many of us who live in a place for so long don't consider its—or our own—history or place in the world.

Moreover, so many of us never do any of the touristy things tourists do when they visit.

What is a *flâneur*?

Well, I didn't know, either, until I became fascinated recently with a woman on Instagram known as The Southern Flâneur who grew up in rural Texas and turned her life upside down by attending Le Cordon Bleu culinary school in Paris, moving to Versailles, marrying a Frenchman and now teaching French cooking online like a modern-day Julia Child. She often takes her followers and subscribers on journeys to the market or through Versailles, the parks and the countryside. It is aspirational and magical.

A *flâneur* literally means a *stroller, lounger* or *saunterer*, but with great nuance and significant depth and meaning. It means that you are a keen observer and documentarian of life and what surrounds you. You are focused on the immediate and not the future. You are an experimenter and keen to make the whole world your home. Moreover, a *flâneur* seeks meaning in life.

My father would call a *flâneur* a *loafer*, and just a year or so ago, I would've likely echoed the sentiment, but I've slowly come to see this way of life not only as nonconformist but perhaps as a healthier way to live. This blogger led me to the Parisian writer Charles Baudelaire, who wrote:

To be away from home and yet to feel oneself everywhere at home; to see the world, to be at the center of the world, and yet to remain hidden from the world… The lover of life makes the whole world his family.

I was taught to focus on schedules and systems. I do that in life and career. I model that to our teachers and students: plan and manage every hour of the day so that you can be most productive.

Over the years, I have begun to feel incredible guilt for the message I'm sending young people: don't take time to let life take you where it goes. Don't be flexible. Control time. Live a strict itinerary. Review that calendar. Color code that notebook. Increase your goals. Be an analytical, not an emotional, observer. Be in charge of the world, not a citizen of the world.

Matt was just like me.

I have been taught to take a vacation and believe that will restore my life's battery. A long weekend will refill my empty tank. I don't even, out of guilt, allow myself to do what I'm doing this day: take time for me.

Today, I have wandered the city. St. Louis is filled with free attractions, a gift to our people and visitors: the St. Louis Zoo, the Missouri History Museum, Grant's Farm. Today, I spent the morning wandering through the amazing collections at the Saint Louis Art Museum. I then walked through Forest Park, the site of the 1904 World's Fair, and marveled at the bridges, lakes and blooming flowers. Then I came downtown to the riverfront and walked through the Museum at the Gateway Arch, learning about colonial St. Louis through the completion of the arch in 1965.

"Ticket?"

I hand the ticket to a man in a navy jacket.

"I haven't done this since I was a little girl with my grand-parents," I say.

He tears my ticket without saying a word.

"Next!"

My heart begins to pound trying to remember what the ride in the tram to the top of the arch is like.

The elevator door opens, and light spills forth. It's then I re-member.

The ride is a bit scary and a touch claustrophobic.

Eight connecting pods hold up to five people. They resemble cramped elevators filled with an orb of light.

I am the first to board, and I take a seat next to the door so I can look out the window. A young mother steps on next and reaches back to take her young daughter's hand. The husband, tall and muscular, takes a step and then stops.

"C'mon, Daddy!" his daughter says.

The man enters the pod and takes a seat by me, his head scrap-ing the ceiling. The door shuts, and the pod begins to ascend. As we move through the leg of the arch, you witness through a window on the door the complex inner construction, the beams and concrete that stabilizes the six-hundred-thirty-foot steel wonder, almost as if you're seeing its X-ray. The tram feels rickety as you ride, and the higher you go the more you can feel the structure sway ever so slightly in the wind.

The father groans, grips the side of the pod and shuts his eyes.

I look at the mother, wondering if she is witnessing this.

He groans.

"Are you okay, Daddy?" the little girl asks.

"Just a little seasick," he says.

"We're not on the water, though, Daddy."

The pod rocks, and the man yelps.

After a long few minutes, the doors open, and the man literally jumps out of his seat and over my body to escape.

"Men," the wife says to me. "We give birth. We raise the kids. We clean their scraped knees and throw-up, and we're the weaker sex?"

She takes her daughter's hand and leads her out of the pod. I follow, heading to the small viewing windows that line the top of the arch. The view west is of St. Louis, and the view east is over the Mississippi River and Illinois.

"I can see the world!" the little girl says, leaning onto the padded space before the windows.

I remember saying the exact same thing when my grandparents brought me up here.

"You can change the world!" Memaw told me. "Girls can do anything."

I take the tram back down to the ground floor and head toward the river. I watch the mighty Mississippi churn, boats and barges moving along its swift-moving current.

I take a seat along the edge of the river and watch the water. Slowly, the Becky Thatcher paddle wheeler churns by.

Like time, the river will never stop. It will never slow. It will keep on rushing toward a point downstream forever.

I stand up and head toward Laclede's Landing, a multiblock, historic area filled with cobblestone streets and vintage brick-and-cast-iron warehouses that are now restaurants and bars.

There is a historic marker about Frenchman Pierre Laclede, one of the fur traders who founded St. Louis and the area's namesake.

How did he make it here?

And was it merely coincidence—after all was said and done—that St. Louis was founded on Valentine's Day over two hundred and fifty years ago? Was it a labor of love? Or did love arrive after his journey?

Legend or reality?
Risk versus reward.

I stop at a bar and take a seat on the patio. I order a glass of rosé and some toasted ravioli. My first glass turns into a glorious second, and suddenly, I feel more alive—or drunk—than I have in ages.

Without thinking, I pick up my cell and call Janice, my principal.

She actually sounds relieved I'm taking a bit more time off.

"Everything will be just fine," she assures me, which is completely the opposite of what she would normally say. "Take your time. We can Zoom until you're back. School doesn't officially start until after Labor Day, so you'll be rested by then. Have fun. Be safe."

She sounds as if she wanted to say *sane* rather than *rested* but stopped herself just in time.

And she said *safe*. For once, I don't want to be safe.

I hang up and call Q.

"Girls' weekend!" I yell.

"Really?" she asks. "You're in?"

"Let's do it. Let's have fun. Let's make it my do-over at forty." I take a sip of my wine. "Let's make it a legendary getaway!"

"Are you drinking?" Q asks. "It's…" I can tell she's pausing to check the time "…earlier than normal to well into a bottle of wine."

I ignore her comment and say, "I vow to do every touristy thing I can do. I'll eat fudge in the middle of the street. I'll have ice cream for breakfast and wine for lunch."

"You're already in training for that," Q remarks.

"I'll wear a bikini and walk the beach without shame," I continue. "No cover-up."

"Now I know you're drunk and just talking crazy," she says.

"I will do whatever I want, whenever I want!" I say. "I am a *flâneur!*"

"I don't know what that is, but I'm hoping it's not a French hooker."

"To new adventures!" I say.

"To new adventures!" Q says with a big laugh.

"And to another glass of wine!" I yell into the St. Louis summer sky. *"Flâneur!"*

"Can you hand your cell to your waitress, please?" Q says. "I just want to have a little chat with her before it's too late."

MARY

July

I glance at the clock on the wall and shake my head as Taffy enters the general store.

Six thirty.

In the morning, mind you.

"So much for a quiet morning," I say with a wink. "And who could possibly think of eating a liverwurst sandwich while they're still drinking coffee?"

"I live for liverwurst," Taffy says, taking the cap off his thermos and taking a swig of coffee. "Got it yesterday for lunch after we talked. Having it on Tuesday. Will have it tomorrow and the next day. Eaten it every day for years. I'm a growing boy. Keeps me strong." He makes a muscle with his arm. "Speaking of years, this is a big one. Have you forgotten?"

"Is this a trick question?" I ask. "I feel like I'm at Doc Ferguson's for my annual memory test. Want me to draw a clock next?"

"It's not a trick question," Taffy says.

"I know darn well what year it is, but I don't want to acknowledge it," I say. "I stopped going to Doc Ferguson at seventy-five, and I stopped thinking about this sixty-fifth anniversary years ago."

"You are one stubborn lady," he says.

I run my knife through a jar of mayo and point it at Taffy. "And don't you forget it."

"And don't you forget the onion," Taffy says. "Lots of it."

"No wonder you're still single," I say.

I chuckle. This is our love language. This has always been our love language. Teasing and tough love with a big dollop of honesty.

And mayo.

I grab the onion and crinkle my nose. I'm still drinking coffee and still thinking of the blueberry streusel muffin I had for breakfast, not...*this*.

You either love or hate liverwurst. It's sort of like with politicians these days: there's no in-between.

I hate it, my mom hated it, but my grandma—like many of the locals and old-timers around these parts—loved it.

I continue making Taffy's sandwich the way my grandma loved it and always made it, the way the Very Cherry General Store has always served it.

We use pumpernickel, a smear of butter on the bread, followed by mustard, mayonnaise, a dump truck of pickled onion, slices of liverwurst, a crank or two of pepper and some fresh lettuce straight from our garden in the back of the store. I slice it on a diagonal, wrap it in cellophane, and place it in a paper bag along with our homemade bread-and-butter pickles and a bag of salt-and-vinegar chips.

"You're drooling," I say to Taffy when I hand him my sandwich.

He sniffs the air like a blue tick hound.

"Yes, I'm making Michigan Treasure Cookies," I say. "I'll throw in a couple of those for you, too."

I head into the cramped, crammed kitchen—consisting of a gas stove and oven, refrigerator and freezer, a butcher's block, sink, dishwasher and a wall of cabinets shoved into every usable square inch of space—and pull open the oven door.

My grandma taught me how to make these cookies when I was a girl, long before they became the official state cookie of Michigan. Essentially, they're a cookie version of my favorite coffee: a cherry chocolate-chunk cookie with cocoa, loads of sugar—brown and granulated—plus tons of butter.

As Ina Garten might say, "How bad could that be?"

Many bakers use dried cherries, but I always use the real deal.

Cherry Mary and the Very Cherry General Store can never skimp on taste or memories.

I slip on an oven mitt—appropriately a Michigan mitten since the state is shaped like one—and pull the cookies from the oven. As they cool, I slide the next batch into the oven and set the timer. I wrap two cookies in waxed paper and head back to Taffy. I slide them into the bag with the rest of his lunch.

"Oh," he begins so innocently, "Virgie wanted me to ask if you were going to participate in this year's Cherry Festival?"

"You came here on a mission this morning, didn't you?" I ask. "Did she pay you?"

Taffy looks at me. "It's just that it's the hundred-and-twenty-fifth anniversary, you know, and as you said, the sixty-fifth anniversary of your cherry championship, and—"

"I know, I know, you don't need to tell me," I say, cutting him off. "I knew that's what you've been hinting at the last ten minutes." I wave a finger at him. "They trot me out every decade or so like a prized pig and then put me back in the barn until they want some media publicity." I stop and ring up Taffy. As I'm totaling, I glance up. "Why didn't Virgie just ask me herself?"

Taffy shakes his head. "You'd have to ask her. But you already know the answer to that. You're scared of her, and she's scared of you. A lot of water under that friendship bridge."

My mind somersaults back to the night we all went to Devil's Elbow. Virgie ran away. I didn't. She's still running, my former best friend, all manufactured confidence on the surface, a frightened turncoat who married well and forgot her history because she's too scared to face her past or present.

My eyes flick to the notice board I have hanging by the post office boxes. A poster of Virgie's multimillion-dollar-home listings stares me right in the eye.

You grew up just like I did, I think. *Poor but proud. You just let money change you. Money made you turn your back on me and run.*

I look at a home for sale not too far from Devil's Elbow. I wonder if Virgie ever returned to look into the horizon at her future? I wonder if she ever heard drums or tried to listen to her soul. I wonder if she's capable of hearing anything but the soft, cushioned sound of money anymore.

The cash register rings.

"Tell Virgie I need to think about it, okay?" I say. "And tell her she knows where to find me."

"After today, I'm staying out of this," Taffy says, handing me a ten and raising his hands in the air as if he's being robbed. "She did say you'd get your own car this year at the head of the parade. You won't have to ride in the same convertible with the Cherry Queen." He stops. "Or a pig."

I laugh.

"Ah, memories," I say. "Tell her it sounds like a bribe. And that I know she's lying."

I hand Taffy his bag.

"See ya later, Mary," he says, the door jingling as he exits.

The sound of the bell catapults me back to the fiftieth anniversary of my cherry championship in which I was placed next to Riley Filmore, the Cherry Queen whose family owns Filmore Farms, the largest pig farm in the surrounding four counties. Rumor has it that her daddy bribed local officials to crown Riley—who was a diva before that word was even *en vogue* and I knew what it meant—the Cherry Queen. I rode next to her on a ninety-degree day in the cramped back seat of a vintage convertible with Prince Oink, a bell around his neck, seated between us as a way for her daddy to advertise his business. A fire truck broke down at the head of the parade, which caused an hour delay. The heat and the delay caused Prince Oink to leave a bag of gold on the seat, which caused his queen to have a monumental meltdown and blame me for all the bad luck.

If there's one thing I cannot tolerate it is tantrums, especially thrown by girls or women who have been taught they can garner attention only by being stereotypes of what men and society expect. My mom and grandma taught me that women are the backbones of our families and the bedrock of this world. We do not—*we cannot*—collapse when things go wrong. We can only become stronger and fiercer in order to survive. We must create wonderful women—and children—ignited from our own flint and built from the clay of our souls.

My mind turns to my son, Jonah, and my grandson, Ollie.

And we must then let our children fly no matter how much it hurts when we only want to keep them in our nest.

Jonah, my baby.

Ollie, my grandbaby.

Maybe a mirage has clouded my vision of you, of what is real.

What *is* real?

Suddenly, I take a seat. Right in the spot where everything changed so long ago.

Summer 1963

The first time my husband Burt came at me, drunk, the night after our wedding, I remembered what my grandma told me.

"Don't do no good to be sweet. You can never talk any sense into a drunk. Just hit him in the head with a can of something. Green beans will do just fine. Or a jar of pickles or preserves. Not enough to kill him, just enough to knock him silly, stop him in his tracks and make him wake up believing he fell."

And so I did.

The next time my husband tried to hit me, after coming home

drunk from a bar, I locked him out until he passed out on the porch and then hightailed it to Virgie's with my baby.

But when Burt started coming at me when Jonah was cradled in my arms, I knew nothing would stop ever stop him.

Except me.

Oh, my mother and grandmother tried to stop him. They threatened him. They yelled at him. They yelled at me. They moved me out over and over.

And yet I always went back.

He loves me, I thought.

He'll change.

He's going to be a father.

But it was me who always returned, unable to make a change, unable to be strong enough.

Until he came for our son.

"This is it!" my grandma yelled at me that night after I went running to her and my mom, shaking, crying, a heaving Jonah still in my arms. My mom and grandma gave Jonah and me a once-over to make sure we weren't hurt. "You're a mother now, Mary. This will never end. We know it better than anyone."

"The three of us married drunks," my mom said. "We didn't have any choice. We were poor. We had to get married. But we thought we taught you better. You learned nothing."

"I loved him," I said. "I thought he loved me."

"He'll never love you more than the bottle," my mom said. "They love the bottle more than us, more than their kids, more than their own lives."

"And no one will do a dang thing about it," my grandma said. "It's a man's world. Men will always protect men. We have to play by their rules. Doesn't mean we can't rewrite them, though."

Grandma looked at me.

"Did you remember to bring them this time?"

I nodded.

"Good girl," she said. "You gotta be ready again, just like you were when you were fifteen. That's how you were able to become the cherry champ." I handed Jonah to my mom. She rocked him to calm his crying. My grandma grabbed my hand. "You're still a champion, Mary. No man can stop you. This will not defeat you. But you gotta stand up for yourself. You're a mother now. We need you to be strong, okay?"

I nodded again.

"This is how I got everything," Grandma said to herself.

She stood at the butcher block in the kitchen. I pulled the papers from the pocket in my jacket. My mom handed her a pen and tablet of paper.

"Let me practice first."

She looked at the papers beside her and then began to write in the tablet.

"This used to be a one-room schoolhouse before it was a post office," my grandma said as she wrote.

"I know."

"Well, you're going to hear it again, so you remember," she said.

My grandma began to tell me how she was the youngest of six girls. My great-grampa wanted a boy, so he made my great-grandma keep trying. "We will have a victory," he said. But when a Victor wasn't born, her mother said, "This is our truth," and Verity—my grandma—was born, much to her husband's disgust.

Same with my mom. Only girls. The family curse, the men said. "No boy to leave our fortunes to," my grampa used to say. "Our legacy."

"Our truth," my mom and grandma said.

"*Our* fortunes," my grandma said as if in a trance. "*Our* legacy."

Despite being the youngest, my grandma was always the leader, the strongest, and she essentially raised her sisters, while her mother kept her father from hurting anyone too badly. And when the teacher couldn't make it to school due to the snow or when the spring mud would shut down a road, my grandma stepped in and taught the class, keeping the kids—and her sisters—safe and warm another day.

That's where she learned how to mimic her teacher's handwriting as well as that of every other student and parent in class when she wanted to write a note home saying how well Nancy was doing in school or a fake note to the teacher stating Johnny would be out sick when he really wanted to go fishing.

That's how Grandma got the family cottage. That's how she got the Very Cherry General Store. That's how we got everything.

Since her family had no boys, her father wrote a will to leave the family cottage and store—which he had run into the ground—to his brother, who lived in a trailer and would have kicked the family out of their own home, lock, stock and barrel. But when my grandma's father came for her mother one night, my grandma picked up a can of beans to knock the beans out of her daddy and then did exactly what she's doing tonight.

She rewrote his will—in his own writing—while he was out cold.

Then she went to school, became a teacher, returned to that one-room schoolhouse and planned her future without anyone knowing.

When her father drank himself to death a few years later, his will was produced, leaving the cottage and the store to the girls in the family.

Forever.

My grandma worked with the state to bring in the post office—and some steady income—and slowly rebuilt and expanded the general store.

"Okay, I'm ready," my grandma said.

The Last Will and Testament of Burt D. Coombs

As she wrote, my grandma talked.

"This was always meant to be ours," she said. "I became post-mistress after your granddaddy died. I added the grocery store to bring in more business in the winter and made it a trading post, and your momma knew more and more people would come to vacation here, so she added the kitchen to make the cookies, sandwiches and potpies in the summer. You already added that orchard out back. Our men would've just drunk and gambled our legacy away."

I watched her write, copying word for word the document beside her in Burt's handwriting, except adding my name where it had never been before, ensuring Jonah would always remain with me. No contest.

"We need two witnesses," my grandma said, signing her name and handing the pen to my mom. "And now the judge."

Even the judge's signature looked the same as the real one.

My grandma studied the fingerprint.

I had taken some cherries from the colander in our sink, cut them in half, tossing the pits, and let the juice flow onto a cutting board. I'd placed Burt's thumb in the juice and created a perfect fingerprint next to the line for the judge's signature. In these parts, Judge Wilcox—a cherry farmer—used that as his legal mark.

"Now Jonah will always be safe when that son of a bitch dies."

Then she looked at me.

"How'd you get this fingerprint, Mary?"

In the distance, an ambulance wailed.

My grandma grabbed me by the shoulders.

"Mary," she said. "You didn't use a can of beans this time, did you?"

"No, ma'am."

"What did you do, Mary?" my mom asked.

"I spit two pits, as if a blizzard were living inside me and trying to escape. One into each eye." I reached out and touched Jonah's pink cheeks. "I think he's blind as a bat now."

"Dear Lord," my grandma said.

"No one saw me. He's passed out. I just ran."

"You ain't scared no more, are you, Mary?"

"No, ma'am."

A siren wailed again.

"He must have called the police, or someone must have seen something," my mom said in a hushed tone. "Hopefully, he won't remember a thing."

"Go on home now," she continued. "Hurry! Put that will right back where it was. Take Jonah, and act like you've been here working. You never saw him. Got it?"

I ran with my baby all the way home.

In the distance, over the sirens, I could hear the beat of a drum.

I keep my eyes shut for the longest time, the silence of the store buzzing in my head. I open my eyes and look around, an irony that is never lost on me. I stand, walk through the kitchen and toward the post-office side of the general store. I must stay busy.

Bins of mail greet me.

I begin to slide the mail into the old post office boxes.

An old post office box, I realize every morning, is a lot like a human brain: you forget how much useless information you stuff inside it.

Junk.

Lies.

Inherited trauma.

I shove junk mail and flyers into the boxes, but though I'm sure it's illegal, I always remove the letters I know are meant to scam and frighten older people into buying fake home or car warranties. I toss them into an empty cardboard box to shred later.

I chuckle when I pull out a magazine sealed in dark paper addressed to one of the local pastors. I don't know exactly what's inside—sort of like the soup they made over in Cross Village at a local diner—but I have a pretty good idea.

"Father," I whisper to myself.

You can learn a lot about a person by the mail they receive.

Bills marked *Overdue!* in bright red lettering addressed to some of the wealthiest resorters, or letters to recent widowers that have been doused in perfume.

The bell on the front door jingles, and I peek through the window of a post office box. I feel like a spy when I'm back here. I've caught people trying to steal. I've caught people lifting the lid right off a cake plate and inhale a half-dozen cookies.

I lean closer to the window and squint. I see purple.

All purple. Head to toe.

My heart leaps.

I release a muffled yelp into the box, my voice echoing around me as if I'm in a canyon.

I leap up and race through the kitchen, my feet nearly sliding out from underneath me on the wood floors.

The woman's back is turned, studying the coffee cakes.

I have to blink twice to make sure it's not Fata Morgana entering my store.

"Francine?"

She turns, and her face lights up.

We greet each other in the middle of the store with a big hug, rocking back and forth, until the bell jingles again and a customer enters.

"What are you doing here?" I ask. "Why didn't you call?"

"Well, I didn't want to bother you," she says. "I know how busy you are."

"There is never a bother between friends. You know that. I could have opened your cottage up for the summer, given it a good cleaning, stocked your fridge with groceries so you didn't have to worry about anything for a few days and just relax."

She nods. Her face is shadowed, and there are deep bags under her eyes.

Francine bursts into tears.

"My first summer here without Bill," she says, her voice a hoarse whisper.

"I know, I know," I say in a singsong voice, holding her, rocking her anew. "It's so hard. But remember, you were lucky to have the love of your life."

Francine holds me even closer.

I have not told Francine everything about my life. My mom and grandma said I should take it to the grave, just like my husband did. But it pains me not to share a secret I worry not only saved my life but cursed it as well.

The woman who came in behind Francine begins perusing the store, turning on occasion to give us a curious eye.

"I own the store," I call to the woman. "She was trying to steal. I punish people with kindness. Go ahead, take something."

Francine giggles, which turns into a big laugh. The woman grabs some bottles of water, a few sodas and ingredients for s'mores, and I check her out. Very quickly.

"When did you get in?" I ask, closing the till. "I didn't see any lights on next door last night. I always walk the beach at dusk."

Francine runs a hand through her hair.

I let my hair go gray long before that trend emerged. I have fine hair that falls just at my shoulders, with a blunt bang, pretty much the hairstyle I've worn since I was a girl. I have to put a little product and hairspray in it to keep my mane from looking as if I just stuck a fork into an electrical socket. Francine's hair is chestnut, a color that is a bit shocking for a woman our age. I know she loves the contrast with her purple outfits, but she's drawn and wan, and the color makes her look even more so. I can tell she's probably stopped going to a salon in the city and began coloring it herself.

Grief can do such monstrous things, without us ever noticing. I know, deep down, it has to me in regards to my son and grandson.

I grieve their absence.

"I stopped at the Camelback Inn," she says.

"That's just a half hour from here!" I say. "Why didn't you call me?"

Francine touches her hair again.

"I... I couldn't bring myself to stay there alone that late at night." She pauses again. "I didn't want to bother you."

Francine's hand shakes. I know I best lighten the situation with honesty, as I do with Taffy, as I do with all my friends.

"If you say *I didn't want to bother you* again, I will brain you." She smiles.

"Sorry. I'm just a bit off-kilter. But I had to come one last time."

My heart sinks.

"One last summer," she adds.

I look at her. Now I realize it's my hand that is shaking.

"Last summer?" I whisper.

"Stock market's down. Home prices are up. We didn't save as well as we should have," Francine says. "I have to plan for my future now. Where will I end up? I don't know how many more years I can make it up here on my own."

"I can always help you."

"I know," she says. "But I don't know how many more years you can make it on your own, either. It's time to plan a little. We're not spring chickens."

"Bock, bock," I say.

Francine doesn't laugh.

"Let's enjoy this summer, okay? One magical day at a time."

Francine nods.

"Speaking of magical days, I also came because I just couldn't miss your big anniversary," she says. "We have to celebrate you this summer. We may never live to see another woman win that contest. We may not be around for your seventy-fifth."

I don't tell her I have yet to decide if I'm participating.

"We have to celebrate you, too," I say.

"Us!" Francine adds.

"To us!"

We hug again.

"You know what this calls for, don't you?"

"Michigan Margaritas on the beach?" she asks.

"Michigan Margaritas on the beach," I nod.

"And do you know what that calls for?"

"Tequila!" Francine says. "Lots of tequila."

I laugh, hard.

"And lots of cherries," I say. "So let's get to picking."

Francine smiles.

I try hard not to think it, but the words fill my mind.

For the last time.

BECKY

August

There are certain rules to which the perfect girls' trip must adhere.

And—being the good elementary-school administrator I am—I printed them out, laminated them, sneaked over to Q's house near Tower Grove Park and stuck them under the windshield wiper of her SUV the night before our trip.

It's hard to break lifelong habits.

I have not been able to sleep for the last few days. Do you remember when you were a kid about to go on vacation—spring break to Florida, or a trip to Disney—and you couldn't sleep for weeks in anticipation? I haven't felt this way—all jittery inside, like I swallowed a gallon of butterflies—in ages.

Since my grandparents used to take me to northern Michigan.

Am I simply excited?

Am I nervous?

Or are both inextricably intertwined?

I have always loved summer. It's a big reason I went into teaching. Summers off. To explore. To relax. To be outside.

The problem was, however, that teachers and administrators don't really get summers off. That was all just a myth we were told. We spend those summer months planning a curriculum, outlining every day of a calendar year, studying the backgrounds of our new students, buying books and supplies, decorating our classrooms and school buildings. A few weeks isn't enough time to recover much less get everything accomplished. And, now, more schools are going all year long.

Moreover, I never allowed myself to experience summer like a kid does. Matt loved his rituals. Dinner at six. Bed at nine. Up at five. A vacation to him was a Cardinals game or two every summer, sitting on our microscopic back deck with a beer looking at the houses that surrounded us, a pizza night out on a Friday.

I love routine. But sometimes that can choke out spontaneity, imagination, excitement. It can choke out the light.

Summer reminds us that there is light, outside and within, and that we should reach for it in order to change ourselves and the world.

I give our students the same speech during assembly on the last day of school every single year. I can recite it in my head.

"Summer is a time for new adventures. Summer is a time to reach for the light you see outside every single day. Summer is the time we recharge. Summer is also the time we grow and change, the time that we rise to great heights just like the sun every single day. I urge you to harness that light, swallow that light, be that light."

And yet I never listened to a word I said.

A light clicks on in Q's house. I take a sip of the latte I got at City Coffee and glance at the clock in my car: 6:42 a.m.

I've been packed for two days, barely slept a wink last night—tossing and turning—and woke at four ready to go. I've been parked in Q's driveway for a half hour.

I see the curtain move in her bedroom window upstairs.

She's seen my texts.

A minute or so later, the front door opens. Q waves, shaking her head. I grab my coffee.

"Remind me never to make you mad," Q says. "And to get a restraining order."

She saunters toward her kitchen in her pajamas. "I need coffee first," she says.

"I got you one, but I drank it."

"You're pretty amped-up about this trip, aren't you?"

"A little," I say.

Q pours a mountain of coffee grounds into a filter and adds water.

"A little? You're like—to use a theatrical pun—a cat on a hot tin roof," she says. "Except the cat drank two quad-shot lattes, and the tin roof is covered in catnip."

I laugh.

"And a cat obviously slept in your hair last night," I say reaching out to touch her tangled mass of red curls.

"At least the cat slept," she says, opening the refrigerator to grab some creame

It's then I notice my list of rules attached to the refrigerator door.

I pull them free as Q grabs a mug and fills it with what coffee has managed to drip into the pot.

"I'm actually excited about something for once." I shake the rules at her and continue. "Let's make sure we have our ground rules set."

"That's not a list," Q says. "That's a scroll." She looks at me and takes a sip of coffee. "Perhaps even a decree."

"So then, be smart and listen to your road-trip queen."

I begin to read my rules.

Rule #1
Plan the Route

Rule #2
Great Playlist

Rule #3
Pack like a Pro

Rule #4
Pack the Snacks (or Stop for Them! Every Few Hours!)

Rule #5
Leave Room for Adventure (on the Drive & on the Trip!)

Rule #6
Say So Long to Your Cell (except for Selfies!)

Rule #7
No Boys

Rule #8
But LOTS of Wine

Rule #9
NO work talk

Rule #10
Secrecy Pact
(What Happens on Girls' Trip STAYS on Girls' Trip)

Last, but most important:

Rule #11
Say YES! To EVERYTHING!

When I finish, there is a long silence. Suddenly, Q nabs the list from my hands and scans it slowly.

"You forgot one, by the way," she says.

"I did not!"

"You did," Q says. "Hair dryer. Always pack your own hair dryer. When you travel as much as I do, you can never trust the terrible ones they have at hotels and rentals. They stink."

I pause, waiting for just the right moment, and then add, "Maybe it's the hair."

Q swats me on the rear with my list.

"Hair is life," she says, turning to pour another cup of coffee. "Now, let me take a quick shower since you arrived before the garbage collectors. And for that rather rude remark, you can move all your own luggage into my SUV."

I look at her.

"Get moving!" she says. "Now we're wasting time. We have a ten-hour drive, but with how much coffee you've already had, that will likely be a twelve-hour drive."

The trip north through the heart of Illinois is like running on a treadmill: flat, boring and repetitive. And yet, there is something beautiful about the cornfields stretching into infinity, crops swaying in the wind, red barns perched against a blue sky, farmhouses with wide front porches, white cotton-ball clouds bouncing over a portrait of America.

When I would take this same route to Michigan with my grandparents, we would make up stories about the people who lived in these houses and worked these farms. My grandma would start a story, ask me to continue, and then we would go back and forth for hours, creating intricate histories of people we would never know.

My grandma sparked my imagination. That spark ignited my desire to teach.

Many people have the misguided belief that teachers simply fall into the profession because they can't do anything else. It was started by George Bernard Shaw who wrote "Those who can, do; those who can't teach," a derogatory thorn that remains stuck in the side of every educator even over a hundred years later.

I wanted to teach to change the future.

But I can't even change my mine.

I grab the list from the front seat.

I can't even stop making lists.

"You really are a teacher at heart," Q says with a laugh.

"I am," I say.

"I'm a teacher at heart, too. Teaching a world of theater people—from technicians to actors—how to stage a play. Teaching is an art."

I nod.

"But," Q says, "what does one of those rules toward the end state?"

I glance down the list.

Number nine.

"No work talk."

"Exactly," she says, "so why don't you focus on..." she looks over for a second "...rule number two."

I click on XM Radio to the '90s music of our teen years, and "Macarena" begins to blast.

We both scream at the same time and begin to gyrate our hips in our seats, imitating the dance craze that swept the nation.

We roll down our windows, moving our hands in the warm, summer air. We pass a pickup filled with kids, and as we zip by them, we yell, "Hey, Macarena! Ay!"

I wake up with a start just in time to see that we're closing in on Traverse City.

"You really crashed after that Twizzlers high," Q says. "I've never seen anybody eat that much licorice in my life. You drool red."

I ignore her and enlarge the map on her dashboard screen.

"Take 72 toward Kalkaska," I say. "Then 131 North!"

Q looks at the map and then me. "Why? Getting off the main highway is going to add so much time to our drive."

I grab my list of rules off the floor and shake it at her. *"Number five. Leave room for adventure!* There's something I have to see," I say. "And do."

Q narrows her eyes, shakes her head and, silently, grudgingly, follows my request, turning the car east to head toward our mystery adventure.

We head north out of the tiny, old-fashioned town of Kalkaska, whose downtown square features a giant statue of a brook trout in honor of the National Trout Festival, and onto a rather quiet country road that seems to lead into the middle of, well, nowhere.

"Okay, driver's patience is wearing thin," Q says. "Where in the world are we going?"

"Final rule," I say, not answering her question. *"Say yes to everything."*

"Including leaving you out here?"

"Ha ha," I say.

I actually don't know where we're headed exactly, which I refuse to admit to Q, but I'll know when I see it. Q taps her fingers on the steering wheel, her sign of growing impatience.

And that's when I yell, "Stop! Pull over!"

Q slams on the brakes and pulls off to the side of the road. For a moment, she doesn't understand, and then I point.

"What is that?"

"The shoe tree," I say.

"The what?"

"Shoe tree," I say. "Get out."

We cross the road and before us stands a huge, old tree whose every branch and limb is covered in hundreds, if not thousands, of pairs of shoes: sneakers ranging from Adidas and Saucony to Reebok, Nike and Keds; flip-flops; high heels; men's dress shoes, sandals; even a few pair of waders. Some of the shoes are inscribed with messages in permanent marker, greetings, love poems, life accomplishments.

"It's creepy but kind of beautiful," Q says. "How did this start?"

"Lots of legends," I say. "One involves a killer and another is about a Depression-era boy who worked outside all winter and never had shoes."

"Not true."

Q and I yelp. We turn, and a girl in a cheerleading uniform has appeared behind us holding a pair of sneakers. Across the road, girls are spilling forth from a parked van. They race across the road, yelling as only teenage girls can.

"One of my friends goes to high school here," the cheerleader explains. "She said high-school seniors started this tradition decades ago as a way to say goodbye to school and leave a mark on the town. You're supposed to make a wish when you add the shoes to bring good luck."

She turns toward her friends. "We're all rising seniors and headed to our last cheerleading camp in Traverse City. We made the bus driver come here."

I turn toward Q. "See?"

"Why did you come here?" the girl asks me.

I smile at her. "To say goodbye to my school and leave a mark."

She laughs and then yells, "Ready? Okay!"

Six girls start to cheer. It is familiar, one I remember from high school.

The girls throw the shoes they are holding high into the air. All six pairs of sneakers—embellished with their names and dreams—catch on different limbs.

They let out a resounding whoop and race back to the van.

The girl stops before crossing the road. "Your turn," she says. "Good luck!"

"What did you wish for?" I call.

"That the rest of our lives is as wonderful as the first part of our lives," she says. "That we remain friends forever. That our lives are legendary."

And then she is gone.

"I take it you brought some shoes in that mountain of luggage you packed?" Q asks.

I nod, and she clicks the remote on her key chain, unlocking the car and opening the trunk. I cross back to the SUV, fish through the luggage and return carrying a grocery bag.

"How many shoes did you bring?" Q asks.

I set the bag down on the ground.

"Have you lost your mind?"

"Yes," I say. "I'm trying to find it again."

I hold up the first pair.

"What are those?"

"My dad's old slippers," I say. "I stole them." I reach into the bag. "Along with this."

"And what is that?"

"My mother's book of carpet samples."

Q cocks her head at me and gives me a questioning look.

I toss my dad's slippers into the air, and they catch on a limb. I do the same with my mom's book, which soars into the sky and then begins to fall quickly, flapping loudly like a drunk turkey. It bounces off a branch, and I think it's going to return to earth—fittingly, right on top of my head as payback—but, at the last moment, it wraps its arms around a leafy branch.

"What did you wish for?" Q asks.

"That my parents might be able to embrace even a sliver of change in their lives," I say. "And be happy for the changes I make in my own."

"That's a big wish," Q says.

"I know."

I pull the last items from the bag. One is a pair of black velvet tuxedo loafers I bought for Matt, and the other is a pair of pink

Manolo Blahnik lurum crystal cocktail mules that I splurged
two weeks' salary to buy on sale at Neiman Marcus.

"Those are beautiful," Q says. "Remember I planned that
surprise evening at the Fox Theatre to see Tony Bennett and a
dinner at the Ritz on the anniversary Matt and I met?" I ask her.
She nods. "When I told Matt to get dressed for a special night—
my treat—he asked how much I spent and how long it would
take to pay it off. He wasn't even excited to go out. He didn't
care that I'd gone to all this effort to surprise him. He didn't
realize I was telling him how much I cared for him." I look at
Q. "He didn't care. He never did. I have to care again…about
life, about love—" I stop, my voice warbling "—about me."

"That's why you wanted to come here," she says.

I nod.

She hugs me.

"Then, throw those shoes, girl!"

I lift my arm to toss Matt's loafers, and Q begins to chant,
changing the cheer the girls just chanted ever so slightly to fit
the moment.

> The B is for Becky and
> The T is for Thatcher
> The P is for perfection 'cause no one can match 'er!
> The M is for Matt and
> The D is for Dud
> so show the world
> You're the best and not St. Louis mud!

"That spells BTPMD," I say.

"Makes perfect sense," she says with a laugh.

I feel like I have superhuman strength—as well as a complete
and total lack of clarity—as I throw his pricey, never-worn shoes
into the branches. They snag at the top of the tree and dangle
in the wind.

I shut my eyes and lift my arm to toss my shoes, but as my arm rises, it meets resistance.

Q's hand is on my arm.

"Not those," she says. "They still have a story to tell."

I smile. "Thank you."

"And if you don't wear them, they'll fit me."

I pull out my cell and, in honor of rule number six, take a selfie, smiling, knowing I'm leaving a piece of my *soul* here for strangers to see.

And, at this moment, it feels good to bare a piece of myself to the world.

MARY

I planted a garden behind the general store the year after my father died. He never listened to my mom's ideas, like my husband never listened to me, and I guess I just wanted to see something grow with a bit of love, nourishment and encouragement. I added the cherry trees after Burt died, because I yearned to see something blossom again along with my son.

The garden not only helped heal my soul, it expanded the soul of the general store.

My husband was, as my grandma called him, a *sumbitch*. The scar on my forehead I keep hidden by my gray bangs is the gift of my youthful stupidity and belief that true love could cure all.

The women in my family all had a history of picking terrible men. It's ironic when people, like Virgie, tell you your whole life you've made bad decisions, but it's hard to make any good ones when you've never had any options.

You want to know the difference between a rich woman and a poor woman?

It's not money.

It's options.

And yet we survived for so long, ironically, largely because the men in our lives died so young.

I plunk a shovel into the ground.

I wasn't present for my husband's funeral. I had him cremated just to make sure any evidence was destroyed. I honestly don't believe I killed him, either. I just blindly helped him along a little bit.

I look out toward the bluff.

That's where they found him the night my grandma changed Burt's will. He'd stumbled out the door I'd left open, blind and drunk, and fell down the bluff and rolled all the way to the edge of the lake. They don't know if he died from the fall or drowned, but I'm glad he went out twice.

Once wasn't enough.

"Looked like he was being baptized," a policeman said.

Everyone thought he'd been jumped by someone that he owed money to, and there were enough of those out there.

I know this isn't the charming Norman Rockwell picture you'd expect when you wander into the Very Cherry General Store, but every story is carefully edited. Every legend becomes a legend for a reason.

I had nightmares about Burt for years, but as the years and horror passed, and my son became a good man who could wake each and every morning with a hug and not a cuss, I began to be thankful not only for my life but also that my grandma first taught me how to spit a cherry pit.

I set down the shovel, ready to pick some cherries, but instead pluck one from a tree and place it in my mouth.

Every story, like every person, has a hard pit at its center. You just have to learn to grow a layer of sweetness and softness around that stone.

I spit the pit, and it goes flying across the yard. I return to picking.

"So ladylike," Francine says with a laugh.

"I've never been the stereotypical woman."

"You don't say." I look up, and Francine gives me a wink. "I tell you what, though, you still got the gift. You ever measure your distance anymore?"

"No," I say, plucking another cherry from the tree. "Too long in the tooth."

"You still have your teeth?" Francine asks. "Lucky."

I laugh. It's the easy laugh that one has with friends.

Francine begins to help me pick, and I can't help but compare her—and all women—to a cherry tree.

Beautiful, pink, often weeping as a girl that slowly grows into a strong, fierce bearer of beautiful fruit before its limbs begin to age and bend. Perhaps that is too stereotypical, but we are mirrored in Mother Nature, and we'd be foolish not to take clues from ourselves in the earth.

Like these cherry trees, I have surrounded myself with women my entire life, and we have created a beautiful orchard.

My garden, like me, is not particularly fancy, nor is my tiny orchard like the rolling ones surrounded by quaint fencing. I have remained faithful to my container garden comprised of rows of Jack Daniel's whiskey barrels, surrounded by boxwood and a small fence to keep the deer at bay. I grow the Michigan essentials: lettuce, tomatoes, spring onions, herbs, asparagus, rhubarb, green beans and strawberries, all of which go into my desserts, sandwiches, soups and potpies. There is a low-lying, wet area beyond the cherry trees that sits close to a ravine that runs toward the lake. I have blueberry bushes there.

It's enough. It's my history. My legacy.

I pick another Montmorency cherry, this time placing it in my basket.

Northern Michigan's legacy is the Montmorency tart cherry, which are the small, bright red cherries, the variety you usually find in your grocery store. They are also the most popular U-Pick cherries.

Any Michigan cherry head knows the history of the stone

fruit around here, and if you're a reigning cherry champion like me, you have to know more than most.

Modern day cherry production began nearly two centuries ago in the mid-1800s by Peter Dougherty, a Presbyterian missionary living in northern Michigan. Though my grandma never knew him, she called him Pastor Pete, as she believed – through his cherries – he brought a piece of heaven to our haven. Pastor Pete planted cherry trees all over Old Mission Peninsula, and – though many made fun of him for his efforts – they flourished, which spurred locals to do the same. Turns out northern Michigan was the perfect climate for growing cherries as Lake Michigan served as both heater in the winter and air conditioner in the summer, tempering Arctic winds in and cooling the orchards in summer. By the turn of the century, the tart cherry industry had taken off in Michigan. Today, according to statistics, the U. S. cherry industry produces more than 650 million pounds of tart and sweet cherries each year with the majority of the cherry production right here in Michigan, which grows about 75 percent of the tart cherry crop.

Thanks to the newfangled mechanical tree shakers, hand-picking cherries has been revolutionized and now takes a mere seven seconds per tree. However, since the shaking is so intense, it shortens a tree's life by seven years.

Ah, the irony.

I'm still old-school with my trees, and I go cherry by cherry, limb by limb, in my garden.

I come to the end of my orchard and run my old hand over the trunk of one of my oldest cherry trees. Most cherry trees only survive some twenty to twenty-five years, and yet, ironically, their health benefits are legendary. My mother and grandmother espoused their good qualities long before medical science and the popularity of tart cherry juice did.

Tart cherries are like the perfect fruit multivitamin, as they contain nearly ten times more vitamin A than blueberries and loads of fiber. Studies show they also contain powerful anti-oxidants that help with anti-inflammation, heart health, cholesterol, a decreased risk for hardened arteries, pain relief and muscle recovery.

Plus, they taste like heaven, perfect for pies and preserves.

And my Michigan margaritas.

"Working up a thirst?" I call to Francine.

"Yep!"

"I'll ask Linda Lou to stay after lunch," I say. I cock my good ear toward the general store and can hear the bustle begin. "I'll get through the rush and then bring you some food and help you get settled."

"When do we drink?"

"Beach at six thirty," I say. "Sound good?"

"I'll be in bed by seven, then," Francine says.

I laugh and look over at her.

"It's good to be home," she says.

Her voice carries toward the lake, a sound as comforting as the breeze off the water.

The sky is clear over the water, and there is a distinct line on the horizon. No mirage today.

My lake may be bright today, but I feel as if my future is as murky as Francine's.

We are the last legacies of a dying era still standing.

Will anyone take our places?

I turn to the store again. What could take the place of this?

"Ready to head in?" I ask.

Francine gathers her basket, and we walk toward the back door. As we head up the steps, my cell rings.

Incoming Call Jonah

"It's my son," I say.

"Tell him *hello* for me," Francine says. "I'll see you later. And I'm taking these cherries. I worked hard for them."

She heads inside, and I answer.

"Is everything okay?"

Jonah laughs.

"Mom, you say that every time."

"It's what a mom says."

"You're the not the typical mom, though."

I think he means this as a compliment, but for some reason, it stings a bit like the sun on my shoulders today.

"How have you been?" I ask.

"Busy," he says.

"You say that every time, too," I reply.

"It's the truth, and I know you're the same running the store. Listen, I know you were hoping we might make it up this summer, but it's just not going to work out. The company bought a strip of condos a block off Lakeshore Drive that we're turning into an urban-living lab."

"Urban-living lab?"

"It's a mixed-use development in conjunction with Chicago universities," Jonah explains. "It's part residential, part retail, with academic centers and entrepreneur space. It has something for everyone and will appeal to everyone from eighteen to eighty. Everything at their disposal, from a grocery store and restaurants to gyms and continuing education along with beautiful, state-of-the-art condominiums."

"Wow," I say. "That sounds incredible." My voice is a bit hollow.

"We're trying to keep people from moving out of the city," Jonah says.

"To places like this?" I ask.

"Mom."

"Sorry."

"And I also wanted to tell you that Virgie called me."

My pulse immediately escalates.

"Why?"

"You know why," he says. "She wanted me to influence you

to be part of the hundred-and-twenty-fifth anniversary. She also hoped I might be coming in order to sway you."

"But you're not."

"I can't, Mom. But Ollie is. I told him to take a couple of weeks off and come see you."

"Yeah!"

"He's been a bit off lately," Jonah adds, a big pronouncement that he makes sound like a casual aside.

"Off?"

"Just removed from work, his friends, me and his mom," Jonah says. "I think some time in Good Hart will do him good, pardon the pun, just like it did when he was a boy."

My heart lifts.

"I'll miss you so much, but I can't wait to see my grandson."

"He's planning to arrive in a few days. He wants it to be a surprise, so act surprised. He's really looking forward to it. You know how much he loves it there."

"Oh, this made my whole summer," I say. "Francine just came back today, too."

I actually jump up and down on back stoop, the cherries bouncing in the basket still in my hand.

"Well, I'm glad," Jonah says. "I want your last summers there to be as memorable as possible."

Silence.

"That didn't come out the way I wanted. You know that. I'm sorry."

"It's the truth," I say. "And I always taught you to be honest, didn't I?"

"You will never die, Mom," he says. "We all need you. Sorry. I'm distracted. Forgive me."

"Forgiven," I say. "I have to get in and help Linda Lou with the lunch rush. And then Michigan Margaritas with Francine."

"You still act like a girl, Mom."

"What good does it do to act and feel old?" I ask. "Old rolls are only good for Thanksgiving leftover sandwiches."

My serious son actually laughs. I hear his phone beep.

"I have to take this, Mom. I love you."

"I love you, too," I say.

I hang up and release a hearty *Woo-hoo!* into the air.

Linda Lou's head pops into the screened door.

"Is everything okay?" she asks.

"Ollie is coming to visit!"

"Oh, how wonderful! I can just tell it's going to be a memorable summer." The bell on the front door jingles over and over again. "And a busy one. I need your help."

"Coming," I say.

Linda Lou races back through the kitchen.

I put a cherry in my mouth, swirl it around and then puff my lips and blow. I watch the pit arc into the air and fly forever, landing at the base one of my cherry trees.

"The old gal's still got it," I say to myself.

At least for one more summer.

PART TWO

"If life is a bowl of cherries, what am I doing in the pits?"

—Erma Bombeck

BECKY

August

A soft breeze—not too warm and not too cool—that smells like summer and sand waft across my body. I pull the patchwork quilt over my body and wiggle my toes underneath it. The vintage, wrought iron farm bed on which I'm sleeping is set against a wall of logs and white chinking. The logs are old and worn, pulled from the woods that surround this cabin, not the prefabricated logs so popular today. A pine dresser painted white—its top découpaged with old Michigan postcards, shiny with marine enamel—is layered in nostalgia: an old minnow bucket turned into a lamp; a wooden jewelry box whose lid is set with beach glass; a duck decoy; a piece of driftwood. The walls are covered in watercolors of the beach, a framed needlepoint, paint-by-numbers of sunsets, dogs and fishermen, and a barnwood sign, warped and cracked, that reads in bright red *Cherries on Sale for a PITtance!*

I sit up in bed and catch myself smiling in the mirror atop the dresser on the opposite wall. I wave at myself, feeling just as I had as a girl when I was on vacation with my grandparents: relaxed, happy, free.

Who is that woman?

Where is that girl?

Are you in there?

I am still youthful-looking, thankful to be naturally and not store-bought blonde and happy for those high cheekbones my mom and grandma gifted me that give my face and skin the illusion its vaulting toward the sky although its foundation is slowly collapsing. But it's my eyes that are different: they are not as bright or as wide-eyed. The lids are sleepier.

I wonder if that's simply age, or if I've let a world of worry and a continent of complacency dominate my life for far too long.

I roll toward the large window in the center of the log wall that faces Lake Michigan. The long arms of pine trees reach for the water, making my blue view of the lake more of a vignette softened by needles of green. My heart leaps just as it did when I was young.

There is something about Lake Michigan that gets in your blood, sticks in your veins, lives in your memory bank. Everywhere you turn in Michigan there is a gift shop selling T-shirts and hoodies that say *Lake Michigan: Unsalted & Shark-Free.*

It's an amusing turn of phrase to be sure, but they're really missing the point. It's the grandeur of the lake, which mimics an ocean. It's the color of the water—especially up north—that is as shockingly blue as the Caribbean, and the clarity of the lake that is so, so transparent that even from this distance I can easily spot massive stones in a rainbow of colors sprinkled along the striated, sandy bottom.

Moreover, much of Michigan's coastline remains unspoiled and undeveloped, handmade just as God intended, with no huge developments to spoil the beauty. The feeling you have every time you come to Michigan in the summer is akin to being the first person in the world to discover it, and all its fun and majesty is there for you and you alone to enjoy.

I lift my head. The lake sighs, and I watch the sky brighten from a deep blue to a bright blue, as if every light in heaven is being turned on for the day. The waves sparkle.

FAMOUS IN A SMALL TOWN

Q did the majority of the driving, despite my pleading to let me take another turn. But her career has made her a complete and total control freak over every aspect of her life, including driving. And if you've ever driven with a back-seat driver like Q, you know what I mean. I still feel as if I need to go to therapy over the two hours I spent behind the wheel. Instead of relaxing, sleeping or reading, Q yelled the same lines at me over and over.

Pass him! Now!

Faster, Grandma! You can drive ten miles over the speed limit without getting a ticket!

Honk at that guy! You can't just let him drive in the left lane forever!

Stop using your blinker! You're not in high school!

I finally pulled over at a roadside stop, channeling my inner Mario Andretti to cross a lane of traffic going seventy-five without using my blinker.

Q, unfazed, merely unfastened her seat belt and said, "Now you stop, after finally learning how to drive?"

I read a novel in quiet for the next hour, mainlining a rather delicious combination of hot fries and Twizzlers. I also drank a gallon of water and a large diet soda just to passively aggressively infuriate Q and make her pull over every half hour.

Such are the dynamics of a long road trip with a lifelong friend.

I hear a buzz, which at first I think is a mosquito that has managed to slip through a screen, but then I recognize it as the vibration of my cell.

Rules number six and nine instantly pop into my head.

Say so long to my cell, save for selfies, and no work.

But what if it's an emergency with my mom or dad?

I reluctantly reach for my cell and my glasses and immediately groan.

It's my mom, and it's definitely not an emergency.

Where are my carpet samples?

One minute later:

You know I need them. How will I ever make a decision?

And then:

And where are your father's favorite slippers? Those brown cor-
duroy ones that he can just slip on with his tube socks? He loves
those. Did you take them?

Finally:

Is this some kind of summer prank?

Perhaps the biggest mistakes of my life were getting my
mother a cell phone and teaching her the basics: how to check
the weather, how to track my location so she doesn't worry
about me and how to text.

I think of walking over to the window and throwing my cell
into the lake, but I don't think my weak shoulder would allow
me to toss it that far. My cell buzzes again.

"You are going to drive me crazy, Mom!" I say to myself.

It's not a text from my mom.

Where did you go? My attorney has been trying to serve you papers. I stopped by your parents' house last night.

I feel like I have a cartoon head, where my eyes explode from
my head and roll around the room, and I swear I can feel steam
spout from my ears and my heart push out of my chest.

As you know, I contributed to many of the luxuries in our house.

Our house?

The eighty-inch television; the new refrigerator that makes cocktail ice; the new dining-room set; the outdoor furniture. I also encouraged you to put more of your money into a retirement account with my firm, and I feel like I'm entitled to a return on my overall investment in you.

What?

I wanted to settle amicably, but the way you've cut me out of your life without so much as a word does not seem amicable at all. Let me know where you are so my attorney can get the papers to you. Just call me, Becky. You're not the girl I used to know.

I look up at my reflection in the mirror.

No, I am not the girl you used to know.

I watch my mouth open in slow motion, and a scream so loud, so mortifying, blasts through the air, sending birds flying from the trees.

I hear a thump and a creak. Footsteps close in on my room.

"Becky? Are you okay?" Q opens the door. Her face is panicked.

"What's going on?" she asks, rushing to my bedside.

The wind catches the door, and it slams shut angrily, as if it's mimicking my emotions. The barnwood sign goes askew.

"There may be no sharks in Lake Michigan," I say to Q, "but that's only because they've crawled onto shore and relocated to St. Louis."

MARY

I heard a joke from a late-night comic a while back, in the midst of winter when a snowstorm was raging, my lights were blinking, and I was carrying firewood from my garage while praying my ancient generator still worked. He said the only food that people seemed to purchase during the pandemic were wine, cheese and chocolate.

"Went to the bread aisle. Stocked," the host said. "Milk. Stocked. Wine? Looked like a pack of college-age wolves had been through it."

I remember yelling at the flickering TV, "Welcome to Michigan!"

That's actually been my longtime joke about summers in Michigan: locals and resorters subsist on three main food groups, including good wine, cheese and chocolate.

I would, of course, throw in fresh fruit and fish as well. There is no summer in Michigan without a stop at a farmer's market or U-Pick for a basket of blueberries, peaches or cherries, or a daily catch from the lake and our famed smoked whitefish dip. And what do we buy at the grocery store? Not cereal. Raclette.

But wine, cheese and chocolate can extend from brunch to dinner in these parts.

That's because we do them all so well.

Michigan now boasts some of the world's (yes, *world's*) best wineries, and breathtaking vineyards dot the rolling hillsides and bluffs overlooking the lake and beautiful bays. The weather is ideal for growing grapes—just as it is for growing cherries—and people from around the world flock here for our beauty and bounty.

Our northern Michigan styled aged Raclette cheese is a pure, pure Michigan treat. Raclette is a traditional herdsman's cheese, handmade here with local milk. It's a silky smooth cheese and comes from the French word meaning *to scrape*.

You will not attend a northern Michigan happy hour or dinner party where our local Raclette and wine isn't served.

"That'll be seventy-eight sixty-three."

I stare at the clerk at Sunset Wines where I buy these summer staples.

"For two bottles of wine that are on sale and a half pound of Raclette?" I ask.

"Inflation," the clerk says and shrugs.

I've been running my shop for so long that I know the ins and outs of the economy's impact on pricing. I've lived through wars, gas shortages, tax hikes and tax cuts and now a pandemic. I know how much I need to mark up products so that I can earn a decent living but customers don't feel ripped off. It's what I call *ethical business* which is much more in line with customers' current conscious consumerism. They are deliberately making purchasing decisions that they believe have a positive social, economic and environmental impact, and I am making business decisions that I believe are fair to them.

But I also know about price gouging, and supply and demand. Resorters will pay any price for the things they love, and they refuse to drive too far to get their summer staples. I rarely come to the so-called big city of Charlevoix in summer due to the traffic. The short drive took over an hour today.

Yes, we locals pay the price.

Literally.

"Ouch," I say to the clerk, handing over my card.

"The wine will help," she says with a smile.

I walk out feeling a little lighter in the wallet, put my goodies into the cooler I always keep in the back of my sturdy Subaru and walk to Charlevoix's main street to shop.

Charlevoix the Beautiful, as locals say, is a charming waterfront community with great shops surrounded by four bodies of water, Lake Michigan, Lake Charlevoix, Round Lake, and Pine River, with boats and blue as far as the eye can see.

I glance up and smile when I see red.

Cherry Republic!

A rustic, turn-of-the-century village—like one you might find at Silver Dollar City in Branson, Missouri —springs to life before my eyes.

Cherry Republic is a store and gift shop. No, that's not even close to being accurate. Cherry Republic is the motherland of cherries. It's the Cherry Capital for cherry products, cherry chocolates and my beloved cherry coffee. And it's all set in a magical land of log cabins and cedar-sided cottages. Cherry Republic hasn't been around as long as the Very Cherry General Store, but it has been around since the '80s and grown like crazy.

Crooked pathways meander under cherry trees and cheery perennial gardens. One path leads to the Winery, where Cherry Republic offers complimentary tastings of "Wine for the Tall and Pop for the Small," and another leads to a restaurant called the Cherry Public House that serves freshly baked pies, homemade cherry ice cream, cherry desserts and craft beer.

But in the center of this magical cherry village is the Great Hall.

An old-fashioned sign in bright red—much like the one that adorns my general store—declares

GREAT HALL OF THE REPUBLIC
This hall is dedicated to the farmers and all the good food they grow.
Without them, there would not be a Cherry Republic, and we all
would be out in the woods right now,
scavenging for grubs and worms to eat

I laugh, as I do every time, when I read the sign.

I open the doors to the breathtaking Great Hall and walk inside. Soaring timber-frame beams evoke the spirit of a century-old cathedral, albeit one that is stocked to the stained glass windows with hundreds and hundreds of cherry products, all free to sample until your heart's content and your belly's bloated.

Visitors meander wide-eyed through the store, walking from display to display, filling their baskets with chocolate-covered cherries, cherry turtles, imperial malted-milk balls, cherry nut mix, sour cherry patches and licorice bites. Then they walk to the jams and jellies, spooning them onto crackers.

They all look like kids again on summer vacation, tongues red, mouths covered in chocolate.

Such a blessing to be reminded of that, no matter our age.

"Mary!"

I jump at the sound of my name. I look over, and Gary, one of the managers, is waving a bag of milk chocolate–covered cherries at me.

"Am I that predictable?" I ask, walking over.

"Is that a bad thing?" he asks. "Give me a hug."

He opens his arms.

"How have you been?" he continues. "How's business?"

"Busy and busy," I say. "You?"

"They say the town and whole area is one hundred–percent booked through October this year," Gary says. "It's crazy."

"People want to be back out again," I say. "They want this. They need summer." I smile. "And I need chocolate. And coffee!"

"I'll be waiting," he says. "You meander, sample and buy."

"Is it okay to eat chocolate cherries before I have cherry margaritas?" I ask.

"Perfectly fine in northern Michigan," Gary says with a laugh and a nudge of his glasses back up his nose. "And you're Cherry Mary! Aren't you made of them?"

He seems to search the top of my head.

"Looking for a stem," he adds with a wink.

I laugh, shoo him off and turn to head toward the chocolate-covered cherry coffee beans. I have only taken two steps when I hear again "Mary."

I look up. Virgie Daniels is standing before me.

"Virgie," I say with no intonation.

Virgie is dressed to the nines. "What are you doing here?" she asks.

"Francine just got into town. I wanted to bring her all her favorites to kick off summer."

"Is she going to sell?" Virgie asks.

"Spoken like a good friend and genuinely caring person," I say, my voice dripping in sarcasm.

"I'm a businesswoman," she says with a sniff. "So are you."

I don't even recognize my former friend anymore. I haven't in a long time.

Virgie is truly a vision among the casually dressed vacationers that fill Charlevoix and flock to Cherry Republic. Most are in shorts, T-shirts and flip-flops. Virgie looks as though she is heading to the Oscars in a body-hugging navy blue sleeveless dress flocked with gold buttons embellished with sailboats on them. Her neck, wrists and fingers are glimmering in diamonds. But Virgie's statement fashion piece is her wig: Reba red, tucked and flipped with waves as soft as the ones you'd find on Lake Michigan on a quiet day. Virgie looks as if she just emerged from a surprise makeover on the *Today* show.

"Love your hair," I say.

I know it's a childish low blow, but I can't help myself.

"Thank you."

Virgie has, I would venture to guess, hundreds of wigs in all styles, lengths and colors. She's northern Michigan's Dolly Parton.

Without the sweetness.

"What are you doing here?" I ask.

"Gifts for clients," she says. "People love kitsch. How's the store?"

She returns my serve with a winner down the line.

"Insanely busy," I say. "My mom and grandma would hardly believe it."

"I miss them," Virgie says. "They built that place."

"Yes," I say, knowing she's trying to push my sailboat-free buttons. "I know how much you miss—oh, what did you used to call them?—oh, yes, *those widows running a failing business.*"

Virgie crosses her arms.

I continue. "I've heard from my family and the entire town that you've been wanting to talk to me," I say. "Why didn't you just call me or drop by the store?"

"I've been so busy," she says. "As you know, I'm one of the area's top agents now *and* chairwoman of the hundred-and-twenty-fifth anniversary of the Cherry Festival. It's hard work making our little area so famous." Virgie pauses, and her eyes soften, at least as much as they can after all the surgery. She drops her voice. "Look, Mary, I knew you'd say *no.* You haven't done a parade or festival in a decade. It's the quasquicentennial of not only the Cherry Royale Parade but also the Cherry Championship. And the Porch Parade has expanded exponentially, too. I want it to be the best ever, my legacy, one that people will be talking about in a hundred years."

"And I'll be the honey that draws the bees?"

"You're the only woman to have ever won the championship. The press is fascinated by that. People are intrigued. Don't do it for me. Do it for all the little girls in the world who believe in that dream on the horizon."

I smile. "You're good." And then I look Virgie right in her mascaraed eyes. "But why should I help you? You didn't you help me when you had the chance."

July 1962

It's amazing what you think to grab when you're running for your life.

An infant.

A blanket.

A flashlight.

The light bounces along the road as I run. A storm is approaching over the lake. On the horizon, I can see—between the openings in the trees—rain falling in heaving gasps in sync with my own.

This is no mirage.

I stumble over a branch that has fallen in the wind, and I can feel my back lurch, hitch and instantly twinge, but I do not go down.

I will not go down.

I ran out of my house wearing slippers, shorts, a flannel work shirt. I have no purse, therefore I have no money, no ID.

Jonah screams.

I wrap him more tightly in the blanket and lean in to whisper to him, so he may hear my voice over the howling wind, remember me as calm and not by the screams I released moments ago.

"Sshh," I say. "It's okay, Jonah. It's okay."

I am a stupid woman. So strong, so smart, so fierce and yet so blissfully ignorant and confident in love conquering all that I allowed myself to be swallowed whole by a whale, allowed myself—unlike my baby's namesake—to remain captured now for three years rather than three days and nights.

A chill slides down my back, and I lift my flashlight into the sky.

The Blue Hour.

The green limbs that cover the road shake in the approaching storm like witches' arms bending down to gather me and Jonah up for dinner. The Tunnel of Trees is a cavern of wind. It is both beautiful and haunting, home and trap, safety and escape hatch.

I feel faint. And then I remember a prayer from Jonah in the Bible, one my grandmother cross-stitched for me that sits above my baby's now-empty crib.

When my soul fainted within me I remembered the Lord: and my prayer came in unto thee.

My entire being may have fainted, but now I am fully awake.

But for how much longer will I fall for Burt's *I'm sorry*s and *I love you*s?

Until I am hurt, or until he hurts his son.

I know I should run to my mother's or my grandmother's, but I am ashamed. Ashamed to have followed their pattern. Love and shame can make you do things you'll regret for the rest of your life.

I turn at a stand of pines and a white fence with a gate spanning the gravel driveway. The gate is adorned with a lavender wreath. I manage to unhinge the gate—shaking, Jonah in my arms—and throw it open. I follow the bouncing light down the long drive until I come upon a beautiful farmhouse with a stone chimney and wide, sweeping porch painted shiny white.

I knock.

Footsteps.

The door opens light spills upon me.

"Mary? Are you okay? Is Jonah okay? Did he hurt you?"

I burst into tears, a heaving mess in this perfect foyer.

"I ran."

"Oh, honey. Come in. Hurry, now."

Virgie ushers me to an oversize chair in the living room next to the fireplace, wraps me in a blanket and checks on Jonah.

"Don't move," she says.

I can hear her rustling in the kitchen.

Virgie's view of Lake Michigan is similar to my mom and grandma's, the cottage I once lived in...that I ran from so I could run to love, run from safety, run from home.

And then run again.

But while our view of the lake has always been filtered by the trees that grew on the bluff and whose limbs draped over our windows and sprung in front of our sight lines, Virgie's husband has the money to remove such nuisances so that view is unobstructed.

Lightning flashes on the horizon.

I can't help myself. I lean forward in the chair, cradling Jonah, and gaze into the distance.

Where are you? Give me a sign.

"No one is coming to save you, Mary."

I jerk upright.

"Except for yourself."

I stare at Virgie.

Over the rumble of thunder, I can hear a pot rattle on the stove, a tea kettle softly whistle.

"I'm warming up some milk for Jonah and making some herbal tea for you," she says.

"I'm leaving him," I say. "For good."

"Good. I tried to warn you. The women in your family have always picked the wrong men." Virgie shakes her head. "You've all believed in this myth that love conquers all, and look at where it got all of you. Alone. Three women—two widows—trying to keep that store alive in a male-dominated world. One day you'll all be crazy widows in a post office that makes sandwiches, cookies and potpies. How is that a business, Mary? But you know what is? *Love* is a business. Men treat us as objects. So how do we make it work to our advantage? Well, I made it work."

Acid burns in my gut.

Virgie stands in her perfect home. On the surface, she won.

She picked the right man, a rich man, one who could erase the memory of how she grew up. Mine stole right from the till at Very Cherry to pay for his gambling and his drinking. And yet...

"I loved him."

"Love has nothing to do with happiness," she says.

I look at her. She is so polished now, with her fancy clothes and hair done at that expensive salon in Charlevoix. Virgie goes to all the big society fundraisers. She is not the girl I knew. She ran that day I saw my future. She ran from her friends. She ran from women right into the arms of a man, and not even for love but for comfort. She's always acted so tough, and yet she was scared of everything, even love. I may be running from my horrible mistakes, but she doesn't even know she's running.

"Can we stay here with you?" I ask. "Just for a little while. I can't go to my mom and grandma's just yet. I need some rest. I need some time. I need a friend."

"You need help, Mary. You're so strong and yet so weak. You believe too much in the good of people. You believe what people say. You help everyone. The world is not good. Look at your life."

Lightning flashes again, and I look out the window.

"Look!" I yell. "Do you see them? The four women. On the horizon. They're still coming."

Virgie walks over to the windows and shuts the curtain with a hard yank.

"Stop believing in local legends, Mary."

Her voice echoes off the artwork and antiques.

"You never saw what I saw! You never heard what I heard!"

She continues. "Those women you said you saw on the lake when we were girls, it's all in your head. You conjured up something in which you need to believe in order to survive. You've forever been running from your past. No one is coming to save you but you."

I start to cry.

"No, they were real. They are still trying to tell me something. I will forever believe in them. What other reason is there to go on in the world?"

"Your son!" she cries. "You have a son, Mary. Not a daughter. And you're no longer a girl."

There is a knock on the door.

Virgie walks to the foyer and opens it. My mom and grandma come rushing into the living room.

"I'm going to kill that sumbitch once and for all!" my grandma says. "Did he lay a hand on you?"

Jonah hears her voice, and his face lights up. She takes him from my arms.

"Are you okay?" she coos. "My angel, it's okay."

"Let's go," my mom says. "You will never step foot in that house again. I told you so."

She pulls me to my feet, and I look at Virgie.

"How could you?"

"My husband," Virgie says, voice low. "I have a family now, too."

"He's changed you. You barely acknowledge me in town anymore."

"Everyone knows about Burt. What if he came here? What if he caused a scene, and the police were called? You need to be with your family, Mary."

"You and your reputation," I say. "Just remember you were named after Virgil, your *father*, not your mother, as you now tell everyone in town."

"Mary," my grandma says, "that is not nice. Virgie is your friend."

"*Was* my friend."

My mother escorts me toward the door.

I turn in the foyer. "You can't just rewrite your entire history, Virgie."

"But you can, Mary. You can. You can stop trying to read

tea leaves and looking onto the horizon for answers. You can change your entire life and future if you choose. But you can't even see past the lake." Virgie puts her hands on her hips and glowers at me. "I'm so sorry for everything you're going through. But you keep going back and back like a lost child. You have strong women to guide you. *Real* women, Mary. Look to them, not some ghosts. And you can't keep acting like an impetuous girl. Grow up. You have a baby. You've spent your whole life literally spitting in the face of society, not acting the way a girl should, and yet you've allowed yourself to be consumed by the men you say you rail against."

"Take that back!" I gasp.

"You think I'm weak. I'm actually the strong one."

"I may let a man break my heart, but I would never let him hurt me or my child," I say, my voice now low. "I may believe in mirages, but I am stronger than you'll ever be, because you'll never see any hope on the horizon. The awful thing about knowing someone a very long time is that you truly get to know them: the good, bad and ugly."

I turn and walk out.

"Being a damn optimist will be the end of you, Mary!"

She slams the door shut behind us.

"I did help you, Mary," Virgie says, knocking me from my trance. "I didn't let you hide from your problems. And the man got exactly what he deserved. An eye for an eye."

Virgie looks at me for far too long.

What does she know?

How could she know?

Finally, she says, "And just look at you now. Strong, independent, free."

"And look at you."

She waits for me to finish the sentence. There is nothing more for me to add.

An impish smile breaks across Virgie's face, and it almost looks as if the Grinch has ventured into Whoville for a summer vacation.

"I joined forces with the men who tried to hurt me," Virgie says. "You simply cut them out of your life because you believed in a mirage." Virgie adjusts her wig just so and considers me—my gray hair, Very Cherry General Store T-shirt and grandma jeans—before continuing. "I mean, just look at your poor son and grandson. They had to get away from you because you still believed in ghosts. Cherry Mary! Famous in a small town! But your boys got tired of simply being infamous in a small town. You still don't see it, do you? You ended up being just as blind as your dead husband."

I can feel my heart rage as if it's in the middle of that storm so long ago. I can feel tears rise, but I stop them and say very calmly, "And your husband had to die to finally be free."

Virgie's face freezes, as if I've slapped her.

"You've run from everything," I continue, very softly. "You're a toasted marshmallow, Virgie. All crispy on the outside, but I know that you're soft inside and the exterior is just a facade."

"I take it, then, you won't be participating this year?" Virgie asks.

I begin to turn when a woman and her young daughter approach us.

"Oh, my gosh! Are you Cherry Mary?"

I look at her for a moment and then finally nod.

"My family has been coming to northern Michigan forever," she says. "My mother still talks about you and your store. We visit every summer." The woman turns to her little girl, who is sporting a face that is absolutely covered in chocolate. "This woman is very famous. Do you know what she did? We've talked about it before, when you got those cookies you love at the Very Cherry General Store."

The girl shakes her head *no* but then nods. "The cherry pit lady!" she says with a giggle.

"Yes!" the mother says. "She did something no other man has ever been able to do in my entire life. Isn't that amazing? She's stronger than any man."

Her words drift in the air, the irony making them hum in my ears.

The mother shakes her head and continues. "This year is the hundred-and-twenty-fifth anniversary of the Cherry Pit Spitting Championship. We wouldn't miss seeing you there for anything in the world. Would we, sweetheart?"

The little girl smiles a chocolate smile. When I don't answer, the girl tugs on the end of my T-shirt and asks, "Am I going to see you, Miss Cherry Mary?"

Virgie crosses her arms and cocks her head at me. "Are we, Cherry Mary? You're still famous around these parts."

I glare at Virgie and then look down and smile at the girl.

"I wouldn't miss it for the world."

"Yeah!" the girl yells.

Virgie beams.

"I'll be in touch," she says, walking away.

I actually notice a spring in the old gal's step.

I walk toward the front door.

"Mary?" Gary calls. "Did you want to check out?"

I turn, forgetting Francine, why I came here in the first place.

"Just need a little fresh air," I say. "And a fresh cherry! I'll be back in a sec."

There is a sign by the front door of the Great Hall that reads

Cherries for Sale!

Big Ones... Little Ones!
Fat Ones... Skinny Ones!
Sad Ones... Funny Ones!

Next to it is a basket of fresh cherries. I pluck a bright red one, lift it to my face and ask, "You must not be big, fat or sad. You must be an ironic cherry. What a day, huh?"

I pull off the stem and then pop the cherry into my mouth, and I am instantly—as I always am—a girl again. The taste of a sun-warmed Michigan fruit—be it a cherry, blueberry, strawberry or peach—eaten fresh on a summer day will always make me feel like a kid.

I walk over to the Pit Spitting Arena.

That's actually what it is and what it states. A large wooden sign hangs over the arena reading *North America's Official Olympic-Size Pit Spitting Arena.*

The Cherry Championship in this area used to be held in Cross Village—and there is still a big national championship in Eau Claire, Michigan, too—but this granddaddy has replaced them both.

It's a simple design really, akin to an outdoor bowling alley. A long sandy strip that you might see for long-distance jumping is lined on either side by a low log fence, feet and inches marked off in white paint along its length. At the head of the strip, underneath another sign outlining the official rules, sit two stumps and a rope. You must stand between the logs and spit your cherry pit without extending your body over the rope. Fresh cherries sit in small baskets, and kids on vacation—young and old—take their turns spitting pits as far as their lungs will let them.

At the end of the arena is a wooden sign with the face of yours truly carved into the wood. It's the picture from my youth, cheeks puffed.

15-year-old Mary Jackson, known as "Cherry Mary,"
spat a cherry pit that sailed ninety-three feet, six-and-a-half inches,
setting the Guinness Book of World Records *in 1958.*
No one has broken the record since.
Will you be the one to do it?

I grab a few more cherries and take a seat on a bench, watching a little boy and his dad give it a shot. The boy's pit flies a few feet, the man's goes spinning out-of-bounds. They laugh. Two older men approach, setting their beers down on the stumps. One takes a bent stance, and his friend laughs so hard the pit falls out of his mouth.

"You look like a crazed giraffe, Bob!" he yells.

His friend begins to laugh, and the pit dribbles out of his mouth.

They take a big gulp of their beers and give it shot.

One of them walks over to the sign at the end and thumps my image with his hand. "What do you think ever happened to this girl wonder?" Bob asks.

"Probably a story, like 'Jack and the Beanstalk,'" he says. "Helluva legend, though, isn't it?"

I watch more men give it a whirl, and—in the twenty minutes I sit there—no girl or woman has given it a try.

I get it. Spitting a pit is not considered a girly thing.

But most things aren't, until women actually enter the arena.

I'm about to stand up and leave when I see two women approach. One is walking, almost like a drunk duck, in a wavering line. The other, with flame-red hair like Mars, is attempting to hold her friend steady.

"Oh, I've got to give this a shot," the drunk woman says with a big laugh, clapping her hands.

"You could always shoot a spit wad in school across the room without getting caught," the red-haired woman says. "And blow a bubble as big as a balloon animal."

"And I can hit my dad in the back of head with the paper off my straw ten feet away," the drunk woman says.

"Guess you've always been full of hot air," her friend says with a laugh.

The drunk woman walks over to my sign.

"Get a load of this, Q," she says. "She set the record sixty-five years ago."

She touches my face.

"I wonder if she's still alive?" she asks.

Very much so.

I can't help but chuckle.

The woman turns and points at me and then at my wooden image.

"I have an audience!" the woman says. "I'm comin' for you, Mary!"

The woman swerves toward the front of the Pit Spitting Arena, picks up a cherry, plucks off the stem and hands it to her friend as if it's a party favor and then pops the cherry in her mouth. She swirls it around for a moment.

Poor thing, I think. *I hope she doesn't fall trying to stay upright.*

"Here's to all the men who've hurt us and all the women who support us!" the drunk woman yells, high-fiving her friend. "And here's to my grandparents, new adventures, the four women and believing in mirages. Fata Morgana!"

Four women? Mirages? Fata Morgana?

The woman inhales with all her might, leans toward the rope, puffs her cheeks and blows. For a moment, I lose the pit. Then I see it arcing through the air, high, so high, and whizzing across the blue sky like a Nolan Ryan fastball.

The pit lands.

Beyond the sandy pit.

Over one hundred feet.

I stand, my heart racing.

The woman laughs as if it's no big deal.

I race over and hand her another cherry.

"Please," I say. "Do it again."

The two women look at me as if I'm nuts.

She repeats her feat, nearly matching her previous distance.

I look at her, waiting for some reaction. She is completely un-aware of what she has accomplished or what this means.

"You have no clue what this means, do you?"

She looks at me and takes a step back.

This drunk resorter could be the cherry Paul Bunyan I've been waiting for my whole life.

She could be the fourth woman I've always seen but never thought I'd meet.

I pull a business card from my purse and hand it to her.

"Come see me tomorrow at my general store," I say.

"The Very Cherry General Store?" the red-haired friend reads.

"Is this a joke?" the other asks, her words slightly slurred.

I look at her, the past and the future finally—*finally!*—crys-tallizing and becoming clear right here, right now, after a life-time of waiting.

"No," I say. "It's not a joke. It's destiny."

BECKY

"Oh, wow," Q says. "That second glass of wine went down really fast."

"It's hot out," I say.

"It's seventy-five."

I motion for the waitress.

"She'll have a glass of water," Q says before I can say a word.

"I'll have another glass of your delicious chardonnay."

Q stares at me. "Despite what you think you might have said, the words just came out *delishus charonnay-heeeyyy*!"

"Okay, Mom," I say.

"I'll bring both," the waitress says, walking away in a hurry.

"Now, that is a future leader!" I say.

We are sitting on the patio of a lakeside restaurant appropriately named Don't Wine about It, facing the lake. The patio is terraced out over the water, and I feel like I'm floating. Perhaps it's the wine, perhaps it's the view, but—after Matt ruined my first day of vacation a day with his pathetic little lawsuit, and I wrangled my anger enough into talking to an attorney Q knows—I finally feel untethered, at least momentarily, from reality.

The setting is so beautiful, the town so quaint, that it feels like a movie set. But it's stunningly, breathtakingly real.

I lift my face to the sun and shut my eyes.

A memory of an old lodge overlooking the lake pops into my head. I can see my grampa sipping a manhattan, my grandma, her face tan, staring toward the water, and they both seemed so happy and content that it made me feel safer than I have in my entire life.

"Sometimes, you just gotta let go, Becky," I can hear my grampa saying. "Sometimes, you just gotta watch the sunset and crawl into sandy sheets exhausted and grateful for a perfect summer day. That's all we have, these little moments in life. Time is but a wave."

And then I see my grandma reaching for his hand and the sun setting so slowly and yet much too quickly.

"Becky?"

Q shakes my hand. "Are you okay?"

I nod. "Just thinking about my grandparents and days like this."

"And I was thinking how nice it is to finally spend a beautiful summer evening on the water with my best friend," she says. "Just as we planned."

I turn toward Q. "I don't want to plan anymore. I just want to be. I just want to let loose and have a little fun for once."

The waitress returns with my water.

"I'm going to have a manhattan," Q says.

My eyes pop. Can she read my mind?

"You know," Q says, the sun across her face, "like you, I've had visions my whole life."

"You never told me this," I say. "Did you see things as a girl like I did?"

"Yes, but different." The water laps around us. "My parents weren't like yours. They fought all the time. That's a big reason why they divorced when I got out of high school. Play-acting was a way for me to escape from the world. Dressing up as a kid, singing. Remember that lemonade stand that I had when you first moved to St. Louis? I didn't start it to make money. I did it to get out of the house and make up a new life in my head."

I reach my hand across the table. "I'm so sorry," I say. "I knew it was rough. I don't think as a kid I ever considered how rough it was for you."

She squeezes my hand and nods.

"When I get on stage, I don't see an audience, a theater filled with seats, or the world the way it is. I see a fantasy world," Q says. "I am in the streets of New York, dancing by the Eiffel Tower or living in a land filled with dancing teacups and candelabras. My visions are of creating a magical world so—like we're doing right now—people can escape reality." She stops and looks at me. "So I could escape reality."

She continues. "Why have I never settled down? Because I'm scared it will turn out like my parents. I know how much coming here means to you, and I want you to understand how much it means to me, too. I'm thankful to be on this journey with such a strong, amazing woman."

"Your Manhattan," the waitress returns, "and your wine."

Q lifts her glass.

"To us!" she says. "To visions! To women! To rewriting our destinies."

A group of ladies at different tables suddenly lift their glasses into the air.

"To women!" they join in, yelling. "Yeah!"

I clink Q's glasses, searching her face and those of the women around me.

Perhaps, I think, *my answer has always been in front of me.*

"Who wants ice cream?"

I race over to an adorable white clapboard ice cream shop whose flashing neon sign blinks *Lake Effect Dairy.* A little cow with a cone upside down on its head sits atop the building. The window is propped wide open, and a woman is just standing there, passing out cups and cones, sundaes and blizzards.

I race over to beat a little girl who's going to have to learn to pick up the pace if she wants to succeed in the world as an adult, and I snag a towering cone as red as Q's hair.

I take a huge bite.

"Oh, my gosh," I say to the woman. "It's so good. Soft-serve vanilla, right? With cherry dip?"

She looks at me.

"I mean, it just has to be cherry, right?" I gesture around at a town literally awash in all things red. "And I used to work at an ice cream store. I know my flavors."

I inhale the cone.

Her eyebrows collapse into the center of her face.

"Who are you?" she asks.

My cone is halfway down my throat when it finally dawns on me that the woman—like the dozen people surrounding her—is wearing a T-shirt reading *2023 Higgins Family Reunion*.

Q grabs my arm and pivots me down the sidewalk as a little girl cries, "My ice cream!"

"I thought they were just handing out free ice cream," I say, taking another big bite of my cone. "I thought it was a promotion. I feel awful."

"Yeah, Dairy Queen," Q says, literally pushing me down the street, turning back to look one more time and give the family an *I'm sorry* wave. "You seem consumed with guilt."

"I will never live that down," I say, finishing my cone. "I really didn't need that shot those women at the restaurant sent over."

"Shots," Q says. "Plural."

"It must be really late," I say.

"It's five thirty in the afternoon," Q says.

"No way!" I yell. I do a little dance in the middle of the street and begin to sing "Workin' nine to five…"

Some vacationers give me a boisterous thumbs-up and finish the lyrics, while some mothers pull their children closer.

"My boyfriend is suing me," I call to a man who looks like he's just heading in from a day at the beach.

"I can understand why," he murmurs to his friend.

Q escorts me across the street.

"I feel like I'm trying to guide a kite in the middle of a thunderstorm," she says. "Let me help you."

"Let me help *you*!" I say. "I have visions."

"I do, too," Q says. "Of you getting arrested."

"Oooh!" I say, looking up, having a moment of clarity. "What is this? Are we in a fairy tale?"

Q laughs. "For being so buzzed, you're incredible literary. It does look like it."

A big wooden sign spins before my eyes.

"*Cherry Republic*," I read. "Is that my stripper name?"

"Good Lord, Becky," Q says. "There are kids around."

"Kids today are way more mature than I was at their age." I point at Q and yell anew. "We worked at an ice cream store together. Nineties girls rule the world! Wahoo!"

I clap my hands and do another jig.

"What's that?" I ask, pointing.

And then I'm off, Q rushing to stay with me.

"What a hoot!" I say, pointing toward a sign that proclaims *North America's Official Olympic-Size Pit Spitting Arena*.

I begin to read the rules and then walk the perimeter of the sandy pit.

"Only a hundred feet?" I say to Q. "That ain't nothin'!"

"You've always been full of hot air," Q says.

"Hardy-har," I say.

"I just can't light a match anywhere near you."

I walk to the end of the pit and read the sign about a girl named Cherry Mary.

"Get a load of this, Q," I say, calling her over. "She set the record sixty-five years ago."

I touch the carved image of Mary's face.

"I wonder if she's still alive?" I ask.

I hear a woman chuckle. I turn. An elderly woman is seated on a bench.

"I have an audience!" I say. "I'm comin' for you, Mary!"

Another laugh.

I head to the front of the arena, grab a cherry, pluck off the stem and hand it to Q.

I pop the cherry in my mouth for a moment, removing all its juicy goodness. It makes the cherry dip cone I just ate taste insanely fake.

I steady myself just at the edge of the rope.

"Here's to all the men who've hurt us and all the women who support us!" I suddenly yell, high-fiving Q. "And here's to my grandparents, new adventures, the four women and believing in mirages. Fata Morgana!"

I hear a gasp from the woman watching, and I wonder if she's lost or if her family sat her here because she's tired and couldn't keep up.

I inhale with all my might, lean toward the rope, puff my cheeks and blow. When I open my eyes, I don't see the pit. At first, I think I likely just spit it straight into the ground, but then I hear another gasp, and I see the cherry stone arcing across the sky, flying, like I'm an Olympic shot-putter.

The pit lands beyond the sandy pit.

I release a big laugh and whoop.

"Do it again."

The elderly woman is standing beside me.

She is holding a fresh cherry out to me as if it's as precious as a ruby.

I nod at Q to do something.

"Are you okay?" Q asks the woman. "Do you need some help?"

Please," she says to me as if her life is riding on it. "Do it again."

"Okay," I say.

I try to remember how I just did what I did, and when I'm ready, I shut my eyes and blow.

I laugh again and high-five Q.

"You have no clue what this means, do you?" the woman says.

Her tone is so ominous and her face so serious that I know she is either completely serious or totally off her rocker. I take a step back as she reaches into her purse.

She hands me a business card. I show it to Q.

"Come see me tomorrow at my general store," she says.

"The Very Cherry General Store?" Q asks.

"Is this a joke?" I ask.

"No," the woman says. "It's destiny."

And then she is gone, moving inside a building marked the *Great Hall*.

Q and I stand motionless, as if we're mired in quicksand.

"Am I drunk, or do I feel like I'm living out the lyrics to that Cher song, "Dark Lady," the one where she visits the fortune teller and things go really, really bad?"

Q touches my shoulder.

"You're definitely drunk," she says, "but this does have a very voodoo feeling. It's like a modern-day *Macbeth*."

"Macbeth dies, right?"

Q laughs.

"You know in the theater world we believe that play is cursed," Q says, her voice low. "We will not mention its title inside a theatre. We all simply call it *The Scottish Play*."

"This is not making me feel any better," I say.

"Maybe it's a good omen," Q says. "Maybe she's the vision you saw and have been waiting for your whole life."

"Or maybe I should heed the advice Cher gave in her lyrics," I say. "Leave this place, never come back and forget I saw that woman's face."

Q smiles. "But remember your road-trip rules, Becky. Leave room for adventure, drink lots of wine and say yes to everything."

"I think I need new rules already," I say.

MARY

"The secret to the perfect cherry margarita is fresh cherries, fresh lime juice and lots of muddling." I hand a margarita to Francine, plop my backside into my red Adirondack chair and plant my feet into the sand. The waves lap at my toes.

Francine takes a sip of her cocktail, and her eyes pop.

"I think the secret is lots of tequila," she says.

"I think you're right. Cheers!"

We clink glasses and stare into the sun that is still high in the sky.

"I'm so glad you're back," I continue. "It's just not summer without you."

"Back atcha," she says.

For the longest time, we sit in silence, as only friends that have known one another forever, can do. Although neither of us are talking, it's like we're having an entire unspoken conversation.

I don't want this to be your last summer, Francine.

Me, either, old friend. But the sun is setting.

Then let's just enjoy this summer day a little bit more before it does, okay?

I call this time of day on the beach the Golden Hour, because the vacationers and resorters head in for dinner, the waves seeming to calm at their departure, the breeze kicks up as the sun lowers, the world smells like sand, water and pine rather than sunscreen, and the entire world looks as if it's been dipped in gold. The waves, the dunes' grass, the masts on the sailboats, the horizon glitter in gold.

Why are things of beauty that are near the ends of their journeys—this day, this friendship, perhaps even my store—always referred to as *golden*?

The Golden Hour.

The Golden Age.

The Golden Girls.

"Everything is gold," Francine whispers over the lake. "I will miss this most."

See? We really do read each other's minds.

I inhale deeply and take a sip of my cherry margarita.

Summer 1964

"There are really only four parts of a cherry: the stem, the skin, the flesh and the pit."

My grandma's lecture has gone on now for over ten minutes. I've heard it many times in my life. To her, cherries are life. Or, at least, they epitomize life.

"Every part of the cherry is useful except for the pit," she continues, "You can even dry the stems for tea." She circles me in a chair at the general store. "Do you know what the pit is? It's hard and bitter. You throw it away. You do not put out your husband's eyes with it."

"No, I spit it," I say. "That's what I've always done. That's what you taught me to do."

"Not in society's face!" she suddenly shouts. "That's now how women get ahead. You're lucky. His death saved you."

"His death made Jonah a boy without a father."

"Good!" my grandma says. "Jonah never had one, and he was never going to have one."

Through the front window, an oval wooden sign reading *The Very Cherry General Store* swings in the breeze.

Most people in town have now forgotten that, when my grandfather was still alive, the store was named after him. But it was his in name only, and just for a short while until my grandma—quite literally—took her future into her own hands.

My grandma was the state's first postmistress. She "inherited" this store and built it back up by working sunup to sundown. No whining. No complaining. Just, as she always told me, "Head down, nose to the ground, pull hard every day, like a mule."

Tourists don't know my grandma's name is Very, short for Verity, which—appropriately enough—means *truth*. My grandmother has always been honest to a fault. She tells it like it is.

She named my mom Geri, short for Geraldine, and I was named Mary. I always hated our names. I felt like we sounded like one of those all-girl singing groups on *Lawrence Welk*. I could even hear his distinctive voice say, "Welcome to the show, Very, Geri and Mary. They will be crooning some of your favorite holiday songs. And a-one, and a-two…"

My mother hands my grandma a black cherry Nehi soda to calm her nerves. My grandma pops the top off with her teeth and takes a long swig. She holds the icy bottle in front of my face.

"Cherries, Mary!" she says. "They hold the secret to life."

Jonah coos in his crib in the corner.

My grandma pulls a chair up next to me.

"There's something you gotta know, Mary." Grandma looks at my mom knowingly.

"What's going on?" I ask.

"The woman at Devil's Elbow…she told us the same thing she told you, when we were girls." My grandma hesitates. "Your mom and I have had the same visions you've had your entire life."

"What?" I nearly knock myself over in the old chair. "Why didn't you tell me?"

"You have a gift of the gab, Mary. We didn't want people thinking we were crazy. That could've killed our store." She drops her voice. "The three crazy woman who run the general store have visions. Why have all their husbands died? Why, those three witches are as evil as the spirit at Devil's Elbow. Stay away from them and that store."

My grandma nods at my mom. "Show her, Geri."

My mother walks directly over to the 1901 National Cash Register and begins to punch in numbers. The numbers spring up on the top totaling four dollars. The large wooden drawer at the bottom I always believed was locked and purely ornamental pops open. My mother pulls something from it, returns and hands it to me.

It is the top of a quill box. The design on the top is of four figures—women—floating over blue water.

"Aponi made it for me when I was just a girl, Mary," my grandma says. "She was just a girl then, too, and I was the only one around who would talk to her. She told me of a legend in which her ancestors believed, a legend of four women who all had the same vision. All were hurt by men. All were misunderstood by society. All were powerful. All were meant to save this area from the destruction of those who didn't appreciate its beauty. All were meant to be united."

My hands begin to tremble. I look at the quill design shaking before me.

"You're scaring me."

"Don't be scared, Mary," my mother says. "Just be aware of your power and your destiny. You showed it as a girl. You let it go as a young woman. Now it's time it returned to you." Mom continues. "Remember what the woman told you. You hold your destiny. Legend lives within you."

"We're trying to help you, just like the woman was," my grandma adds. "She said you would be the last girl, but that there will be another who will join you. But it may take a lifetime."

She pulls the quill lid from my hand.

"We thought the fourth woman would be your baby," my grandma says, her voice barely audible. "That was not to be."

"Who is the fourth woman?" I ask.

"We don't know," my grandma says. "Your mother and I may never know. We believe that is your destiny."

"My destiny? To do what?"

"To save this store," she says. "To save this family."

"To save our beloved homeland," my mom adds.

"Or maybe just to save yourself," Grandma says.

"That woman handed me a quill box when I saw her as a girl," I tell them as if in a trance. "When I removed the lid, it was empty. But when I looked into it again after seeing the women on the horizon, it was filled."

"With what?" my grandma asks.

"Cherries."

The gold begins to fade, and the world becomes real again.

"Yes, I will miss this most," Francine says.

I cannot deal with reality right now. Nor can I deal with visions.

I just want to be.

So I change the subject.

"You would not believe my day," I say.

I begin to tell Francine about everything, from my run-in with Virgie to the drunken vacationer who eclipsed my record. When I finish, she is silent for a moment.

"Am I crazy?" I ask her.

"For believing in your intuition?" she finally asks, her voice crisp as the breeze. "Despite all the bad, you've always believed in the good in people, Mary. And so have I. I think that's why we're friends. But you've always been a little bit stronger than the lot. You've always been able to see into the souls of people."

Francine looks thoughtful. "May I tell you something I've never shared with anyone, save for my minister?"

I pivot in my Adirondack and take a sip of my margarita. I nod.

"I caught Bill cheating on me."

"Bill? No!"

"It was decades ago," Francine says, "after Hope was born. I know now that I had postpartum depression, but there really wasn't much diagnosis or discussion about that back then. I could barely bathe and get dressed, much less keep the house clean and care for three kids. It was like I was living in a fog." She takes a sip of her drink and continues. "I remember a crisp spring morning when the windows were open and the cold air was turning warm, and I could feel a bit of me coming back to life, too. I was loading the kids into the car to run errands for the day, and I was retrieving all of Bill's dirty shirts to take to the dry cleaner. I smelled perfume. I pulled one of his shirts to my nose and inhaled. And then another and another. It wasn't just any perfume, it was Opium. Have you ever smelled Opium?"

I think back in time. I nod.

"Mystical," I say. "Earthy. Seductive."

Francine nods and sips her margarita. "Exactly. And I hadn't worn perfume in months. I smelled like spit-up, baby powder and Cheer."

I nod.

Francine continues. "I called all my friends, and they said, 'You're being crazy. Bill would never do that. He loves you and those kids more than anything.' I called my doctor, who told me I was just being hormonal. 'Women get like this,' he said. But I couldn't get the thought—or scent—out of my head. So I did what any crazed wife and mother would do. I went directly to Bill's office with my three children in tow. When I made it to his office, his secretary stood to greet me. Mrs. Moore, who'd been there for ages, had suddenly been replaced by a young, very pretty redhead."

"Who smelled like Opium?"

"Story as old as time," Francine says. "I turned and left, furious, unable to think straight. I drove directly to a jewelry store on the other side of town and asked a young man working there how much he thought I could get for my wedding ring. Out of the blue, he started to flirt with me."

"You don't have to sell it," he said. "You could just take it off when you need to."

"Oh, my goodness, Francine!"

"Oh, my head was spinning, Mary. I wanted to teach my husband a lesson. I not only wanted to divorce him and take him for everything he had but also have payback." Francine shakes her head. "I drove around all day with the kids, his stupid shirts sitting in the back seat filling the car with Opium. I drove back to that jewelry shop and waited for that man. When he walked out and saw me, he waved. He started to approach the car, and all of a sudden I threw it into Drive and took off. I started crying so hard I had to pull off the side of the road. I realized I didn't want to be a coward, too. I didn't want to live with this shame and agony the rest of my life like Bill would. I drove to our church and had a talk with my pastor. Do you know what he said?"

I shake my head.

"He said I could have had that affair, and it would have felt great for a fleeting moment, but it would have all been a fantasy. None of it was real, nor would it ever be real. He told me what likely would have happened is that I would have entered that jewelry store, and that man would have pushed me against the jewelry case, and—in the middle of everything—the glass would have collapsed underneath me. That's when I understood, Mary. So much of life is an illusion. We create this image of what a perfect life and family is supposed to be. And when it doesn't turn out that way, we seek distraction or perfection, but it will never be that way. The glass is going to crack at some point in our lives. We just have to decide if we're going to be the ones to get cut or to clean it up and move on."

I can only stare at my friend. Her revelation has left me speechless.

"I decided to clean up and move on," she says.

"Did you ever tell Bill?" I ask.

Francine shakes her head. "But he knew I knew. And we learned to live with that. And I did love him, as much or more than anything in this life. Family is good, bad, ugly, imperfect, happy, sad, warts and all," she says.

Without warning, I begin to blubber and tell Francine the story of my husband and what I did, a secret I kept from my best friend out of shame. She takes a seat in the sand and holds my hands until I am done.

"I'm so sorry, Mary," she says. "For everything you went through. I heard some of the gossip in town, but I never wanted to believe it. Just like you couldn't believe Bill would do such a thing. I didn't want to ask you, either, dredge up bad memories. I just thought you left an abusive man and your husband drank himself to death. I'm so sorry."

I wipe my eyes.

"We're not crazy, you know," she continues. "No decision a woman in trouble makes is ever easy, especially when there are children involved. We both did what we thought was best for them and, hopefully, for us. You didn't kill your husband, Mary. He did it himself. And I didn't make Bill cheat on me. That was all on him."

Francine stands and heads back to her purple Adirondack.

"The world tells women we're being irrational, or overly emotional, when our gut tells us otherwise. But we're not. We're simply dialed into the one thing that separates us from everyone else—our instinct. And that's always what saves us in the end."

Francine lifts her glass. "To women's intuition!" she says. "And cherries!"

We watch the sun slowly melt into the lake, along with the ice in our glasses.

BECKY

There is that moment when you've had too much to drink the night before and you start to wake up, your head is pounding and your tongue is stuck to the roof of your mouth. Before you open your eyes, you pray that it is still the middle of the night and you have hours left to sleep. And then you feel the light on your face—like I do right now—and you know: *it's gonna be a long day.*

I open my eyes.

Sun pours through the window.

I groan and roll over. They call it hangover for a reason.

I can feel my cell underneath me somewhere, and I search for it among the sheets and blankets. I hold it in front of my face, squinting to read the time: 8:18 a.m.

A much longer day than I imagined.

I hear the waves lapping in the near distance, and I know I could drink all of Lake Michigan right now—its unsalted entirety—and still be thirsty. I sit up and notice a bottle of water on the nightstand along with two aspirin. I smile. I know Q placed them there after I passed out. I take the pills and a long drink and try to dissect last night.

Wine.

Shots.

Stolen ice cream.

Cherry spitting.

Talk of visions.

I take another sip of water.

And there was an old woman who said I was her destiny, right?

"Just a normal girls' weekend," I say, my voice husky and filled with sarcasm.

My cell flashes. I pick it up.

"Hello?"

"It sounds like I'm talking to Norma Desmond."

"Why did I hire an attorney with a Broadway obsession who thinks he's Henny Youngman?"

"Because Q recommended me?"

"Of course," I say. "Long night. Please don't make it a longer day."

"It's eight in the morning," he says. "Actually, seven here in St. Louis. Early bird gets the worm."

"Worm," I say, groaning. "Tequila shots. Make it stop."

"That's my goal," he says perkily. "So I spoke with Matt's attorney. As I already said, Matt really has no real claim here."

"Then, why he is suing me?"

"He's just trying to get your attention."

"This is a great way of showing it."

"You're an elementary-school administrator," Larry says, his voice slow and deliberate. "What do little boys do at that age when they like a girl?"

I shake my head.

"They hit them, tease them or provoke them," I say. "That's how they show affection."

"And that's exactly what Matt is doing. His attorney pretty much admitted that. Look, the guy misses you. He knows he screwed up. He's just trying to rattle your cage over a claim to a fridge that makes cocktail ice and a new couch because that's the only way he knows how to get your attention again."

"Well, that's incredibly childish."

"The only thing that's different between a boy and a man is his age."

"You should be a writer," I say.

"I am," Larry says. "Working on a thriller. Most attorneys want to be novelists."

"And most elementary-school principals want to be retired."

He laughs.

"I not only think you're going to be okay," he says, "I think you're going to be better than you ever have."

"Are you also a soothsayer on the side?" I ask.

"Being an attorney has given me a good read on people," he says. "Let me talk again with Matt's lawyer. I'm going to play hardball. I'll tell them you're going to countersue, them on defense. Listen, Matt has no claim considering it's *your* name on the mortgage, contents are covered by *your* insurance, and he moved out on his own. He's simply filled with remorse. Just try and go have some fun today. Take a nap on the beach. Forget about all this for now."

"Do you think Matt will want to talk to me?"

"Probably," he says. "Do you want to talk to him?"

"Not really. But will it make all of this go away faster?"

"Probably," he says. "And it'll probably save you both a lot of money. I charge by the quarter hour."

"Talk to his attorney," I say.

"Okay. Good-bye, Becky."

I get out of bed feeling slightly better and take a shower to rid the cobwebs from my head. When I emerge from my bedroom, Q looks surprised.

"A shower? And a smile? Did you dream last night never happened? I mean, you even slept through all the thunderstorms."

"Oh, it happened," I say. "But I just got some good news."

I bring her up-to-date.

"Things are looking up," Q says. "Now we just have to go see an old woman at a general store to find out why exactly it's destiny for the two of you to talk."

"Can I just have a cup of coffee first?" I ask. "And a few hours at the beach. It's our vacation."

"This feels very *Andy Griffith*."

Q looks at me.

"What? I watch it on TV Land while doing paperwork. Believe me, it's more soothing than classical music."

"I get it," Q says. "I still watch *Saved by the Bell* and *Gilmore Girls* when I need to escape."

I laugh.

Q stops on the narrow path leading to the beach and looks around. "This is very nostalgic, very *Andy Griffith*, isn't it?"

There is a forest of pines that encircle the log cabin where we're staying, and the air is drenched in their scent. The sandy path beneath us is covered in needles, a virtual carpet. Another circle of trees, this of sugar maples, rings the pines. I turn to take in the view.

Two rocking chairs, quilts tossed over their arched wooden backs, sit on the front porch, and the logs of the cabin—which have become shiny over the years from the harsh winters— shimmer in the light glinting through the pines. The door is a happy red.

The cabin sits down a long winding gravel driveway off the main road in an ecological area that is known in these parts as a *sugar bowl*. The house, quite literally, sits atop a giant bowl made of sand. In the sun, the sand glimmers, making it resemble a sugar bowl, much like the one my grandma used to keep on her dining-room table for her tea and coffee. A coffee table book on the area in the cabin said this bowl was most likely carved by glaciers and once existed as a small lake separate from Lake Michigan.

Q heads down the path—a virtual pack mule carrying a folding chair on her back, a beach bag filled with lotions, towels, snacks and books, a cooler filled with drinks, a massive straw hat floating atop her red hair. I am strapped down with the same. Why two women need so much for just a few hours on the beach is beyond me, and yet our routine and preparation never changes and seems vitally important not only for a good day on the water but also for a great day making memories.

We follow the snaking trail down into the midst of the bowl, and the temperature rises. The wind is cut off here, and the sand boils in the sun. I begin to perspire profusely, sweat dripping off of me as if I've just gone through a car wash.

"The sand will be drunk in a few minutes after your perspiration sinks in," Q says with a laugh.

I stop to catch my breath.

"Coming?" Q asks.

"Go on," I say.

"Glass of wine will be waiting for you," she says.

"Ha ."

Q traverses up the other side of the bowl. And then it is silent.

It is spectacularly beautiful to be standing in the middle of a massive, real-life terrarium. It is also spiritually and physically overwhelming to be reduced to a tiny fragment of the world and reminded of just how small each of us really is.

The wind whistles across the dune, making the sand sing.

Pops used to whistle as we walked to the beach, and I feel as if he's with me right now.

Slowly, I climb the opposite side of the sugar bowl, my feet churning up the sand as I walk. It is a fairly large dune, and I have to keep trudging to move forward. Finally, I can feel a cool wind kiss my face. When I look up, Lake Michigan is spread out before me.

I have been to both coasts, and the Atlantic and Pacific Oceans are stunning in their beauty, but there is just something about Lake Michigan.

Sailboats float across the horizon at a rapid clip, while other sit anchored throughout the lake. From a distance, the boats look as if they are sitting atop glass.

But it's not just the water that makes this area so spectacular. The dunes rise over the lake as if they're mothers keeping watching over their newborn babies. Aspen trees arc toward the water like divining rods. Dunes grass waves in the wind as if the lake is whispering her watery secrets to the earth. And the sand lies in a golden, unobstructed band as far as the eye can see.

I scamper down the dune to the beach.

"Thank you for making all this happen," I say when I reach Q.

"Thank you for not getting arrested last night."

"I'm serious," I say. "Thank you. I need this."

Q smiles. "You're welcome. Me, too."

She pulls a beach blanket from the bag and whips it into the air. Q unfurls it onto the sand. I laugh when I read what it says in bright blue letters: *There Will Be Drama!* Underneath, in smaller letters, it continues *and singing and dancing and music and jazz hands, of course!*

"My theatrical beach towel," she says.

Q grabs a sunscreen with triple-digit SPF and covers her entire face. She then applies a 55 over her entire body. She catches me watching her.

"I'm the color of typewriter paper," she says. "My people were Victorian queens who exploded into flames on a sixty-degree day."

I point at the message on the towel.

"After last night, it's my turn for a little drama," she says.

Q places her flip-flops on two corners of her towel to secure it from the wind and places the bag and cooler on the others. Finally, she puts her beach chair on the towel.

"No wonder your productions are so good, considering how much planning goes into everything."

She narrows her eyes and takes a seat with a big sigh.

I simply grab a towel, lay it on the sand and lie down.

"When you work with children, you just want everything to be as easy as possible."

"Oh, believe me," Q says, pointing at me, "I do work with children."

I laugh.

We are lying about ten feet from the lake's edge, and there is no one even close to us. I scan the beach. I can barely make out the people through the mist.

Yet another amazing fact about Michigan: it has the longest freshwater coastline in the world and the second-longest total shoreline, right after Alaska. All this means you can come to the beach nearly anywhere in the state and find a place all to yourself.

Which can be comforting to a woman of forty.

In St. Louis, without any fresh water like this close by, I'm relegated to hitting the public pool, along with every teenage boy and girl in the city. The last time I went with Q, and we removed our cover-ups to take seats on the loungers near the pool, every youthful eye was on us as if the parents had arrived on the set of *Euphoria*.

"I will not feel this judged even by Jesus when I enter the Pearly Gates," Q had whispered to me, before—in her inimitable style—she had stood, walked to the edge of the pool and yelled, "This is what cellulite and stretch marks look like, kids! Get ready!" before diving in with a monstrous splash.

Q places her straw hat over her face. "I'm taking a little nap," she says. "I was up most of the night making sure my best friend was alive."

"Dramatic much?" I ask. "I'm going to sweat out my alcohol,

drink some water and join you for a little shut-eye, too. Good night, Mary Ellen."

"Good night, John-Boy."

Within a few moments, I can hear her softly snoozing.

I drink some water and then lie back and stare into the lake.

I blink, and sunspots float in front of me.

And then four dots settle onto the horizon over the water.

Slowly, they move toward me. As they do, the dots elongate, take shape, morph into four women floating across the water. They are coming directly toward me.

I blink again and shake my head, hard.

The image does not disappear. In fact, it becomes clearer.

The women look the same as they did in the mirage I saw when I was a girl. Only, today, I swear I can make out their faces more clearly than I ever have. They aren't women. They are girls. Holding hands. Youthful. But... *Not happy. Not at peace.*

Who are you? I wonder. Why are you here again? What do you want?

I think of my grandparents' scrapbook gift to me so long ago.

The first photo in the album is one Pops took on a sultry day in Charlevoix. I am pointing toward the horizon, stooped on the beach, my grandma beside me, showing her what I saw: the four women.

"It's not real," my grandma said. "Just a Fata Morgana."

"Fata Morgana," I whisper out loud.

I sit up and grab my cell.

I scroll and scroll through the thousands of images I have stored on my phone until I find the picture of the letter my grandparents wrote me so long ago. I took it years back when I was feeling down, after Matt had broken up with me for the first time, and I needed support from those who were no longer with me.

We often create a beautiful mirage of how we want life to be. We fool ourselves into thinking it's perfection. So many in our lives will see us as mirages: how they want us to be, or live, and we will bend our optic light to create that image for them. But it's not real. And there will come a day when the weather will change, when the sun breaks out, the clouds clear, and the mirage fades. You will need to be clear-eyed enough to see it, strong enough to shape-shift and grateful to understand you can create a life that is not a Fata Morgana. But that starts now. Don't create an image and life that pleases others. Don't set your feet in concrete or you'll never be able to move. And yet it's okay to see beautiful things on the horizon, to believe in them, to strive to reach them. One day, you will return to northern Michigan—with or without us—and I hope you will always see the wonder and magic possible in the distance.

I can hear a girl, in the distance, her words carried on the wind, yell, "Mommy! Mommy! Look!"

I glance up, half expecting this child to have seen what I am seeing today—to make sense of what I'd seen so long ago—but the water is calm as glass.

I get up and walk toward the lake, edging in up to my knees.

I move through the water, staring at my feet, bending to peer at the pretty rocks and stones that wash onto the shoreline every morning and evening. I used to spend all afternoon on vacation rock hunting with Memaw. She'd carry a homemade picker she'd cobbled together by attaching a small, vintage colander to the end of a favorite walking stick to save her back from bending over so much.

"What are we looking for?" I'd always ask.

My grandma would stop and point at all the avid rock collectors walking the beach in search of a particular rock: Petoskey, Leland Blue, stones embedded with fossils, lightning stones.

"The rock that calls to you," she'd say. "Everyone's out searching for something particular, but they're missing the magic of what's directly in front of them."

I smile at the memory as I walk.

So much of our lives, as my grandparents tried to tell me after finding their peace in retirement, is spent searching for the thing we've been told we want or should have. So much of our lives is spent trying to be like that perfect rock we see in the water. An image gets in our heads and remains. And, without ever realizing, we conform to an image and reality that is probably no more real than what I just saw on the horizon. Then we spend our lives trying to fit in, to become that image, to make it real, though it may have nothing to do with us.

When we moved to St. Louis, all I wanted was to be liked. The curse of any child is to be unique, different. I had a role model in uniqueness in Q—I mean, her nickname is essential in making the word *unique*—but my parents tended to override her unconventional wisdom, and they taught me the path of least resistance would be the best.

Don't pursue business. Girls become teachers.

Why pursue a principal's job when you're so happy as an assistant principal? You don't need that pressure.

Matt's a good, steady guy. Why do you need sparks when that might only lead to a fire?

I know this sounds terribly archaic. What parents would dish out such antiquated advice? But the Catholic Midwest where my parents grew up was quiet, conservative, not progressive like the coasts.

Moreover, no one would want to be me, I always thought—an average-looking girl with a decent sense of humor, good grades and the ability to keep her wilder self in check—so I should just be invisible. I teach my kids to believe in themselves, and yet I don't take my own advice.

My mom and dad were so upset at my grandparents' newfound wild side and adventurous nature when they turned sixty.

"We don't even know them anymore," my dad would say. "We don't know who they've become."

I am finally beginning to realize they just become who they always wanted to be after letting every expectation go. How were they able to unlearn the fear that had controlled them their whole lives? How did they drown their own stasis and comfortability? How did they—at seventy—skydive, quite literally, into a new reality?

I know my mother and father wanted me to be some version of them because my grandmother shared a story they never told me.

My mother was accepted to college in Chicago. She was so overwhelmed by the city and the experience that she called my grandmother every night begging to come home.

"No," my grandma told her. "Give it time. It will all be okay."

But my mother didn't want to give it time. She got on a Greyhound and returned home. When my father met her at church, he promised her that life would never be scary, that she would always be safe, and when he asked her to marry him, she said *yes* immediately.

"She never really left home," my grandma told me. "She never grew up, she never dealt with her anxiety, her fear, her loss of dreams. She disappeared into that ranch house and became as entrenched as the carpet."

I see a flash of bright blue shimmer before my feet as I walk. I lean down.

Beautiful beach glass. It is a glorious blue, like ice.

I hold it up to the sun. *Is this another sign?*

My grandma taught me that beach glass is really just broken shards of glass that have been smoothed over many years, thanks to the tumbling and rubbing against the rocks and sand in the lake. Glass bottles and construction materials were discarded into Lake Michigan, which served as a sort of washing machine for the glass, turning broken bits and sharp pieces into rounded, softer, frosted objects of beauty that people seek to collect.

The broken and discarded, the overlooked, can become something entirely new and completely amazing over time, I think. We just need our pain to be smoothed.

I think of last night and the old woman.

We just need to expel the hard pit that lives inside us.

All of a sudden, I turn and wade back to Q, who has rolled onto her side and is still sawing logs.

I pull from my beach bag a book, pen and vintage postcard I picked up while shopping yesterday before dinner and take a seat on my towel.

My mother has called and texted me, oh, about a hundred times since we left, not to ask if I'm having fun but if I'm alive, when I'm coming home, if the school understands where I am, if I've talked to Matt.

If I talk to my mother, I know I will lose it, so I decided to take the old-fashioned route of communication my grandmother used with her: a postcard.

"Maybe it will force her to see what she's missing," my grandma used to always say as she wrote. "Michigan. Summer. Life. Fun." She'd look at me and shoot me a wink. "Us."

I haven't mailed a postcard in forever, and it sort of seems so silly, but—staring at the card—it also seems so personal and sweet.

Too many of us never mean what we say, or we use too many words to say what we mean. But a letter, a postcard, it forces us to choose our words carefully. They are a mirror to our soul.

Featured on the front of the card is an old black-and-white photo of a girl buried up to her waist in the sand, her hands over her head, the lake behind her.

Good Times in Good Hart! it reads in big, white vintage type.

I turn the postcard over and begin to write.

Dear Mom and Dad:
I am having a good time in Good Hart! So far, I've:
  *Walked on the beach
  *Had dinner on the water
  *Laughed until my sides hurt

*And thought a lot about Pops and Memaw and being a girl again

I stop, editing out, as any good reporter or writer would do, essentials that are not pertinent to the story I'm telling. Things like Matt trying to sue me for ownership of our large-screen TV, getting insanely drunk, stealing a child's ice cream cone, spitting a cherry pit a really long way and having to go meet an old woman who might lock me in her basement.

I love you both so much, and I hope you can feel the lake breeze all the way in St. Louis.
XOXO,
Becky

I glance up from the postcard. Four older women are walking the shoreline, laughing. As they disappear into the misty haze down the beach, I look over the lake.

The four images are coming toward me over the lake again.

I lie back, shut my eyes and fall asleep.

I dream that I can skip a cherry pit all the way from the lakeshore until it disappears into the horizon.

MARY

"Ope!"

I hurriedly turn off the mixer, scan the bright yellow mixing bowl beside me and repeat my Michigan mantra when I mess up. "Double ope!"

The trash can is filled with beautiful cherries. The mixing bowl is filled with pits.

I lift the paddles and scan the batter.

"Half the town would have been walking around without teeth," I say to myself in the quiet of the general store's kitchen at dawn.

My mind whirs to my impromptu run-in with Virgie, and I can't help but smile at an image of her smiling without her front teeth or, better yet, having her jaw wired shut.

Such has been the last twenty-four hours of my life. Everything, like my batter, has gone crazy.

I grab the mixing bowl and dump its contents into the trash can.

I begin to measure the flour and butter once again, starting from scratch.

I did not sleep well at all, and my mind is as foggy as the air over the lake out the kitchen window, an ominous haze that creeps toward the general store at its own leisure, devouring everything—the water, the bluff, my cherry trees, my gardens—while leaving only a shroud of mystery.

That is how I feel this morning: cloaked in fog and mystery.

We had thunderstorms overnight, and cool air has moved over the warmer lake water, causing a line of fog to form a misty curtain this morning.

After Francine went back to her cottage, I remained ensconced in my Adirondack on the beach, unable to move. I watched the sun set on a day that I had long awaited but never thought would arrive.

Am I crazy?

Or completely sane?

I couldn't help but deconstruct my frayed friendship with Virgie, my reluctant acceptance to be a part of the Cherry Festival, Francine's bombshell, my admission, my memories of my mom and grandma and—above all else—that drunk woman at Cherry Republic.

All of this had shaken me to my core, so much so that when Francine stood to leave, I couldn't even get my legs to work. I was dizzy, felt ill, unable to stand.

And then to believe that the woman I had waited my whole life to find—the woman who I've envisioned, the woman I believed could save my store, my future, my family legacy, myself—might actually be a drunk blonde resorter? Well, that did nothing to bring on a peaceful night's sleep.

My Fata Morgana is a chardonnay clown?

Was everything I was told and believed in simply something to cling to—like a life preserver in the lake on a red-flag day—to help me survive all these years?

And then, to top things off, on my way to bed, my neighbors Geoffrey and Moira stopped me as I was heading up from the beach. They called to me through an inconvenient wind-burned clearing in the pines—caftans billowing in the lake breeze off

their deck—as they sipped wine while similarly dressed couples with layered hair, false eyelashes and bee-stung lips danced
to—*what do the kids call it these days?*—ah, yes, electronic music.

"We see your neighbor is back."

I tried to ignore them, reaching for my cell phone too late, and
parroting like an idiot into the receiver, "Hello? Hello? Johnny?"

I have no idea who Johnny is, by the way, or how I even came
up with the name. *Misery makes for strange bedfellows.*

"Oh, I'm sorry," I had said. "Yes, her name is Francine."

"I've heard about her husband," Moira said. "Sad. We're so
sorry. She must be devastated."

*Have you ever met someone who can try to utter the nicest sentiment
in the world and yet it comes out without any real sincerity whatsoever,
as if they were ordering a large order of fries in a drive-through?*

I began to count, wondering how long it would take them
to segue to the real reason they have bothered to talk to me for
the first time all summer.

One, two...

"Do you think," Geoffrey starts, "that your friend would be
interested in selling?"

Wow, that was fast.

I began to open my mouth, but Moira took over, her voice
purring like a leopard's.

"We could keep it all on the DL without any realtors getting
involved. Cash deal. Market value. Would save her and us a lot
of money in extra fees."

"She just wants to enjoy summer right now," I said.

"We notice her family no longer visits," Geoffrey added. "It's
such beautiful property."

"Such a shame," Moira said.

"What would your intentions be with the property?" I asked,
being simultaneously nosy and polite.

"Intentions!" Moira said with a laugh. "You are such a doll.
Such an old-fashioned doll. Well, our intentions with the prop-

erty would be to turn it into something amazing. It would be an ideal spot for a yoga or retreat center. Or we have friends who would love to tear it down, build their dream home and live next to us in a summer paradise."

"We've already drawn up plans," Geoffrey said with great confidence and zero irony. "So, of course, have our friends."

Moira glanced toward Francine's cottage. "It's in such ill repair."

No, it's not. It just requires a little love.

"This is residential property, though," I said.

"Anything can be rezoned," Geoffrey said. "Easy these days. And your property values would skyrocket."

"But then I'd be next to a business with revolving clients, people coming and going all day, a parking lot, traffic, folks on the beach." I stopped. "Or people I don't know."

Silence.

"Why can't people just enjoy what they have?" I asked. "Why must everything must be torn down, improved, monetized?"

"The world is evolving," Moira said. "Changing. You either adapt and change, or disappear."

Her words sounded like a threat, but—again, coming from her—seemed as flat as a coffee cake without baking powder.

I drop the measuring spoon I am holding and jump at the sound.

Am I simply a stubborn and stupid old woman who refuses to change, or am I the only domino refusing to fall, the only thing standing in the way of keeping history from collapsing?

Widows' Peak.

I catch a glimpse of myself in the kitchen window.

Hi, there, old gal.

I wave at myself, a cloud of flour puffing from the measuring spoon and becoming one with the fog outside.

I tossed and turned all night. In the pit of my gut, I've felt as I've been running across quicksand these last few years, desperately staying just head of the inevitable.

I've always felt as if my son was just waiting for this old gal to die so he could have a little peace. I know that's not true, but I also know I clouded his childhood—and that of my grandson—with my talk of our family's female legacy and what I believed was waiting on the horizon.

I think of the poster, the deed, the first dollar on the wall beyond me.

I think of my husband.

Perhaps I have been blinded by the past.

Although Jonah has never come right out and said that he'd like to get his hands on the cottage and general store in order to do something grand with it, his busy career and the fact that he visits so rarely makes the selfish part inside of me feel as if his interest is solely in the properties' value and not the importance they hold to me.

I'm not an idiot. I know the land value of this store and my cottage.

My mother always joked she was worth more dead than alive. I used to laugh, but it's not funny now. Do we really need another retail space with an insurance company, mattress store and coffee shop? Do we need a lakeshore mansion overpowering the landscape?

Change is *not* always good.

I shake my head at myself.

My mother's and grandmother's curse to me, I'm now convinced, is that I would sound like them the closer to the grave I got.

The fog envelops the window.

I shake my head again.

I know once the sun rises, it will fade, like my own fog.

Sometimes, it just takes a little time for things to clear so you can see the world again.

I take a swig of my coffee, shut my eyes and allow that world to still.

When I was young and large thunderstorms would roll in off the lake, I would run to my grandmother, trembling, and leap into her arms as she sat reading in her chair.

"Is God mad at me?" I would ask, thinking the booming, echoes and reverberations across the great lake were his voice calling me out for something mischievous or unladylike I had done as a girl. I even believed my visions were wrong.

My grandmother would set her book down on the little log table that sat next to her chair and the stone fireplace. "No, Mary," she would say. "It's just Mother Nature. She's having a bad day like all mothers do sometimes."

She would tell me to shut my eyes and count between the thunder boomers. The further apart they were in time, the more distant the storm was, the calmer the world was becoming.

"Just wait until you hear your soul sing again," my grandma would say.

I would keep my eyes shut until that moment when the rain immediately stops, as if a faucet has been shut off in heaven, and all of a sudden the world stills, and the birds began to sing.

"Everybody has storms in their lives, Mary," she would tell me, rocking me on her lap. "I've had too many to count. You just have to be patient enough to wait them out. And you have to be smart enough to understand their importance."

"I hate storms!" I would say.

"But they feed the earth, our cherries and our gardens," my grandma would say. "And they force us to stop and remember what calm sounds like."

As I grew older, my grandma used to take me outside onto the road.

"Gotta face your fears head-on!" she'd say. "Learn you can stop any storm right in its track before it knocks you down."

She'd hand me a cherry and tell me to spit it right into the coming storm.

"Blow!" she'd yell over the wind swirling down the Tunnel

of Trees. "Blow, Mary! Center all your anger and your nerves right into that pit, and blow just like the Big Bad Wolf! Blow the bad away! Blow, Mary, blow!"

I hear a mourning dove coo—my family always referred to them as *rain crows* for being harbingers of a storm's beginning and end—and then a robin sing its loud, liquid call.

Cheerily, cheer-up, cheerio!

I open my eyes and glance out the window. A fat robin, big and bright-eyed, is sitting on the branch of a pine. It has its head tilted and is looking directly at me.

"Hello," I call to our state bird.

The robin calls again, but this time I hear its song differently, the way my mom and grandma used to always sing back to it.

Cherry, cherry, cherry-oh!

It nods as if taken by my change of lyrics and takes off.

I take another swig of coffee and start pitting cherries once again.

BECKY

Q opens her sunroof, and I stand on the passenger seat and stick my head out the top.

"Hey!" she says. "Watch my leather!"

I must not just see this seated in a car, I must be a part of it. I am enclosed in a tunnel of trees.

"I've forgotten how pretty this is!" I yell, my hair flying.

"I know! This might be the most beautiful thing I've ever seen," Q calls to me over the wind and the music.

The trees' branches and limbs have created a canopy—a virtual ceiling of green—that extends over the road. Slants of light dance across the road, which twists and turns this way and that. On one side, ferns grow as big as bushes, and on the other, the lake appears in breathtaking peeks through the trees.

I take a seat again.

Every mile or so, an old cottage or art studio will wave from a clearing, but it's truly a magical hardwood forest.

The trees whiz by, a flash of brown and green. It's like revisiting a scrapbook and flipping through the pages, your history a blur.

"So this is the Tunnel of Trees?" Q asks. "Beautiful! What a history!"

Yes, I think. That's exactly what is so pretty and evocative about this feat of nature: its history. A family still standing strong after all these years.

"We need a convertible," I say. "Should have stolen my dad's."

"Is this it?" Q suddenly slows the car.

A sign says *The Very Cherry General Store*.

"Yes!"

Q pulls into the parking lot.

"Speaking of beautiful," Q says, "is this place for real?"

The general store isn't just quaint. It's I'm-Doris-Day-out-for-a-ride-in-the-country-in-a-convertible-and-I-have-to-re-move-my-scarf-to-take-in-all-the-cuteness-of-the-place-my-boyfriend-just-brought-me-to quaint.

A bell on the screened door jingles as we enter, and then the door bangs shut.

"Oh, my gosh," I say. "The screened door even sounds like a screened door is supposed to."

"This place is a total throwback," Q says.

On one side of the store, a group of locals is picking up their mail from the post office. In the center, a throng of a vacationers is perusing all the homemade baked goods, their faces pressed up to the domes, noses fogging the glass. A long line of people waits behind a barnwood counter, many studying the chalkboard featuring the day's sandwich and potpie specials.

"Tomato sandwiches," I say, pointing at the board. "Home-made chicken-and-veggie potpies." I rush up to the baked goods. "Muffins, cookies, coffee cakes. I've gone to heaven!"

A couple of people turn to look at me, and I wave sweetly.

I grab Q by the arm and whisper into her ear, "Do you see her? Where's the old lady?"

Q scans the store. "Maybe she's in the kitchen or putting out the mail. It looks like the type of place where you have to do anything and everything at any given moment."

"In other words," I say, "it's like working in a school."

Q laughs. "Just be nice. Her kids probably run this place, and they didn't realize grandma got loose last night and visited her own statue until she got home last night eating chocolate-covered cherries and rambling on about a drunk woman who could spit better than an angry llama."

I laugh out loud.

Q continues. "Be cordial…"

"Like a cherry?" I quip.

She rolls her eyes. "Just be cordial so we can get on with our day and our vacation. I want to picnic on the beach tonight. I don't think we should be seen in town again until the Most Wanted posters of you stealing a little girl's ice cream cone are taken down."

Q grabs a small basket and beelines toward the shelves in the back of the general store. "We need a few things so we don't have to eat out all the time."

"We packed enough to feed an army."

"Well, the army ate all the chips when they were drunk."

A few more people turn to look at us.

She scoots away and begins to place vacation essentials into her basket: Pringles, French onion dip, aspirin, Gatorade. I meander over and check out the old cash register. I feel as if Mr. Potter from *It's A Wonderful Life* might suddenly come to life behind it and admonish me for being frivolous with my pennies.

And then I see her.

The old woman from last night, who—now that I'm sober, and in the light of day—seems much more youthful and spry than I remember. She is attractive, her hair in a sweet style that seems appropriate for her, not too young and not too old. She is wearing jeans, tennis shoes and a floral, short-sleeved top with a cute collar, topped by an apron reading *The Very Cherry General Store: run by women since 1874!*

I stare for much too long at her apron, the words taking me by surprise but also causing the world to stop around me. She catches my eye. Without missing a beat, she raises a finger in my direction, an indication to wait until she's ready, and scurries over to deliver mail to a group of locals before racing over to the counter to take over from a frazzled girl. I stare as she begins to make a half-dozen sandwiches from scratch while relaying orders to her staffer for potpies, sides of coleslaw or potato salad, and cookies, all while bagging and chatting with each person as if they are a member of her family.

"Cherry Mary!" a woman exclaims when she reaches the counter. "I wait every year for this moment!"

"First week of vacation, Jill?" Cherry Mary asks her.

"First week of my life," she says. "I don't feel like I come alive until I smell the water and the pine and come into your store."

I smile.

"The usual?" Cherry Mary asks. "Liverwurst for your husband, extra pickled onion, and a tomato sandwich for you, with a side of slaw and a dozen Treasure Cookies to go?"

"You remember?" the woman says with a big laugh. "Every year?"

"Can't remember to turn off my coffeepot or where I parked my car, but my customers? I never forget."

I watch this woman everyone calls Cherry Mary work at a pace I haven't seen since Q and I manned the window at Ted Drewes. There is a pace in which you work in retail—no matter if it's food or clothes—and it gets in your veins. I've always had to watch my tongue around coworkers who dally or just want meander through their days.

"Next!"

I look up. The line has cleared, and the woman is waving at me to approach the counter. I glance over at Q, who is practically drooling onto the cases of cookies and cupcakes.

"Hi," I say, a bit too enthusiastically. "I'm Becky. Becky Thatcher. We met last night."

"Thank you so much for coming. Means the world. Sorry

about the wait." She suddenly stops and looks at me curiously. "Becky Thatcher? Are you pulling my leg?"

"I'm not," I say. "And, to make matters worse, I was born in Hannibal, Missouri."

She laughs, hard.

I continue. "My parents didn't see the irony, I don't think."

She wipes her hands on her apron and then extends one. "Everyone calls me Cherry Mary," she says, nodding to a poster behind her with that moniker in faded type. "You saw this face last night." Mary hesitates. "If you remember."

This time, I laugh.

She continues. "I actually think Becky Thatcher is a better name than Cherry Mary. At least you're named after a famous literary character. I sound like a Nehi soda."

"That's you, right?" I ask, glancing at the framed newspaper article. "Just like the carving of you. See, I remember."

"Was," she says. "Still is. I can explain. Do you have a few minutes to chat?"

"That's why I'm here," I say.

She turns to her helper at the counter. "Do you mind handling things for just a few minutes, Erin?"

The girl's freckled face freezes. "Sort of."

"Just yell if you need anything," Mary says. "I'll be right back."

"Don't go," the girl says.

I hide a laugh.

"It's okay," Mary says. "You'll be just fine. If you need to delay, just tell everyone about today's cookies or the history of the place. Okay?"

Erin doesn't answer.

Mary motions for me to come behind the counter and follow her into the kitchen. I hurry over to Q.

"If I'm not back in five, I'll be locked in the basement," I whisper. "As any best friend in any horror movie would do, you have to come find me." I stop. "Even if you die."

She waves me off.

The tiny kitchen smells like freshly baked Snickerdoodle cookies. Mary leans against the butcher-block counter.

"Why are you here?" she asks.

"To see you."

"Not here, but in Good Hart."

"Vacation," I say. "With my best friend."

"No," Mary says. "What really brings you here?"

The way she says that—as if she can cut through the nonsense and see into my soul—gives me goose bumps.

"Um, well, I broke up with my boyfriend," I say. "I thought he was going to ask me to marry him. Turns out, I don't think he ever really loved me. Now he is trying to sue me for custody of a fridge and some furniture."

"Now you're talking," she crows. "What happened?"

"I had a meltdown on a playground and told him to move out," I say. "And then I ran away from home." I stop to reconsider my words. "I actually ran away from life."

Mary narrows her eyes to consider what I've told her.

"My husband tried to hit me when I was a young mother," she says.

"What did you do?" I ask.

She studies me for a minute.

"I blinded him with a cherry pit," she finally says. "And then he died."

I think of calling for Q, but she says, "But I never ran away from life. It just made me confront it head-on. I think that's the direction you're going in on the compass of life."

Goosies again.

"Men," Mary says with a wink, as if to ease my nerves.

"Men," I repeat.

The sounds of an unfamiliar world envelop me: the soft

clamor of shoppers in the general store; the hum of the oven; the gentle rattling of the cookie tins stacked on top of it; a robin singing its heart out outside the back screened door; the buzz of bees just outside the open kitchen window; the crash of the waves from Lake Michigan in the distance.

And though these sounds are unfamiliar, they are as deeply comforting as the sounds from my life: a spring rain outside my bedroom window; the giggles of children in the hallways; my mom's humming as she made soup; the muted sound of a Cardinals baseball game coming from the living room; my grandma singing a Sinatra tune as she drove me to the grocery store.

"Have you ever made a Michigan Treasure Cookie?" she asks out of the blue.

"I've never heard of them."

She smiles. "That's because we put them on the map."

"As an elementary-school assistant principal, I'm more used to taking cookies away from children, handing them apples to appease their parents, and then taking their contraband back to my office, closing my blinds and eating it while I softly cry."

From the depths of Mary's stomach, a deep guttural laugh emerges, which slowly evolves into a roar.

"This sounds like a big step up, then," Mary says, wiping her eyes.

"Oh, it is, believe me," I say. "Especially the not crying alone."

"You're funny," she says. "That's one of the traits I love most in people. I believe a person who doesn't know how to laugh at herself doesn't really know herself."

Mary grabs an aqua-colored colander and dashes out the kitchen, the screened door banging shut behind her.

"Follow me!" she calls.

By the time I catch up, she is standing in the midst of a small orchard of cherry trees whose limbs are drooping in beautiful red fruit. The trees, dancing gently in the breeze, look like a young girl flushed from a day in the summer sun.

I join her and begin to pluck the warm, firm cherries directly from the branches, and—in a matter of moments—the big old colander is filled to the brim. Mary zips across the vast lawn and the hill and back into the kitchen, moving with the excitement of a kid out of school on the first day of summer vacation. I dash after her to keep up. I am out of breath when I reach her. Mary has already washed the cherries and has the colander sitting atop a giant cutting board on the center island.

"Have you ever pitted a cherry?"

I stop and think.

My mom always used those canned cherries for her desserts. Maraschino cherries didn't have pits. And the with cherries my grandparents bought at farm stands on vacation, I'd just chew and spit the pits right out the car window as my grampa drove.

"I actually don't think I have, if you can believe it."

Mary picks up a cherry.

"There are different ways to do it," she says. "Many today use a cherry pitter." She pulls one from a drawer in the island and punches out the pit. A big explosion of red hits her apron. "This is the easiest and fastest way. Problem is there's often a lot of splash-back, as you can see, and some wasted fruit." She wipes her hand on her apron. "And then there's the twist and poke methods."

"The twist and poke?" I say. "That sounds like a dance my elementary-school kids would do for an open house."

Mary grabs a toothpick from a drawer. She pops the stem off the cherry and sticks the toothpick into the fruit. "The twist method requires sticking something thin into the cherry, hitting the pit and then twisting it until it's out."

She pops out the cherry, which resembles a mangled mess by the end of the process. "You're going to need a lot of practice to get it right," she says. "And then there's the poke method."

Mary reaches into another drawer and fishes out a thin pastry tip used on a piping bag for decorating. She grabs an old soda bottle, places it on the island, and then inserts the tip into the stem hole, driving the pit down and into the bottle.

"Wow," I say. "Amazing."

"But you still have to chop the fruit, so it's just another step. Wanna know my way? The way I've done it my whole life? The way my mom and grandma did it?"

I nod.

Mary places a cherry in the middle of the cutting board and an empty bowl beside it. She grabs a gleaming paring knife and presses the flat side onto the cherry until it pops.

Splash!

An explosion of red juice explodes onto the cutting board and a small spray hits her apron. She picks up the cherry, pries it apart with her hands and tosses the pit into the empty bowl. She repeats this process a few times.

Mary stops and hands me the knife. "Your turn."

I take it rather hesitantly and press softly into the cherry.

"No," Mary says, grabbing my hand. "It's a firm cherry. You have to really take charge."

I do as I'm instructed, and upon my cut, the cherry explodes, soaking my white T-shirt with red juice.

"Makes quite a mess, doesn't it?" she says. "Too late for an apron now." Mary looks at me. "Keep going. Show me what you've got."

I begin pitting cherry after cherry, until there's a large mound on the cutting board. Mary leans in and scoops the chopped cherries into a separate bowl, carefully lifting the cutting board and pouring a river of red liquid into the cut fruit.

"You can use any gadget you want," Mary says, "but you still have to chop the fruit. Pitting cherries is just like life. You can try to take the easy way out, but in the end you realize there really is no easy way. So why not just get your hands messy and have a little fun along the way?"

I wipe my hands on a tea towel and smile.

"Now, let me show you how to make the batter for the cookies."

Mary begins to pull ingredients from the cabinet, and I watch her work—quickly, by memory only—smiling as she measures, pours in chocolate chips, mixes. When the dough is done, she hands me a spoon, and we begin to drop the mixture onto the cookie sheets.

"May I ask you a question?" Mary asks.

I nod.

"How did you learn to spit a cherry pit like you did?"

I shake my head and shrug my shoulders. "I don't know," I say. "I've always been able to whistle, I could always blow a bubble with gum bigger than any kid in school, and I've always been able to shoot the paper off a straw and hit my dad in the back of the head from a mile away. My best friend, Q, who's with me, said I could hit a kid in the back of the head all the way to Auntie Anne's Pretzels on the other side of the mall while sitting at Orange Julius. I had no idea it was a skill set until I got here."

Mary smiles.

"It's a big, big deal in these parts," she says. "Mostly because it's something a woman isn't supposed to do. It's something a woman isn't supposed to try. It's something a woman was never supposed to win." Mary smiles. "Until me."

"That's amazing," I say.

"You have to enter the contest," Mary says as soon as I finish.

"Oh, I don't think so. I'm just here on vacation. That was all just a drunken spectacle, as you saw."

"No!" Mary says firmly.

Her tone catches me off guard.

"It's destiny!" she insists. "You have to enter this contest. My entire life has led to this moment." She stops. "Please. Do it. For me."

"I'd have to think about it," I say, hesitantly.

She points at her apron. "Women weren't supposed to be the

ones running this store, either, but we have been, since it began."
Mary looks at me. "It's destiny."

I stop spooning and narrow my eyes. "What do you mean?"

"It's destiny that a woman be a part of this general store," she
says. "It's destiny that a woman be the one to break my record."
Mary reaches out and puts her hands on mine. "It's destiny that
you are here right now."

Once again, my body explodes in goose pimples.

My eyes grow wide. "I'm sorry. I don't think I understand."

"Fata Morgana," Mary says. "I heard you say that last night before you spit that stone. Our visions are the same. Four women.
I've seen them coming toward me my whole life, ever since I
was a girl."

I suddenly drop the spoon I am holding.

"I've waited my whole life for you," she continues. "My whole
life."

I open my mouth to tell her about my visions, my grandparents, the scrapbook and their message to me, but behind me I
hear a man's voice say, "Surprise!"

Mary looks toward the door.

"Ollie!"

Mary rushes over and hugs a handsome young man with curly
hair and piercing eyes.

"This is my grandson, Ollie," she says, stepping back. "Ollie,
this is my new friend, Becky."

He surveys me with an inquisitive gaze but then smiles.

"I've always wondered if *I'm* actually the fourth woman,"
Ollie says, "but I don't look so great in a wig."

I laugh uncertainly but sense a sad tone in his joke.

"It's nice to meet you, Becky," Ollie says to me. He turns to
Mary. "I see you're busy, Grandma. I think I'm going to take a
walk, maybe hit the beach. My back's a bit stiff from the long
drive."

Ollie heads outside without waiting for a reply.

As the door swings open, I can hear the lake call in the distance, sirens singing to me as they have my whole life. But I still don't know if they're calling me here to the shores of Lake Michigan or luring me to crash on the shores of a place I remember only as a girl.

MARY

I already know where Ollie will be.

When I catch up to him, he is seated in the giant tree swing my mom and I built for him when he was little. After spending all year in the city, Ollie loved the quiet and charm of Good Hart's summers. Swimming, rock hunting, biking through the trees and reading—right here in this swing—made for a wonderful summer and one he wanted when he grew up. While other friends were traveling to Europe, starting corporate careers or moving with their jobs, Ollie preferred to return to the lake.

"Want me to push you?" I ask.

He ducks his head but does not answer.

Ollie has always been this odd mix of boyishness and masculinity, child and grown-up, push and pull, big city and small town…

Father and grandmother.

I move behind him. He lifts his feet off the ground, and I smile inside.

I give Ollie a gentle push, and he begins to swing. I step aside, and he pushes off with his legs, going higher, higher, the whoosh of the swing merging with the hum of the cicadas.

It feels as if nothing has changed.

It feels as if everything has changed.

I move around in front of the tree swing and watch my grand-son. His dark curls are much the same as they were when he was just a boy: bouncy, shiny, edging into his eyes. He spent his teen years trying to alter those family genetics, shaving off his hair one summer for freshman football, growing it into an awful mullet another summer and then straightening it one year to resemble a surfer.

His dark eyes are mirrors to his every emotion, stormy as a summer thunder boomer over the lake one moment and as beautiful as a chocolate iris the next. He's always been a pale boy with pink cheeks that flush red whether he's upset or ex-cited. Ollie is a big boy—a linebacker in high school—and he looks as if he's been hitting the gym of late and gulping down that protein powder he so loves. Although he is now thirty-six, Ollie still looks like a boy. I like to think he gets that youthful spirit from me.

The wind from the swing swirls my hair around in circles. Ollie goes higher and higher, and I have to stick my hands in the pocket of my apron to keep from reaching out and stopping him in order to protect him from getting hurt.

Too late, I think.

Finally, he slows, digging his feet into the ground.

He refuses to look at me, instead focusing on the narrow path that leads down the bluff to Lake Michigan. Through the green, there is a window of blue. He will talk when he's ready.

Ollie has always been emotional, the exact opposite of my son, who bottled everything up tight as a drum and refused to talk about any of it. If he didn't acknowledge it, then it wasn't real, from his drunk, dead father to his kooky, headstrong mother. I used to joke that Jonah should have become a janitor because he likes to sweep everything away.

But Ollie's emotions are as big as his body, and he has always been caught in that terrible middle ground of needing to share what he's feeling but unable to do so in a house that wouldn't acknowledge it. His mother is a good, kind soul. So is my son. Despite all of my turmoil, we provided Jonah a rather idyllic life, and yet he experienced a great deal of shame. Small towns gossip, whispers spreading from one person to another, generation to generation, like a breeze through the branches. You often don't even realize how loud a sound has been building until it finally arrives at your doorstep. A boy living without his father—no matter how terrible a man he was—is still hard, and I know that. And a boy with a father like Burt, well, that's even harder. Rumors hurt. The truth is even harder. But Jonah's spent his whole life trying to make everything so perfect—like the condos and developments he creates—that there's no room for imperfection. I have always felt that same internal pressure pulse from my grandson.

"My whole life, every time I've come here and looked out at this lake, it's brought me peace."

Ollie's voice catches me off guard. I pivot toward him. He meets my eyes after a second and continues.

"You see images of women out there, grandma. But I have visions, too. Do you know what I see?"

I shake my head.

"You."

My heart flutters in my chest like a hooked fish in the bottom of a johnboat.

"I came here to have a nice summer break and to encourage you to participate in the Cherry Festival."

"I am, sweetheart."

"Good!" he says. "This whole town should be celebrating you! I want to celebrate my grandma, too, and also have some fun just like I did as a kid. I loved spending my summers here."

Ollie waits until I look at him again.

"I loved spending my summers with *you*," he emphasizes.

"Me, too," I say softly. "More than anything in this world."

"Can I ask who the woman is you were talking to in the kitchen? Maybe I'm jumping to a big conclusion here, but I walked into find you telling a complete stranger that you've waited your whole life to find her." Ollie looks me right in the eye. "That kinda hurts, Grandma, because I feel like I've waited my whole life for you to say the same thing to me."

"Oh, Ollie," I say. "You know how much I love you."

"I do," he says, "but I just feel like I've never been part of your vision for the future."

"Honey, you've never said anything about it since you were a very little boy," I say, genuinely surprised.

"I know. But it's the main reason I'm here."

My heart flip-flops again.

Ollie continues. "It's just that I walk in to surprise you only to find some strange woman in the kitchen. I just don't want anyone trying to take advantage of you and your...situation."

"She is not taking advantage of any *situation*, Ollie. I met her yesterday and asked her to come over."

"But you think she's the woman you've dreamed of finding?" he asks. "The fourth woman on the horizon?"

I shrug. "I don't know," I say. "But I watched her break my cherry-pit record last night. I've never seen anything like it. She certainly seems like the one."

Ollie smiles, shaking his head.

"This is what has been so hard for me and Dad," Ollie says. "You've waited your whole life to find a mystery woman who could spit a cherry pit farther than you ever did. I just need to know why. For what? To take over the general store? To be the daughter or granddaughter you never had? To fulfill the family female legacy? Dad and I love you, more than anything, but it just seems like we've never been enough."

"Ollie, please," I say, moving toward him. "It has nothing to do with you or your father. It just feels like my destiny calling, no matter how crazy that sounds. It feels like a question

that needs answered. Who knows, maybe it all has something
to do with you. Maybe it has nothing to do with me. Maybe
you two were meant to meet. I just know that sometimes you
have to have faith, no matter how much common sense tells
you not to believe."

I look out at the window of blue and sigh. "I'm an old woman,
Ollie. I want my life to have meant something. I want this store
to carry on after I'm gone. I'd love my family to have all of this.
But you have to understand you and your father have never really seemed to want anything to do with this, and that hurts
me, too. I don't have a lot of runway left to plan. Sometimes,
I feel like you and your father are just waiting patiently for me
to die so you can pawn all of this off to the highest bidder and
turn everything I love into lakefront rental condos."

The pink flushes from my grandson's cheeks.

"Is that what you really think of me and Dad?" he asks. "I
would never...we could never..."

"I just don't know where you two stand because you've never
told me. I truly don't mean to hurt you, but I hope you understand where I'm coming from here."

"And you're willing to trust some stranger who's probably
stalked you online? You don't understand the way the world
works today. I'm just trying to protect you."

"I went through hell to save this family. So did my mom and
grandma. I worked my entire life to give Jonah—and you—a
world filled with options. I never had that. I just had options
that a world of men gave to me." I can feel my heart pounding
in my chest. I take a step forward and a deep breath to steady
myself. "What options are you and your dad giving me? Neither of you have ever said a word about wanting to keep this
store or the cottage in the family, much less any finite plan for
the future. My trust leaves you both everything. But to do what
with? Do you have any idea how that makes me feel at eighty?

It's like treading on quicksand. I have no firm ground on which to stand as I near the end of my life."

"I know, Grandma. It's part of the reason I came home. I feel…lost. I came here to, hopefully, find myself again," Ollie says.

He jumps off the swing and heads toward the path to the bluffs. Ollie turns.

"I just want to hear you've waited for me your whole life, too."

"I have," I call after him. "I never meant to hurt you. I'm so sorry."

He stops right in the middle of the path, framed by the trees, the sky, the lake, the sun shimmering over his head like a light.

Say it back, I think, Say I'm sorry, too. Please.

And then Ollie is off, jogging down the bluff.

In the distance, I see him kick off his shoes, dump the contents of his pockets, tear off his shirt and jump into the lake.

He begins to swim toward the horizon.

The women are back. The women are closer.

And Ollie is swimming directly toward them.

BECKY

I rush out of the Very Cherry General Store. Q is standing in the parking lot shoveling containers of cookies, cupcakes, muffins and coffee cakes into the back of the car.

"What was all the commotion?" Q asks, completely unaware of what just transpired. "I thought you had probably been dragged to the basement, but I couldn't save you because the poor girl at the counter was having a breakdown." She gestures into the trunk. "I was ordering so much, using actual money, and she didn't know how to make change. She asked me what the shiny thing was, and I actually had to say 'A nickel.'"

I stare at her, unable to put my emotions into words.

"I know, I know, I look like Little Debbie," she says with a laugh. "I couldn't resist. Did you know that Cherry Mary woman makes all of this stuff herself? I'm convincing myself this will be healthy, that I'm carb-loading for our walks to the beach."

When I don't laugh, Q finally stops talking.

"What happened?"

"I actually don't know. I think Mary's grandson came to visit and was upset that I was talking to her."

"I know one thing," Q says. "He was so hot. He looked like one of those European soccer players but stockier."

Q touches her red hair. She always touches her hair when she talks about a man. I first noticed it in elementary school when Todd Grimes put a Valentine in her homemade mailbox.

"I didn't notice what he looked like," I say. "Only how hurt he sounded. It sort of broke my heart."

"Right," Q says. "You didn't happen to notice the only guy in these parts the last few days not wearing Dockers or fixing his dentures."

"I guess he was okay-looking," I say.

"Okay-looking? Did you fall and strike your head recently? He was H-O-T hot."

"I feel like I'm in a dream," I say. "Mary asked me to make her special Michigan cookies with her and then taught me how to pit a cherry, but then she told me she had been waiting her whole life for me to arrive here, Q. She told me she's had the same vision as I've had her whole life, since she was a girl like me. A Fata Morgana of four women walking toward her on the horizon. It was surreal." I hold up my arm. "I still have goose bumps."

"Is this all because you spit a cherry pit farther than she did?"

"I actually think so," I say. "I think it has to do with something deeper, though, about a woman being able to do something better than a man, be it spitting a cherry pit or running a business like this for so long." I turn and look back at the store. "It was like my whole life led to this trip and this moment. I think she was ready to share more, but we got interrupted by her grandson. I think she feels I'm part of some predestined plan. It just all ended so strangely, like a cliffhanger on *The Real Housewives of Good Hart*. She went running after him."

"I should do the same thing," Q says. "I played soccer in high school."

"You don't even know if he plays soccer," I say. "You've already created an imaginary story in your head."

"Just like Cherry Mary," Q says with a wink.

Suddenly, I hear Mary's voice cry, "Ollie! Stop!"

The bell on the store's screened door jangles, and then the door bangs shut.

Ollie races into the parking lot, shirtless, his pale skin glistening, his ringlets wet and dripping water.

"Speaking of visions," Q says to me in a stage whisper. "Good golly, Ollie."

Ollie beelines toward a car on the other side of the parking lot. It has Illinois plates.

"Stop!" Mary says, racing out the door.

Ollie grabs his key and clicks the remote. A beep echoes through the lot, and he begins to open his car door.

"Stop!" Q suddenly yells. "In the name of love!"

Ollie turns in our direction, squinting in the sun. And then he comes over, stops in front of us and wipes the T-shirt across his chest.

"Lucky shirt," Q murmurs to me like a ventriloquist, mouth shut. "Hi, Ollie. I'm Q." She is touching her hair.

Ollie doesn't even look at Q. He directs his stormy eyes on me.

"So who are you, anyway?"

"My name's Becky," I say. "Becky Thatcher."

"How appropriate," he says, rolling his dark eyes. "Becky Thatcher. Didn't you ruin Tom Sawyer's life, too?"

"Ouch," Q says.

"Who are you?" I ask.

"I'm the grandson of the woman you're trying to take advantage of," he says. "And I'm not going to let that happen."

"*Excuse* me?" I say, my voice rising. "Your grandmother invited me here. You need to apologize."

"I'm not going to let you waltz into town and manipulate an old woman for her money."

"I would never take advantage of anyone, especially a woman her age. That's despicable even to suggest."

My voice is at a very high octave. People are staring. Mary has stopped a few feet away.

"I won't let some crazy woman near my grandmother!"

"Crazy?" I yell. "You haven't met crazy yet, Ollie. I mean, what kind of name is that? You sound like something from *Finding Nemo*."

He snorts at me.

"You can't just throw around terms like that at women," I continue. "We get that all the time. When women get emotional, we're *crazy*. When we decide to break up with a guy, we're *nuts*. When women want to make big changes in our lives, we're *hysterical*. When women date more than one guy, we're *loose*. When men do those same things, you're described as *headstrong, not ready for a relationship, career-oriented* and *players*.'"

I take another step toward Ollie.

"The word *crazy* comes from the word *craze*, derived from the Middle English word *crasen*, which means to become cracked, diseased or deformed. In the 1500s, that word described *cracked* people who were deranged."

My fingers fly around my head making quote marks around those dangerous words.

"*Crazy* has such negative connotations," I say. "Calling someone crazy suggests there is something wrong with them. It blames them. Mental illness is never a person's fault. And being emotional is actually a good thing."

"How do you know all of this?" he asks.

"I'm a teacher. And I was an English major. Teachers and English majors know everything."

"You're putting words in my mouth," Ollie says, deflating just a bit. "I just came here to see my grandma." He turns toward Mary. "I just wanted the town to recognize her accomplishment."

Silence.

In fact, it is silent so long that I can hear the cicadas moan in the nearby trees, the wind tilting each branch toward the next, as if they are whispering to one another, passing along gossip about all that's occurred today.

Suddenly, I remember what Mary said to me earlier.

You have to enter the contest… It's destiny.

"That's what I want, too," I finally say.

Ollie looks at me and then his grandma.

"I'm so sorry," he says. "I overreacted. I just could never live with myself if I let my grandma get hurt."

"Aww," Q says.

"I understand completely," I say, softening at his heartfelt words. "And, to be honest, the last twenty-four hours have been anything but normal. I still don't know what's going on, but I do feel like I was supposed to meet your grandma."

I hesitate.

"In fact, I've been so moved by her story that I want to honor her legacy by entering the cherry competition."

Mary yelps her approval.

"I'd love to be the first woman since your grandmother to make history."

"Well," Ollie says, "I think I'll enter, too. I'd love to keep the championship in the family."

"Then, may the best man—or woman—win!" I say with a big smile.

I jokingly poke my finger the middle of Ollie's chest for emphasis.

Oh, no.

It's a good chest.

Thick and shiny, like marble.

It's like the new bathroom countertop I installed a few years back in my home.

But way hotter.

And attached to a man that makes Matt now look like Garfield the cat.

My finger hits muscle and just stops. I try to move it, but it lingers on his chest, as if I'm a paper clip and he's a magnet.

"Well, this is an unexpected turn of events," I hear Q whisper in her ventriloquist way, lips shut, a murmur only I can understand.

"I guess I'll see you at the cherry competition," Ollie says to me. Then he goes over to Mary and gives her a hug. "I'm sorry for being a hothead, Grandma. I'm going to go unpack. I'll see you back at the cottage."

Ollie gets into his car and drives off.

"I'm so sorry about all of that," Mary says. "We've always been very close. He's just being protective."

I nod. "I can understand how it could be off-putting to walk in and hear your grandmother saying she's waited her whole life to meet a total stranger."

"Ollie has a way about him," Mary says.

"You can say that again," Q says.

I give her the evil eye, and she moves toward the car.

"My cookies are melting," she says. "Better turn on the AC."

"Speaking of which," Mary says, "if you want to come back and try making those cookies again, I'd love to have you."

"I don't know if that's such a good idea," I say. "I don't want to overstep any more than I already have."

"I know in my heart and soul that we were meant to meet."

Silence again. The trees whisper.

"I'll think about it," I say. "Thank you."

"And I'd love to help you train for the Cherry Championship."

"Train?" I laugh.

Mary tilts her head as though she's listening to the trees. "Believe me, you'll need all the help you can get, especially when the nerves set in and the men try to distract you."

"Distract me?"

"They don't want another woman to win," she says. "They never want a woman to win."

"I'll think about that, too," I say. "I just don't want to cause any more upheaval around here. I mean, what else could go wrong, right?"

The screened door on the general store flies open.

Erin, the overwhelmed young girl who had been working at the counter, stops on the front stoop and cries, "I can't take it anymore!"

She takes off running across the parking lot, throws open her car door and leans her head against the steering wheel.

A lonely honk fills the air.

"And...end scene!" I can hear Q say from the car.

PART THREE

"That's the hard part of overdosing on cherries.
You have all the pits to tell you exactly how many you ate."

—Andy Warhol

MARY

August 1958

The only sound I can hear is my heart pounding, louder than any drum emanating from Devil's Elbow.

The limbs of a giant sugar maple part in the breeze, and a glint of light temporarily blinds me. Sunspots fill my eyes, and they dance and drift until there are just four remaining, drifting closer and closer, until they are gone, inside of me.

I glance over at my mother and grandmother.

My grandma's head is bowed in prayer. My mother is clutching her handbag so tightly I'm amazed it hasn't disintegrated.

My grandma looks up and winks. My heart and mind stills.

Murmurs begin to fill my ears.

My own voices, my own fears.

First girl to do this...

Part of that all-women general store...

All married to drunks...

This should be good for a laugh...

Why is she standing up there?

I recognize that last voice. I skew my eyes just so without moving my head. Virgie is whispering to the town's rich girls, who she's managed to befriend in high school by doting on their every whim and serving as their errand girl. She runs to the pharmacy to retrieve their makeup, she sprints to the general store to pick up sodas and snacks, she's the one they make pump gas at the station, giggling as the attendant stands by watching her do it.

I don't even know my former best friend anymore.

I'm still the same rabble-rouser wanting to do the things girls aren't allowed instead of playing nice with the girls who play by the rules.

"Forty-two feet, eleven inches!"

The deep, gravelly voice of Baritone Bob, our local radio deejay and announcer for the Annual Cherry Pit Spittin' Championship booms across the fairgrounds.

"Let's give Wilbur Jenkins a big round of applause! Next up is..."

Baritone Bob pauses for much too long. The microphone squeaks, and a riffling of papers echoes forth.

"This says *Mark*," you can hear him mumble. "I got eyes. That ain't a Mark." More shuffling. More whispering. "Rules don't say a girl can't enter. Just never have." More microphone squeaks. "I got it. Okay, well, next up is Mary Jackson. You heard that right. Looks like Mary will be the first girl to enter the contest. Let's hear it for Miss Mary!"

A smattering of applause is mixed with a chorus of boos and a few belly laughs.

I walk toward the rope and steady myself in front of the sandy pit. A little girl, Betty Trimble, wearing a red gingham jumper, walks up with a basket of cherries. She curtsies, I pick a perfect cherry from the basket, and she skips off.

Just as I am about to put the cherry into my mouth, I hear a man yelling.

"Leave me alone! That's my girl! Mary!"

I pivot. My father, stumbling, weaving through the crowd. He stops when he sees me. He yanks a flask from the flap on his overalls and yells, "Cheers, Mary!" before taking a long pull.

My father turns toward the crowd, many seated in folding chairs or on big blankets.

"My little girl decided to embarrass her old man today!" He laughs. "Her whole family. Her whole town." One more drink. "I tried to stop her." He scans the crowd and stumbles toward my grandma and mom. "But these two encouraged her. No, they taught her to break tradition. So let me just save her—and all of us—a lot of time, trouble and embarrassment and just take her with me right now. A girl shouldn't be allowed to do this. We all know that. She's just going to humiliate herself. The only reason she's here is that she lied. Mary signed up as *Mark Jackson*. Check the records. I know. *She* forged my signature."

He turns and points at my grandmother.

Many in the crowd gasp, and a few begin to boo. The two men stationed at the end of the pit to record distance look at each other helplessly.

"Let me just take my little girl," my father says, moving toward me. "No harm, no foul. Just a prank."

My father leans toward me.

"You'll pay for this," he says quietly, a big smile on his face for the crowd, his breath thick with whiskey.

He grabs my arm.

"Over my dead body."

I look up. My grandma is standing in front of him.

"Move, old lady," he says, "before I have to move you."

"Over my dead body."

My mother stands before him.

"You will pay for this, too," he says.

"I've paid enough already to keep this family going in the eyes of society. I want you gone, you mean, pathetic drunk."

"Move!"

"Over my dead body."

I look up, and Aponi, the old woman from Devil's Elbow,

is standing before my father. She raises her walking stick and pokes my father.

"Witch," he says. "Witch!" he yells.

"Leave!" she says. "Before I call on my ancestors to make you."

My father's eyes grow wide, he turns and—as he has done my whole life—simply disappears after creating havoc.

I am shaking.

"Don't let them see you cry, Mary," my grandmother says. "You show them what you got inside you. You show them what we all have inside us. Tune everything out, just like I taught you. Channel all that anger into the pit, and blow it into the wind, okay?"

And then Aponi leans into me and whispers, "Fata Morgana. Your destiny now lies in your own hands. Just close your eyes, envision the horizon, turn fable into reality." I look at her. "The legend lives within you. Change history."

They move away.

"Stop her!" a man yells.

"No!" a woman calls. "Leave her be!"

I see Virgie whispering to her friends. She cannot look at me.

I take the cherry and place it in my mouth. I eat the fruit and then move the pit around in my mouth.

I shut my eyes.

Envision the horizon.

I see four women.

But illuminated in the sun is one woman.

Me.

I can see myself clearly. I am radiant, transcendent.

This is not a special cherry, nor a magical one. It is simply a cherry. The same as any other man in this contest received.

And I am simply a girl, no more special than any other.

But it is the ordinary person who must step into the light to do the extraordinary.

I open my eyes.

Four dots float, then disappear. The sun crosses my face.

"Fata Morgana," I whisper to myself.

I inhale and blow the pit as if in a trance.

The world disappears. The pit arcs into the air. The crowd stands, gasping.

"Ninety-three feet, six-and-a-half inches!" Baritone Bob yells. "That's a new *Guinness Book of World Records* distance, folks! Can you believe what we've all just witnessed! Let's hear it for Cherry Mary!"

I turn to look at my mother, grandmother and the old woman. They are crying.

Little girls rush me, hugging my legs, asking me to autograph their programs.

Women of all ages begin to chant, "Cherry Mary! Cherry Mary! Cherry Mary!"

The old woman lifts her walking stick into the sky and strikes the air with it over and over and over.

In the distance, I hear the beating of drums.

BECKY

I am sitting on the beach, my legs crossed, pen in my hand and a postcard propped on a book in my lap, but I just can't stop watching Q mainlining sugar.

"Don't stare at me!" she says, cramming one of Mary's cookies into her mouth. "I'm not a zoo animal. How rude."

"I can't turn away," I say.

Two beautiful young girls—perfect skin, tight stomachs—walk by and glance over at us.

"Yes, I'm eating sugar," she says to them. Q gives her a thigh a slap. "This is what's waiting for you!"

One of the girls lifts her cell and takes a picture. I laugh.

"They'll title that *Chips Ahoy Lady on the Beach* on TikTok," I say.

"I'm sure it'll go viral," Q says, her mouth still full of cookie. "Speaking of viral, I swear I could feel a connection between you and Ollie, even after that disastrous introduction."

I stare at her again.

She places a hand over her mouth. "What? It's one cookie!"

"One?" I raise my eyebrow at her. "You know I teach kids how to count."

"Well, counting is overrated," Q says. "Back to my comment."

"There was a spark," I admit. "I just didn't know if it was a romantic spark or an I'm-going-to-burn-your-house-down spark. It hurt my feelings he would think I was taking advantage of his grandmother. You know how close I was to mine. It was insulting. And then he called me *crazy*."

"Pot, kettle," Q says.

"Hardy-har-har," I say. "He just really pushed my buttons for some reason. Mary was the one who asked *me* to meet *her*. She's the one who said we were destined to meet. I didn't do anything to start any of this. I just came on vacation."

"I know," Q says. "And so did he. Just imagine how he might have felt. Call me an X-ray, but I can see both sides."

I give her a look. "That makes no sense."

"I just wanted to divert your attention," she says. "But the way you touched his chest! Girl, I felt like I was watching *Twilight*, except with older people and a female vampire who used to go to a Catholic girls' school."

"I just feel like Mary needs a friend," I say. "I feel like we were meant to be friends. Like you and I were."

I glance over at Q. Despite her quick humor and outward bravado, Q is still a little girl with bright red hair and too big a personality who had a hard time making friends.

Until I came along.

We were waiting for one another.

Destined to meet.

And that happened on a whim, too.

I can't shake this feeling deep in my gut—which I readily admit has often been wrong in the past—that I have been waiting for Mary to come along, too.

My instinct with hurt people has always been better than my instinct with men.

I can tell when a child in school is sad simply because her head is bowed as she walks the hall or he doesn't have the same bounce in his step when the cafeteria is serving pizza. I'll call them into my office and ask how they're doing, and often before the question is out of my mouth, they start to cry.

Sometimes, they're sad because their parents were mad at them. Or someone they like has called them a *doofus*. But usually they're sad because of a fight with a friend.

I look at Q.

I think of Mary.

Despite my breakup, my issues with my parents and the grind of my job, I can't imagine getting through any of it—or life being bearable at all—without my best friend.

I reach out my hand and grab Q's.

"You will always be my best friend," I say.

She nods.

"Back atcha."

Q looks out at the water. "And I guess if we have to make room in our circle, it might as well be with a Golden Girl that makes Bea Arthur seem like Shirley Temple."

I laugh.

"Okay, write your card," Q continues. "I love that you won't call or text your parents, but you're willing to get in a time machine and send them a postcard."

"You know my parents," I say. "Any change in anyone's life portends disaster. I'm not ready to hear that right now. I'm sure my mom has candles lit all over the house and is going to church three times a day to pray for me to come home and return to normalcy."

This time, Q laughs.

"At least your parents care," she says. "Remember that. They might drive you batty, but what you have is a blessing. You understand that when you've never had it." She reclines her beach chair all the way back until it is parallel with the sand. "I've got to sleep this sugar off. Wake me when I drool."

"You're always drooling," I say. "But when you start doing it in your sleep, I'm going to call those girls back over to record it."

I position my pen on the card, and before I can even write *Dear Mom and Dad*, Q is snoring.

I stifle a laugh and stare at the postcard.

Q bought it for me yesterday. It is a vintage photo of the Very Cherry General Store, a black-and-white picture that has been hand-tinted and brought to life in brilliant, shocking color. Three generations of women stand in front of the store holding out cherry pies. Heavy, green limbs of the surrounding trees frame the photo. The photo is so evocative it feels as if I'm dreaming. Suddenly, my heart jumps, and I hold the postcard close to my face.

Mary!

She is just a girl, but I can still see her features clearly: the eyes, the nose, even the haircut is the same.

Is that her mother and grandmother?

They all resemble one another, but there is something more deeply connective there than is just on the surface. Each woman is staring directly at the camera sporting a look of sheer determination that suggests *I'm not going anywhere!* more than *Hey, look, I just baked a pie.*

Their shoulders are squared, and there is a hint of a smile not only on their faces but shining in their eyes. They seem to be looking not simply at the camera but through the photographer, as if transfixed on the horizon.

I pull the postcard even closer to my eyes.

Mary looks as if she's searching for that fourth woman.

Am I her?

My cell trills, and I jump. I pick it up, stunned that I have cell service on the beach. There is a text from Mary.

Meet me tomorrow morning. It's urgent.

I set my cell down on the towel.

My heart hiccups. I think of the connection I feel to Mary,

the story I yearn to hear from her, and yet I cannot come between a grandson and his grandmother.

My cell trills again.

Please!

I look at the postcard once more, and this time I hear my cell ringing.

Without thinking, I pick it up.

"Hello?"

"Becky? Oh, thank goodness. You're alive!"

My mother.

"Hi, Mom. Why wouldn't I be alive?"

"Well, you're just so far away doing goodness knows what with goodness knows who."

"I'm on a girls' trip with Q in northern Michigan," I say. "I'm not skydiving over a volcano."

"Oh, Becky! I just saw a video on—what do the kids call it, ClickClack?"

"TikTok?"

"That's it!"

"Why are you on TikTok, Mom?"

"Anyway, a woman skydived directly into a volcano while some disco song played," she rambles. "It was horrifying. Can you imagine how her mother felt watching it?"

"No need to worry. That was probably fake, Mom," I say, trying to reassure her. "I imagine it was a staged video set to the song 'Disco Inferno.'"

"Is Q's hair still so red?" she asks.

I can actually follow my mother's train of thought: *Volcano... inferno...red.*

"Why are you calling, Mom?"

"Well, we got that postcard, and your father and I were a little worried."

"Why?"

"You just sounded depressed about missing Mom and Dad."

"I wasn't depressed," I say. "I was actually feeling inspired and happy, thinking of Memaw and Pops and how much fun we used to have here. I miss them. I miss those times. It's nice to recreate them for a little while."

"Well, you know what your father calls a vacation?"

I inhale sharply.

"A vacation from reality," she continues.

"That's not true."

"Well, it is, young lady, because you've been on one," my mother says. "You held back the truth from us."

"What?"

I suddenly realize a huge part of my life has simply consisted of saying *What?* To my mother.

"I think there's someone here that can shed a little light on that."

"Becky?"

No, she didn't!

"Matt!"

"How are you?"

"What do you want, Matt?" I ask.

"My attorney said you wanted to talk. You didn't call."

"I'm sorry," I say. "I'm on vacation and have been distracted."

"With another guy?"

"I am so not doing this right now," I say. "And you should not be at my parents' house. We broke up. This is wrong in every possible way."

"I missed them," he says. "I missed you."

"Stop!" I yell, so loudly that Q snaps awake and wipes her mouth.

"Matt?" she mouths.

I nod.

"You cannot do this," I continue. "You strung me along. You

didn't ask me to marry you, and then you sued me for a TV and refrigerator that you cared about more than me."

"I didn't really do anything wrong, Becky. Just stop and think about it." He is silent for a second to give me pause, I guess, to reconsider. "I'm a nice guy who liked things the way they were."

My focus pivots to the photo on the postcard.

What did these women overcome in their lives to be together? To own this store? To face the world, shoulders back, faces etched with determination?

Matt may not have tried to hurt me, and I may not have blinded him with a cherry pit, but he is not a nice guy no matter how many times he says it to convince me and himself. He hurt me, over and over and over again, a loss of my soul by a million paper cuts.

And I let it happen.

Me.

I stare into the eyes of Mary's mother and grandmother.

The look in her grandma's eyes mirrors the pride, drive and optimism my Memaw's had after she forged a new start to her life after retiring as an executive assistant.

But the way Mary's mom looks into the camera is so much different than my mom, who—in holiday photos and candid pictures—is always looking away, embarrassed to be the focus of attention, hands fluttering, already on the move, wanting to disappear into the kitchen.

I suddenly remember two moments from my past, jagged memories that were so painful that they left layers of scar tissue, and recalling them right now feels like I've just cut myself with a sharp blade.

There was a seminal moment in the summer after my first year in college when I wanted to switch majors from education to business. I was required to take an intro to business class, and I had been quite taken by it. I talked to a counselor about the major and even began dreaming about earning my MBA. When

I asked my mother and father for advice, my dad said, "Women should be teachers. Men should handle business."

When I searched my mother's eyes for help, I could see there was a flash of anger, but she ducked her head and repeated, "You will make a wonderful teacher and mother."

I never told my grandparents until years later.

"She only knows the limits of the world," my grandmother sighed sadly, "not the possibilities. Don't hold it against her. Show her the way."

And when I was looking to move up in my career and interviewing with other schools and districts about becoming a principal, I had an epiphany: perhaps changing jobs wouldn't solve my career frustration. Perhaps I should start my own consulting business. When I excitedly approached Matt with my plans—including a business model, projected clients and income—he looked at me and said, "I don't think you're equipped to go it alone. I don't think you're equipped for risk. And I certainly don't think you're equipped to fail."

But it was me who let it happen.

Me.

"I forgive you, Matt," I say quietly. "But I don't ever want to talk to you again. And I don't ever want you to set foot in my parents' house again. It's not right."

"You're making a huge mistake, Becky."

"No, Matt, I'm the one who made a huge mistake for staying too long with someone who didn't appreciate me."

Q's eyes widen. She lifts her arms into the air and gyrates as if she just scored a touchdown.

"And if you want that the TV and the fridge that makes cocktail ice you never used once to make cocktails so badly, they're yours," I say. "You can take them. You have a week. And then I'm changing the locks. For good. And then I will sue you for all the years you lived with me and never paid a cent." I take a breath. "We all need to move out of our comfortable, little boxes. Now, put my mother back on the phone, please."

"What are you doing, Becky?" my mother scolds.

"No," I say. "What are *you* doing, Mom? This is incredibly hurtful and disrespectful to me. Matt hurt me. He never wants to marry me, which, remember, is what you wanted. He never wants to have children, which, remember, is something you wanted, too. And I realize now that Matt has held me back in every possible way, and I'm happy we broke up, and that I've moved on. Now you need to do the same. He is not your family, Mom. I am. He is not your son. He is not part of my—or your—future. I love you, but if you continue to allow him to be a part of your lives, then I can't be a part of yours."

My mother gasps. "You don't mean that, Becky."

"I do," I say. "And now I'm hanging up."

Q stands and walks in circles around in the sand as if she's dizzy. And then she simply falls to the ground, as if it's all been too much and she's passed out.

I end the call.

"Where has this girl been all my life?" she says.

Buried, I don't say. *Under layers of self-doubt.*

I stand, help Q to her feet, and we both go sprinting across the beach and dive headfirst into Lake Michigan, the water washing away...

Everything.

When I pop my head out of the water, I am facing the horizon.

MARY

When you live a cottage life along the lake, there is a sense of peace that comes based solely on light.

Michigan is a kaleidoscope of light, changing by the minute, an ethereal magician gifted with the ability to cast a blue lake gold, a pine glowing red, the sand pink.

I rise before dawn, as I have nearly my entire adult life, to have coffee with Mother Nature and wake as she does.

For my effort, she rarely disappoints.

The first light of dawn is a glorious spectacle, a rim of light—of hope, really—that slowly spreads across the horizon. For a while, it is but a sliver of a glow, much like that of an old TV as it warms up. But then—*bam!*—it explodes across the sky, and the smudges grow into finger paintings and then into jaw-dropping portraits of surreal color.

A heron with wings of purple.

A moored sailboat with masts of orange canvas.

A jumping fish, scales of bright blue.

A sugar maple whose leaves are Day-Glo green.

When you start your day in this way, it aligns your soul in harmony with wonder.

I take a sip of my coffee.

I need, no matter my age, to reclaim my wonder.

I need to reclaim my light and direct onto those who need it.

That is why when that little girl looked at me, I decided to participate in the Cherry Festival. That is why I must do what I am doing this morning.

I nod to myself as the sun continues to rise.

By noon, the world will be drenched in sunlight, everything as bright and shiny as a newly washed window.

The Golden Hour will burnish the lakeshore, the Blue Hour will make the mundane magical, and sunset will dazzle, a bowl of rainbow ice cream melting into the last light of day.

I finish my coffee and head upstairs to shower and ready myself for the day. I pull on a favorite long-sleeved T-shirt, worn soft as a feather, featuring an image of the general store that reads *Have a Very Cherry Day!*, a comfortable pair of jeans, a pair of athletic socks and sneakers—outfitted with an insole as thick as a stack of pancakes—and glance out my bedroom window before heading back downstairs to leave. I smile.

Francine's lights pop on, a soft glow illuminating her cottage.

I witness countless stunning illuminations throughout my summer days and have been blessed to be witness to them my whole life in Michigan, but one of my favorites is seeing the lights come on in a neighbor's cottage. It could be the first night they arrive after a long drive, or it could be first thing in the morning.

The light always stills my heart. I know my friends are nearby and safe.

Mostly, that light gives me hope.

It lets me know that I am not alone.

Yet.

In so many ways, this external light fills the darkness I feel internally.

I've been alone a long time. It scares me to do the math, realizing that I may live a larger portion of my life alone than I did with family beside me.

What is the one thing we truly want as parents and grand-parents? We want to know that our children and grandchildren are happy and healthy, safe and loved, but we also want to know that our lives have meant something, that they mean something to our children and grandchildren, that our legacy will be carried on in some way.

I look out the window beyond Francine's cottage through the pines to the new home Taffy continues to expand.

And yet all I sometimes see is history being clear-cut. Sometimes all I see is light being extinguished.

I see a puff of smoke and smile that Francine has started a fire on this summer morning. Our northern Michigan mornings often start chilly, even in the dog days of summer, and many wake to cottages that feel like iceboxes.

I stand and stare out the window.

How do you restart a fire that has been out for too long?

How do you reignite that light?

Does it take someone else to start it, or can we do it ourselves? Or is it a team effort?

I head downstairs and sneak over to the guest room. I put my ear to the door. I can hear Ollie snoring softly.

I heard him come in very late, and I figure he'd been out at Phil's Bar & Grille, reconnecting with some of his summer friends and trying to kick off his vacation in the right way. I grab a pen and notepad in the kitchen and write him a note, leaving it on the counter under some muffins I brought home last night. I walk to my car and begin the short drive to work.

The world—the light—changes again as I head toward the Tunnel of Trees. At first, from a distance, the tops of the hard-woods burn bright in the morning sun. But as my car enters the tunnel, there is an eerie glow, an iridescent green like the light-ning bugs in these parts. The sun cannot penetrate the depth of the branches that smother the road, and daylight barely trickles through, but it does make the leaves glow, and I feel as if I've left the earth and am driving in another universe.

I feel safe again.

These trees have been around longer than my grandmother and mother. They will remain long after me. I roll down my window and can smell their sweet scent, the pine, the bark, the leaves. I stick my hand out the window and let my fingers dance in the cool air as I did as a girl. I lift my arm and can feel the branches reach for my hand. The road winds and bends like a lazy river, and light glances through the dense foliage, a Biblical painting come to life. Shafts of light dance, and as I drive through them I can't help but think they are heavenly stand-ins for my mom and grandma when I need them most.

Each bend brings a surprise: a bluff overlooking the deep blue of Lake Michigan, a log cabin tucked under a tent of oaks, maples, birch and cedars, a mother deer and her babies having breakfast off a buffet line of lush, low canopy.

There is no center line on the road. In fact, the road narrows and seems to disappear around every bend.

This is where I learned to drive. My grandma drove a 1958 Buick Special Riviera, aqua-blue and white, which was big as her personality. Steering the car felt like navigating a space shuttle with a kite string. The beautiful beast would drift left and right, limbs swatting at its exterior, and my grandma would yell, "Keep her straight!"

"There's no line!" I'd yell in a panic, sweat beading on my face. "How do I know where to go?"

"Stop looking so far ahead," she'd tell me. "Just keep your eye on the right side of the road. Stay focused on what's right in front of you."

And that's exactly the philosophy that has kept me going for so many years.

But now, at my age, I realize there is little road in front of me.

A car zooms around the bend, going much too fast, and I can see the surprised driver jerk the car at the last moment to avoid me.

Locals like to say *M-119 is not a road for those in a hurry.*

That's a philosophy that doesn't fit the mindset of the flurry of tourists who descend upon our area every summer and fall to escape the city and get a taste of our bounty and beauty. They zip down this road as if they are late for work, believing they have slowed down simply because they are not in their own world for a moment but forgetting what it truly means to disconnect. I actually have to stay more alert and concerned for my safety driving on this road during the height of tourist season than I do in the middle of winter when the road is blanketed with snow.

I emerge from the Tunnel of Trees, and the general store is dead ahead. Although it is morning, and the world is brightening, the little store is still dark.

I pull into the lot, unlock the door and begin turning on the lights.

Old-fashioned schoolhouse pendants pop on throughout the store.

My final, and perhaps, favorite moment of light in the day comes when the Very Cherry General Store wakes up. The post office boxes shimmer, the cake domes glimmer, the old cash register glows, the old pictures come to life.

I head into the kitchen, still turning on lights, and immediately start another pot of coffee and click on the oven to pre-heat. Today I am making my grandma's luscious pink cherry chip cake—a labor of love if there ever was one—along with peach muffins and the crusts for some veggie potpies.

I pull butter from the refrigerator and sugar and flour from the cupboards. I line up peaches and begin to peel and chop them before pitting the cherries and saving all the juice, a necessary ingredient for the cake and the reason for its spring-tulip color. I start on the muffins and pie crusts first.

An hour or so later, I hear the crunch of gravel, the bell jangle and the screened door slam.

"Grandma?"

"Back here!"

Ollie appears in the door of the kitchen. He's wearing a Cubs ball cap and still looks half asleep, still so much like a little boy to me, even though he isn't.

"Good morning, Grandma. I love starting my day with you."

"And they start early around here, don't they?"

He nods.

"Want a cup of coffee?" I ask. "And then you can help me pit more cherries."

He grabs a mug and pours himself some coffee. Ollie begins to pit the cherries, quickly and deftly, just like I taught him so long ago.

"You're making the cherry chip cake, aren't you?" he asks.

I nod. "Your favorite."

A slight smile crosses his face. He ducks his head, the brim of his cap shadowing his face.

I used to make this cake for Ollie on his birthdays, the first night he'd arrive for the summer or any special occasion. He loved the airy white cake dotted with cherries and the thick butter-cream cherry frosting, even though it was pink.

I'd always pour myself a cup of coffee and Ollie a glass of milk, cut two pieces of the cake and take a seat at the dining-room table—just the two of us—and I'd ask Ollie to tell me all about his year at school as well as his hopes and dreams.

"One day, I'm going to live here forever with you, Grandma, and we're going to run the general store together. The two of us together forever!"

I know he was just a boy, and kids say things they don't mean, but that forged a place in my heart and has lived there forever.

Did I ruin his dream? Or did he just grow up?

How do you honor the past while trying to erase all of its mistakes?

"Where are you going?" he asks as I head out of the kitchen.

I return carrying a domed cake plate. Underneath, an already completed cherry chip cake glimmers in all its pink frosted glory.

Ollie's eyes sparkle.

"Want a slice?" I ask.

"Cake for breakfast? Absolutely!" I cut a perfect piece of cake and place it on a Desert Rose dish. I hand him a fork and then head to the fridge and pour him a glass of milk.

"Just like old times," I say. "And I'm eighty, so all of my times are old."

He laughs, eats a big forkful of cake and then shuts his eyes, savoring the sweetness.

"Just like I remember," he says.

I grab a stool, pull it to the butcher-block counter and take a seat.

"Talk," I say. "Why are you feeling lost? Your father said you weren't yourself of late."

Ollie nods a few times as if to say *He noticed* and then takes another bite of cake.

"Do you know why people in the city don't bake?"

I shake my head at my grandson, not understanding his question.

"There's a bakery on every corner," he says. "You can get any dessert you want—German apple cake to chocolate cupcakes—any hour of the day. It costs more, it tastes great, but it's not the same as this."

Ollie takes another bite.

"You forget what it's like to take simple ingredients and create something extraordinary," he continues. "You forget to take the time to slow down, pit cherries and talk about your dreams like we did when I was a kid."

Ollie takes a sip of his milk.

"I forgot, Grandma," he says. "Everything. That's why I'm here. That's why I wanted to come back this summer."

I nod. "Go on."

"I've come to a point where I feel as if I've been walking in shadows my whole life, caught between a strong grandmother who became famous in a small town and a strong father who simply felt infamous in this small town."

"Oh, Ollie."

"You and Dad have cast great shadows on my life. I've always felt like I've been forced to make a choice between the two of you, between city and country...between baking for joy and buying for convenience when I didn't even know what I wanted."

"I didn't know you were feeling this way."

"I have realized lately that I was blaming you or blaming Dad, but it's all my fault, Grandma. I got complacent. Maybe that's not even the right word. I got tired. So I just gave up," he says. "There's a lot of pressure in this world on men to make money, conform to convention, be the creator of buildings, maker of money, ruler of the world, but what if my joy is..." he sweeps his arm around the kitchen "...this?"

"I came home to surprise my grandma," Ollie continues, "but I also need to surprise myself. I need to recapture what I had as a kid, to see if maybe I can stop being so afraid of baking something all on my own. You taught me never to blame anyone, Grandma, to look at what anyone can do to forge his own path. And I hope that you can see me as me, not an image of Dad. Just little ol' Ollie, the kid who wanted to be like his grandma more anyone in the world."

I gesture for Ollie to come over, and I hug him with all my might.

"Thank you for coming," I say. "And thank you for sharing that."

Gravel crunches in the distance.

Ollie looks up and glances at the clock.

"A customer already?" he asks. "Must be Taffy, huh? Picking up both breakfast and lunch, right? I haven't seen him yet. I'll go surprise him."

I hear the bell jangle and the door bang shut.

"What are you doing here?" I hear Ollie ask.

"What are you doing here?" Becky counters.

Ollie returns to the kitchen.

"Grandma—" he starts.

"Trust me," I interrupt him. "I just want you to try and look at me not as some crazy old character from a novel but as a woman who's always followed her instincts and heart." I stop. "And that it's always turned out for the best."

Ollie sighs and heads into the general store.

I hold my breath and follow, hoping new light can eliminate the shadows, chase away the darkness and bring my plan to life.

BECKY

Mary comes out of the kitchen, wiping her hands, fingers stained red, like some sort of rural Lady Macbeth.

"Umm," Q starts, a look of concern on her face.

"We've been pitting cherries," Mary explains. "Nothing sinister." She flashes her hands at me and Ollie. "And I'm sorry for not telling you both that the other was coming this morning. I just didn't know any other way to do it."

Mary's eyes look sunken this morning, her skin the color of dried oatmeal.

"Do what?" Ollie asks.

"I was touched that you both wanted to enter the Cherry Pit Spitting Championship this year to honor my anniversary," she says. "And it would be the ultimate irony and compliment if one of you won. Imagine, another woman setting the record, or my own grandson. It would make the perfect full-circle moment."

A smile has crossed Ollie's rather attractive lips that look as pink as cherries this morning.

"*But,*" Mary continues, "there's a way to win. It takes training and focus, and I'm the only one who can teach you." She looks at me and Ollie. "And maybe in between you'll both not only learn a little bit more about the history of me and this place but also each other. Maybe you'll understand that you are both here for a reason and that you were both brought here for me. Deal?"

Ollie and I look at each other and nod.

"Deal," we say in unison.

"And that secret to winning, which was taught to me by my grandma, starts right out there."

Mary points. I look outside.

"In the Tunnel of Trees."

We all look at one another again.

"This is like a bad Western," Q says.

Mary laughs. Ollie actually cracks a smile.

"Okay," I say. "I'm in."

"Me, too," Ollie says.

"May the best man or woman win," Mary says.

The bell on the door jangles, and a man comes sauntering inside as if he owns the place.

He has longer hair, has on worn Dickies and is sporting a tool belt around his hips and sunglasses on the back side of his head. He looks like he's on one of those HGTV shows, in this instance *The Country Contractor*.

"I feel like I just walked in at the wrong moment," he says.

"You actually walked in at just the right time," Mary says. "Ollie!"

"Taffy!" Ollie yells.

The man grabs Ollie and gives him a big bear hug, lifting him off the ground and spinning him in a circle.

Taffy

"When did you get here?" Taffy asks, setting him down. "We need to catch up over beers at Phil's."

"Anytime, buddy," Ollie says.

"And who do we have here?" Taffy asks.

"This is Becky," Mary says. "She's visiting from St. Louis, and we've become fast friends."

"It's nice to meet you," I say, extending my hand. "And this is my friend, Q."

"Q?" he asks, shaking her hand and lifting an eyebrow. "That's an unusual name."

"Really, Taffy?" Q says with a dramatic wink.

He laughs. "Well played."

"What do you do?" Q asks him.

"I'm a general contractor," he says. "Build and renovate homes."

"Tries to talk young buyers out of tearing down historic cottages," Mary adds. "I've known him since he was a boy who tried to steal all our saltwater taffy."

"Now it's all making sense," Q says. "I've known Becky since she was a little girl. I felt like we were destined to meet and become friends forever. No one like her."

Mary nods her head, and Q smiles at her.

Ollie watches us, and the light glints through the screened door, making him look as if he sees me in a new way.

"What do you do, Q?" Taffy asks.

"I run a theatrical company in St. Louis," she says. "In essence, I build imaginary worlds just like you build dream houses."

Taffy smiles. "I like that," he says.

"What can I do you for today, Taffy?" Mary asks.

"Why don't you teach me, Mary?" Q says. "Show me the ropes around here. I can fill in for a bit while you try to teach Thelma and Louise here not only how to spit a pit but also how to get their vacations restarted on the right foot."

"I think I like you," Mary says to Q.

"Back atcha."

"You two are entering the championship?" Taffy asks, clearly surprised.

"Yes," we say at the same time.

"You got your work cut out, Mary," Taffy says. "Your legacy is on the line."

"Virgie asked me to participate," Mary says. "So I'm going to give her a show."

Taffy bends over, slaps his knees and roars with laughter.

"Who's Virgie?" Q asks.

"Long story," Mary says.

"Go on," Taffy says to Mary. "I'll show Q how to make my sandwich and run the store. I've got time. Moira and Geoffrey won't be up for hours, anyway. I'll cut them some slack for once and won't start sawing outside their bedroom window at dawn."

Taffy heads behind the counter into the kitchen and returns with a loaf of homemade bread and a sleeve of liverwurst.

"Ready?" he asks Q.

"Yes, sensei," Q says. "Teach me the magic of mayo."

"This way!" Mary says ushering me toward the door and directly into Ollie, who has yet to move.

Our skin touches. Mine is cool, his is warm. I can't help but look at Ollie's bicep. I want to move, but I cannot. My arm explodes in goose pimples.

Ollie doesn't move, either.

"I would not eat liverwurst if it were the last thing on earth," I hear Q say. "This looks like something Hannibal Lecter would enjoy."

"You need to learn the ways of northern Michigan," Taffy says. "Next lesson will be how to make a pasty and a potpie."

"That sounds like a lyric to a song in a new musical," Q says.

"Good luck!" Mary says as she grabs a container of cherries off the shelf and ushers us out the door, my friend's laughter echoing in the general store.

"Wait here!" Mary says, handing me the cherries.

She heads around the store and returns with two construction cones.

"Grandma?" Ollie asks. It is as much a question as it is a concern. "What are you doing?"

"Follow me!" she calls. "To the Tunnel of Trees!"

MARY

I place a traffic cone in the middle of the road just beyond the entrance to the general store's parking lot. I hand another cone to Ollie, who places it on the ground in front of him.

"Ollie," I say, my tone serious. "We only have a short window of time."

"Grandma," he repeats in the same tone.

I stare at the cone he set down. It is a literal sign—in blaring orange—of the barricade that has long been between us. I must remove it for both of us to move on fully.

"This is illegal," Ollie finally says.

"It's not illegal," she says. "It's creative. You just said you need to start thinking unconventionally. If my mother, grandmother and I had been conventional women and played by the rules, I would never have won the Cherry Championship, and I wouldn't have this store. So will you let me teach you how to be unconventional?"

Ollie nods.

"Can I teach you how to be unconventional, Becky?"

"I think that's exactly why I'm supposed to be here," I say.

I grab the cone and begin trotting down the road. I place it just beyond the curve where the road disappears. I set it down and when I stand up, the trees spin, the tunnel a vortex. I am out of breath, my face clammy, and I grab the top of the cone for support.

"Are you okay, Grandma?" Ollie calls.

I nod, smile broadly and wave for the two to join me. "Not enough coffee yet! Come over here, please!"

They trot down the road, their footsteps in sync as if in marching band. It's downright adorable.

"Okay, so the sheriff will come by eventually and say, 'Mary,' like I'm a child, but she will understand," I tell them. "She's been around these parts as long as I have, and she knows the things women have to do sometimes. Now, we have to hurry before the tourists come barreling down the road and realize there's actually no road construction."

"What are we doing here, Grandma?"

"I'm teaching you how to spit a pit."

"We know how to do that, Grandma. What training is necessary?"

I laugh.

"May seem silly to you, but anything in which you wish to succeed requires discipline and training," I say. "If there's anything I should have taught you by now, it's that."

"I still don't understand why we're standing in the middle of the road," Ollie says.

"Listen," I say.

The wind begins as a soft whistle, but it picks up slowly and steadily as it rounds the bend. Our hair ruffles in the wind, and the limbs above our heads rattle.

"You're each going to spit with the wind, and then we're going to the other side to spit against it," I say. "You have to be ready for any distraction at any moment. It could be someone coughing or laughing, a child screaming. You have to be ready to overcome all the tricks your mind will play on you when pressure sets in. Doesn't matter if it's spitting pits or life."

I turn to Becky and reach for the cherries. "Ready?"

The two look at one another tentatively and nod.

"Who wants to go first?" I ask.

Ollie steps forward and grabs a cherry.

"Wait," I say, heading down and into the middle of the road about ten yards.

Ollie steps into the middle of the road, steadies himself, inhales and blows.

I eye the spot the pit lands before it bounces. I take the tape measure from my apron pocket—the one that Taffy gave me years ago that seems to stretch into infinity—and measure all the way back to where Ollie is standing.

"Fine first effort," I say. "Roughly forty-one feet." I look at him. "With the wind." I turn to Becky. "You're up."

Becky grabs a cherry. She glances over at me, and I can read her mind: Ollie's attempt, with the wind, was less than half of what she achieved.

I know she's better than Ollie. She knows she's better than Ollie. But there's always the chance that someone will care so little about all the work, effort and hardship that got you to this very moment, and they will ruin it for you in the blink of an eye.

Becky purses her lips and just before she is about to release the pit, I pull an air horn from my apron and blow it. Becky's eyes pop, she screams, and the pit dribbles out of her mouth.

Ollie grabs the tape measure.

"Eight inches!"

"That was not fair!" Becky exclaims. "Why did you do that?"

"You have to be prepared for anything," I say.

"An air horn?" she asks. "C'mon!"

Becky begins to look at the two of us, her head bobbing back and forth. "That's just downright mean." She stops. "Did you two plan this? Am I some sort of pawn in a game you're playing?"

"No!" I insist. "I just want you to be prepared."

"For what?"

"For life!"

"I'm leaving," she says, stomping down the road. She turns, and her eyes are filled with tears. "I thought you were nice. I thought you were my friend."

My heart stops.

"I did that for you, Becky." I grab my air horn and blow again. Becky stops. "Come back. Please!"

Becky stops in the middle of the road. A breeze tickles the trees, and Becky lifts her head to the tunnel above her as if listening to their giggles. Finally, she turns, as if she has heard their wisdom.

"Thank you," I say. I take a deep breath. "I have to tell you a story."

In a rush, I exhale the story of what my father did at the Cherry Championship that has lived within me for decades.

Becky is in tears again when I am done.

"Why didn't you ever tell me that?" Ollie asks. "What didn't Dad?"

"I never told him," I say. "Too painful."

I pluck a cherry and hold it in front of them.

"Cherry trees start as seeds," I say.

I pop the cherry into my mouth, eating the fruit and depositing the pit into my hand. I hold that in front of them.

"The seeds become the pits found in cherries," I say. "The seeds are planted, they grow into trees that bear fruit, which matures and falls to the ground, bearing more seeds. The cycle begins anew with the seed ready to be planted."

Ollie and Becky glance at one another.

I look up at the trees and continue. "What I'm trying to say is that it's the same with family. Too often, the seeds become pits within us, and they harden over the years. A cycle begins anew, and we hope, pray, believe and try to ensure that seed won't become a pit, but it's impossible when we repeat the mistakes of our family."

I inhale and blow, the pit arcing along the Tunnel of Trees, before landing in the road and bouncing until it comes to rest at the foot of an ancient hardwood.

I take Ollie's hand. "I've had that pit inside me my whole life," I say. "Because of my father and my husband. My inability to deal with that has turned my beautiful seeds—you and your father—into pits, too. I'm sorry. I'm trying to change. It's hard for an old woman to change."

I motion for Becky to join, and I take her hand in mine, too. "I feel like you have that pit inside you as well. I feel like I've seen you on the horizon my whole life—just like that old woman at Devil's Elbow showed me when I was a girl—and have been waiting for you so I can…" I hesitate, letting go of her hand, grabbing another cherry and chucking it as far as I can "…let go of everything that's haunted me."

I look at the two of them. "I think the two of you were meant to meet somehow. More than anything, I don't want the two of you to leave Good Hart with a taste in your mouth that's more sour than the tartest cherry. I just believed in a vision that could bring us all together at the end of my life, a vision that could heal us, a vision that could allow us all to exhale that pit inside us once and for all. I was trying to connect my past to our future. But maybe I'm just a foolish old woman. Maybe I've always been a foolish woman."

"You are not a foolish woman, Mary," Becky insists. "Maybe you're the grandmother I lost and have found again. Maybe you're the mother I needed. I do have a pit that needs to be removed from inside of me."

"Grandma, you're the reason I'm here. You're the reason I always come back. I think maybe I heard you and the wind call me this summer."

The trees spin.

"Thank you," I say. "I think I'll just go for a little stroll this morning since Q and Taffy are at the store. I don't take time for myself often enough."

"You do that, Grandma," Ollie says. "We'll get everything and meet you back there. And thank you for the lesson today."

"Don't know if it did much good," I say.

"It did," Becky says. "Focus. Faith."

I smile.

"Air horn," Becky and Ollie say, laughing.

In sync.

"Thank you both for being here this morning."

I follow a footpath into the woods, going deeper and deeper, disappearing so as not to worry them about how I'm feeling. I don't stop until I am out of the breath, dizzy again, my aged body hugging a giant sycamore whose bark is as ancient as my skin.

What do most people do when they are choking?

They walk away out of embarrassment rather than asking for help.

You are a foolish old woman, Mary.

I close my eyes, and the trees sing a lullaby in a voice as soft as my mother's when she would rock me to sleep as a child.

BECKY

"If we were teenagers, we would so be arrested," I say after Mary's confession and departure.

Ollie and I are walking down the road carrying the two construction cones, the container of cherries and Mary's air horn and tape measure. Cars slow to take a closer look.

"I feel like we're the visual punchline to a very bad joke," Ollie says.

I laugh, releasing a loud whoop.

"Wow," he says. "You have a memorable laugh. And by memorable I mean *frightening*."

"It's sort of my calling card," I say, "like Elaine's dancing in *Seinfeld*."

This time, Ollie laughs. "A gift *and* a curse," he says.

I glance subtly at him as we walk. Since yesterday, it seems as if the clouds have lifted and the sun has returned, like I'm seeing a clear, blue sky for the first time in my life.

The magic of Michigan.

The grandeur of a grandma.

We stop on the stoop of the general store and set down our odd collection.

"Have a seat," Ollie says. "I'll be back in a sec."

The screened door bangs shut, the bell jingling, and—within seconds—Ollie is back, heralded by the same rural symphony.

"Ever had one of these?" he asks, taking a seat beside me on the steps.

He hands me an ice-cold soda. I read the label. "Vernors?" I ask, shaking my head. "St. Louis is a beer town, so if it doesn't say Bud or Busch on it, I probably haven't had it."

"Well, nothing says summer in Michigan like an ice-cold Vernors," he says. "It's Pure Michigan. Locals say it's the gingeriest ginger soda in the world."

I pop the top and take a big swig.

"My nose is tingling," I say with a chuckle. "Honestly, I can feel the ginger tickle my throat and nose."

"It was invented by a Detroit pharmacist," Ollie says, taking a long pull of the soda. "Mmm, you can taste the ginger. My grandma always said her mom and grandma used it to ease stomachaches, and she mixed it with lemon juice and served it to me hot whenever I had a summer cold. I have to admit, it worked."

"So you believe in Michigan lore, then?" I ask, nudging him with my elbow, an involuntary gesture that takes us both by surprise.

He takes another drink of Vernors and kicks a small stone off the step with his sneaker. Ollie traces a line with his finger through the condensation on the soda, drops of water racing to the bottom, making it appear as if his Vernors is crying.

"Oh, Michigan lore is very real," Ollie finally says. "The lake, the trees, the history, the sky, the sunrises and sunsets all seem to want to share a secret with you."

"And that is?"

"I'm still trying to figure all that out," Ollie says. "I'm still trying to figure myself out." He looks at me. "My grandma is lore around these parts. Everyone knows her: the first woman to win the Cherry Pit Spitting Championship. The woman whose record still stands. The woman who is the third generation of women to run this store. The woman from the family of women who all married these bad men. The woman who sees things on the horizon."

My eyes grow wide. "You know about that?"

Ollie nods.

"Always been a part of our story," he says. "And around here, the whole town talks."

Out of the blue, Ollie begins to sing, *"Everybody dies famous in a small town."*

His voice is deep, a beautiful bass, all country coming out of this city boy.

"Know that song?" Ollie asks.

I shake my head.

"It's by Miranda Lambert," he continues. "Love her. Love that song. It just sort of sums up growing up here with my grandma."

"You're a little bit country," I warble like Donnie and Marie Osmond used to do, "and I'm a little bit rock and roll."

"You sing better than you laugh," he says, nudging me with his elbow.

"I had a good teacher in Q," I say, hearing her and Taffy's voices drift outside.

For a moment there is silence, and then Ollie says, "I always wondered if there might be room for a man to take over this place, and all that lore, all that small-town gossip, sort of made me question if I should even be a part of this. Or if she even *wanted* me to be a part of this. And then I come here to find you here. Despite everything I thought all these years, perhaps my grandma was right. Perhaps that missing piece, that fourth woman—*you*—will finally complete this mysterious puzzle."

My heart somersaults.

"I loved my grandmother more than anyone else in this world, too," I say. "Memaw…"

"Memaw?" he asks.

"Pops and Memaw," I say with a laugh. "That's what I called them."

"Of course you did, Becky Thatcher."

I smile and continue. "Memaw worked her whole life, nine to five, before she retired and had the ultimate epiphany: she completely reinvented her life in order to find the joy in it before it was too late. She's the one who brought me to northern Michigan as a kid and captured me seeing the same mirage of four women on the lake that your grandma has always had. Her message about not living my life for others made me stop and rethink everything. She's the reason I'm here right now. I would never dream of taking advantage of your grandmother because she reminds me of my own. In fact, I came here seeking that same independence and joy for life. I came here to reinvent myself. I came here to be a *flâneur*."

"A what?"

"A passionate stroller through life, for the first time. I'm tired of being everything the world expected of me and not at all the woman I dreamed of being."

"I feel exactly the same way."

Ollie is looking at me now as if seeing me for the first time. It's a lingering, intense review, and I cannot meet his gaze, so I take a sip of my soda, letting the ginger tickle my throat.

"I broke up with my boyfriend before I came here," I say. "I thought he was going to ask me to marry him."

"How'd that go?"

"Not well," I say. "I fear that, years from now, many St. Louis schoolchildren will be in therapy."

I roar in laughter.

"If not from your breakup, then surely your laugh," he says jokingly.

"Ironically," I continue, "it was the best thing that ever happened to me because it made me realize I'd spent my entire life accepting conditions on the love I received. Unconditional love,

I've learned, is the hardest thing in this world to give and re-ceive. It's love *without* any conditions. My boyfriend loved me only if I stayed exactly the same and things never changed. My parents have shown me love only when I did as they expected. But I let all of that happen because I never loved myself uncon-ditionally. I had conditions on how I treated myself, always put-ting the world ahead of my own dreams. That's not the place I wanted to be anymore, so I ran away here—to the place I loved as a child—to try and find that unconditional acceptance my grandparents showed me. I think I found that instantly upon meeting your grandma."

I lift my eyes and meet Ollie's. His eyes are as curious as a child's, open, searching, exploring. Though it is morning, there is a five-o'clock shadow on his face, and his muscular arms are outlined in the sun.

"I have no idea why I'm telling all of this to a man I just met," I say, unable to take the silence any longer. "But it just sort of feels like kismet, as if we're already in sync with each other's thoughts."

"No," he says. "Thank you for sharing. I was just telling my grandma that I feel as I've been caught between her and my fa-ther much of my life, trying to please both, but pleasing neither and definitely not myself. I really don't love working for my dad. It's never what I dreamed of doing."

"What did you dream of doing?"

He nods back at the general store.

"I just thought it seemed foolish," he says. "A pipe dream. Something a man isn't supposed to do."

"I think we have a lot in common, actually," I say. "I don't know if I love teaching any longer. I certainly don't love ad-ministration. I've tried to please my parents, then my boyfriend, but rarely myself. I feel like I'm a hamster just going in circles my whole life, pretending to be happy but trapped on a wheel inside a cage."

Ollie places his hand on my back and rubs it gently to soothe me. I lean gently into the pressure.

"My grandma's right, you know," he continues. "If we don't expel all of this pent-up emotion, the seed turns into a pit, and it hardens our hearts. It stops us from growing, even though we want to take root."

I nod.

"Do you perhaps think she feels as if—and don't get mad at me for asking this, please—you haven't given her a reason to believe the seed is ready to take root?"

Ollie dips his head.

"Just hear me out," I say. "She's eighty. She's alone, especially all winter long." I turn toward the general store. "This is her entire life—her entire being, her entire existence, her everything, everything she's fought for—and I think she believes it's just going to fade away when she's gone. I think she worries her own son and grandson will just demolish all that she and the women in your family have worked so hard to create. I don't mean to overstep any boundaries here, but I've seen a similar pattern in my own family. My grandparents loved my parents but felt as though they really didn't want much to do with their lives, which is why they showered me with so much attention." I turn back to Ollie. "I finally started to listen to their voices decades later."

The sun shifts through the tunnel of trees, light forcing its way through the thick branches, glints of light illuminating the tiny road.

Ollie doesn't stop me. I continue. "My grandparents told me that we create a mirage of how we wish our life to be, a false image of perfection that we hope will make others like us. Few of us ever really discover who we are meant to be. Few of us rarely look on the horizon and believe that something magical is coming our way." I take a deep breath. "Maybe you've created an image of yourself just to please your father. Maybe you need to know it's okay to see and believe in beautiful things on the horizon and then strive to reach them."

"I have guilt about making a change because I do have a good life," Ollie says. "A happy life. I'm blessed and loved. I don't take that for granted."

"So do I. But that doesn't mean it's a complete one."

"My dad looks to the future, my grandma lives in the past," he says.

"What do you like?" I ask.

"Both."

"Then, merge the past and the future."

"Are you a psychic?" Ollie chuckles, turning his gaze upon me again.

"No," I say. "I'm just an assistant principal, which means I basically solve the world's problems every day while eating pizza and corn off the same tray."

He laughs. "That food combination never made sense."

"And yet it's the one thing that still endures."

For the longest time, the only sound is the wind through the trees.

"Listen," Ollie says, shutting his eyes. "Really listen."

I shut my eyes, too.

"This is the sound of my childhood," Ollie says. "You'd think it would be the waves crashing into shore, but it's this. I used to sit here on the stoop as a kid and listen to the wind in the trees. It was only a few years ago that I realized this is the one place where it wasn't the wind that I was hearing, it was the trees. The wind was merely the conductor, but the trees were the symphony."

I cock my head, my ear toward the Tunnel of Trees.

The trees sing, whistle, giggle, chat.

"They sound like a family," I say.

I feel a hand on my bare leg and open my eyes. Ollie is staring at me.

"Exactly," he says. "Maybe my grandma was right. Maybe we were destined to meet. Maybe we were meant to be famous in a small town, too."

"Or infamous in a small town," I say, "depending on how we do at the cherry competition."

"Legends don't become legends without some truth and history, right?"

His hand is warm. My heart begins to race.

I listen to the trees.

"Maybe they've been trying to tell you something your whole life," I say, "but now you're just ready to listen."

MARY

I stand on the porch outside of Francine's A-frame, holding a hot Crock-Pot with my famous baked beans. My hands are ensconced in oven mitts printed with a map of Michigan. We sell them in the general store, and they are a popular gift for vacationers who want a reminder of their visit to our beautiful state, but my mitts are worn and a bit scorched on the ends, just like the woman wearing them. I wonder why I have never bothered to grab a new pair for myself.

"I'm just like the cobbler's son," I laugh to myself in the quiet, the lake sighing behind me.

Figures move in front of the large windows that front Francine's home, and the A-frame winks at me.

I smile and wink back. The door opens. Francine smiles.

"I can always sense when you're nearby," she says. "Friends know that about one another, don't they?"

"They do," I agree.

She ushers me inside and toward the kitchen. I place the slow cooker insert on a trivet made of polished lake stones.

Today, most people would call her decor *retro*. Her kitchen is dotted with the original appliances—a jadeite green refrigerator and oven that match the jadeite glass collection perched on her wooden shelves, and a multicolored, oval rag rug lies before the farmhouse sink.

"This way," Francine says. "Everyone is in the living room."

She puts her hand on my back and guides me out of the kitchen.

What is about the touch of a friend's hand that instantly calms you, erases all those years and makes you feel as if time has stopped, you are young and there are still memories to be made?

I too often forget the simple majesty and meaning of an A-frame until I step foot under the soaring ceiling. Francine's home arcs toward heaven, knotty-pine wood everywhere, dark beams and trusses holding it all in place. The front is all glass, truly a window on the world. The sun glints off the lake and fills her home with a light so bright I need sunglasses. The wood in her home shimmers. I feel as I'm living in a beautiful glass terrarium, surrounded by nature.

Francine's home is filled with finds. She loves to go junkin', and she has discovered Saarinen tulip tables at estate sales, brutalist coffee tables at antique malls, and—once—two Eames chair on the side of the road with a Magic Marker sign that read Free!

Her architecturally simple home is even more beautiful with the minimalist furniture with which she has artfully decorated it. My cottage, on the other hand, is a flood of heirlooms, artwork and memories.

Layered, as Francine so beautifully and sensitively describes it.

I cannot imagine anyone else in this home but Francine. I cannot imagine anyone tearing this home down to build an oversize monstrosity on the lake.

"I never imagined my home would feel so alive again," Francine says. "A dinner party was a wonderful idea."

Two sleek sofas in a nubby upholstery flank a glass coffee table. Taffy and Ollie occupy one sofa, Q and Becky sit opposite them.

"I know," I say.

Francine's purple soul seems to shimmer before me in the

lake's light. She nods as we look into one another's eyes and she opens her arms, and we hug.

"And I never imagined you could have assembled such a disparate group of folks like this in the same house much less on the same couch," I say. "Two were strangers only weeks ago, and two didn't like each other much just days ago. Now look."

"You saw it, and you made it happen," Francine says.

"Well, you made tonight happen," I say. "Thank you."

"Just know you're the strongest woman I've ever known. And the best friend." Francine rubs my back. "Speaking of strong, what would you like to drink? No Michigan margaritas, but we have lots of Michigan wine."

"I'll take a glass of Pinot Blanc, thank you."

"Perfect for tonight," Francine says.

An antique sideboard serves as a makeshift bar, and Francine pours a glass for me and her. Ollie scoots into the middle of the sofa, and I take a seat next to him, while Francine squeezes next to Q.

"Cheers!" Francine says, lifting her glass.

"Cheers!" everyone responds.

I take a sip of my dry, crisp wine.

"Rule number eight of a girls' trip," Q says. "Lots of wine!"

"Amen to that!" Taffy says. "So how long exactly is this girls' trip of yours?"

Q and Becky glance at one another, considering his question.

"Cosmically undecided," Q says. "Rentally—is that a word?—through Labor Day."

"We still have lots of time together, then," Taffy says.

My eyes widen at Taffy's enthusiasm, and I glance at Q. She lifts a brow and smiles.

"You certainly did a great job at the store," I say. "I still can't thank you enough for stepping in to help."

"My pleasure," Q says. "I loved it. And I know that Becky wants to try her hand at it, too."

"You do?" Ollie asks, cutting me off with the same question I was going to ask.

"I do," Becky says. "There's something so beautiful about what you do there. And if I can deal with angry, entitled parents every day of my life, I certainly think I can handle happy, entitled vacationers."

Music drifts through the open windows on the side of Francine's house.

"Speaking of *entitled*," Taffy whispers to me.

"So I understand that you and Ollie will be entering the Cherry Championship?" Francine asks. "You have some very big shoes to fill."

"Very big," Ollie says. "But I think I'm ready. How about you, Becky?"

"Me, too," she says with a wink. "We've had a good coach."

I watch the two of them, and I cannot help but notice that something has shifted. Not long ago, this exchange would have been laced with underlying tension, but their current banter is not only friendlier but more personal.

I take a sip of wine and surreptitiously glance at my grandson.

His cheeks are flushed, the telltale sign he is either angry or smitten.

And he is certainly not angry. A grandma knows.

"I'd be happy to help you one day at the store, too, Grandma."

"I'd love that," I say.

"So," Q continues, "Taffy was telling me all about the Cherry Championship, but I've seen signs for other events, too."

"Yes," Francine says. "There's also the big Cherry Parade in Traverse City as well as the Very Cherry Porch Parade."

"The what?" Becky asks.

"It's a way for the community to demonstrate its cherry spirit," she says. "Been around as long as I have, if not longer, right, Mary?"

I shake my head. "Folks decorate their homes, porches, yards, windows, storefronts with all things cherry."

"Have you ever won?" Becky asks.

"Oh, I've never entered. I don't have time for that," I say. "And I think I show my cherry spirit in other ways."

"Oh, you're full of spirit, all right," Francine says. "And a little bit of the devil."

"Ain't that the truth," Taffy says.

"It's not nice to pick on an old woman," I say.

"Well, the grill should be hot by now," Francine says. "Let me go throw the sausages on—we have a feta chicken, spicy brats and some plain ol' hot dogs—so come on out in a few minutes. We'll have dinner on the deck overlooking Lake Michigan."

Francine exits, and Taffy stands, too. "Let me help you."

"I never dreamed I'd be sitting in a beautiful lakeside home having dinner with such an incredible group of people," Q says. "I couldn't have written or cast a better summer play myself. It's just what we needed, isn't it, Becky?"

Becky nods, takes a sip of her wine and glances out the window toward the lake.

"It is," she says, as if to herself.

With the sun beaming upon her, Becky looks as if she's been dipped in gold, a statue a sculptor has created to honor the beauty of youth.

And yet, I can feel that Becky is much like me: a woman who never believed she was beautiful, even in the glow of her youth. She is a woman, like so many, who is seeking to find her voice in a world that listens to those of any other save for those who have been kissed by the sunshine of life, loss, experience and hard work. We only admire the faux image anymore.

I follow Becky's eyes toward the lake.

What does she see out there? Her grandparents? The four women? Or simply the end of another day, the closing of another chapter in her life that she doesn't want to end?

We often are our best on vacation. We go to the places we dream of being, the destinations we would prefer to live. We do the things we always wish to do but that time never allows. And we go with the people we love.

I watch Q chat with her friend.

And often we see ourselves—and each other—in a new light.

On those vacations, when we look into the horizon, when we lift our faces to the sun, when we raise a glass to the stunning sunset, what are we seeking?

What are we seeing?

I know.

We are experiencing an external picture that has been buried deep inside of us, one we only allow ourselves to witness on special occasions rather than every day of our lives. We are seeking a glow that illuminates us and makes us shimmer with excitement for the day that is to come, rather than be filled with dread.

We are seeking the spark we had as children.

I turn and notice that Ollie is staring at Becky as she continues to chat with Q and gaze out the windows.

I smile to myself.

They each came here on vacation to rediscover their inner child.

None of that is a mirage, and yet we believe it is in our lives.

Society tells us we deserve only two weeks of magic and happiness a year. And then we turn our heads from the horizon and return to our drudgery.

"Grandma?"

Ollie's hand is on my arm.

"It's time for dinner."

He helps me up. As we make our way outside, a cell phone trills.

"My mom is like a bad comic," Becky says to Q, stopping in her tracks. "Her timing is always off."

"You don't have to answer it, you know," Q says. "She's just going to make you feel bad."

"I can't do that," Becky says. "I left it in such a bad place the other day." She holds out her phone. "I never should have taught her FaceTime. I'm so sorry, everyone. Excuse me." She moves toward the windows in the living room. "Hi, Mom."

Becky is quiet as she listens. She paces. I can see her fade from this place as she steps from the sunshine into a darker part of the house.

"I'm so worried about you, honey," her mother is saying. "And where are you right now? It looks like you're on the set of that weird show you made us watch a long time ago. What was that? *Mad People*?"

"*Mad Men*," Becky says.

"So depressing. And the way those people drank. I can see wine in the background. Are you drunk?"

"Not yet."

I stifle a laugh.

"When are you coming home?" her mother continues. "Is Monique holding you hostage up there?"

Q lifts her wineglass and polishes off its contents. "Cheers, Betty!"

Ollie laughs.

"And those postcards you keep sending," she says. "I just don't understand the allure of Michigan. What do you do all day? Sit in that sun and stare at the water? Those swimsuits girls are wearing these days should be illegal. Aren't you always cleaning up sand every time you turn around? And all those cherries. They stain everything. And your father's tummy gets upset when he has too many. You know him and stone fruit."

Becky's eyes are the size of UFOs. "Mom," she keeps saying, over and over again, like a five-year-old trying desperately to get her parent's attention. "Mom."

"Let me say hello," I finally interject.

"Really?" Becky says.

"Are you talking to me?" her mother asks.

"I want you to meet someone," she says, turning the screen toward me. I wave.

"Hi, Mrs. Thatcher. I'm Mary Jackson. I own and run the Very Cherry General Store in Good Hart, Michigan. I just want to let you know what a blessing it has been to get to know your daughter. Becky is wonderful and so talented."

"My Becky?" she asks, touching her hair and looking around her kitchen as if searching for her daughter. "Well, she has a job that she needs to return to that won't be there forever, and a home that needs tending and—"

"You're supposed to say *Thank you* when someone compliments you on your daughter," I say.

Betty stops as if seeing me for the first time. "How old are you?"

"And those are questions we don't ask out loud," I say.

Q bursts into laughter.

I continue. "But I'm eighty."

"And you still work?" she sounds confused.

"I do," I say. "Every day. I love what I do. I'm blessed."

Betty seems uncomfortable. I watch her walk to the kitchen sink and grab two dish towels, make her way down a narrow, beige hallway, open a door and toss the towels into a washing machine.

"How is Becky doing? Is she okay? She's just been through so much."

"I'm right here, Mom," Becky says, turning the camera back on herself. "And I'm having the time of my life. I've been learning not to live my life in the pits."

"Well, all of this laundry is the pits, Becky," her mom says.

Becky moves toward me, and we watch her mom reach for a gallon of liquid detergent while juggling her cell. "And I have to get your father set up for the ball game. You know how he likes a beer in his lucky Cardinals mug and a bowl of popcorn. Oh, and the dining-room curtains need to be closed at dusk. We have so many strange people walking the neighborhood that we don't know, and I hate that they can just look right in our window. You know I have to masking-tape them shut now. I don't live in a zoo. Not to mention—"

Suddenly, she looks up and sees me watching.

"Becky, you are embarrassing me."

"Don't be embarrassed, Betty," I say. "We all have to do laundry."

She chuckles nervously.

"What have you done for yourself this summer, Betty?" I ask.

She sets the detergent down and looks into the camera, nervously searching the world with her eyes.

"What do you mean?"

"Fun stuff. Have you read a book, gardened, gone to the theater to see a show that Q has produced, gone on a vacation like your daughter, even just taken a nap or had lunch with a friend?"

"I don't have any friends," she says.

"Everyone needs a best friend," I say. "We're having dinner with my best friend right now."

For a moment, Becky's mother stills. She leans against her washing machine in her minuscule laundry room and sighs. "How nice," she finally says. "May I see your view?"

Becky turns the camera and walks toward the window.

"My goodness," Betty says. "The green of those pines against the sky and water. Oh, your grandmother loved that, didn't she?"

"She did, Mom," Becky says. "You would, too."

"Well, I better get this laundry going. And your dad is calling. I'll talk to you later."

"I love you, Mom," Becky says to her cell that no longer has anyone on the other end.

I walk over to her, place my arm around her waist and whisper, "She loves you. You know that, right? Just has a hard time showing it."

Becky smiles and nods, and we head to a glorious dinner. As Francine serves dessert—a warm blueberry crisp with French vanilla gelato—we hear a faint rustling followed by a soft "Hello?"

Our neighbors, Geoffrey and Moira, appear from a path that leads to a small lawn. They are draped in colorful, patterned caftans that billow in the lake breeze as if they are birds about to take flight.

"We heard a party," Moira says. "Was our invitation lost?"

The table emits a collective, uncomfortable giggle.

"Hello, Taffy," Geoffrey says.

"We are so deeply sorry about your husband," Moira says, moving up one step toward Francine. "I know how hard this must be."

Francine looks like a deer in the headlights.

"We've been telling our friends all about this place," Geoffrey says. "And since you're having a party..."

More rustling and then two couples appear on the steps as if they've been waiting in a green room for the host to introduce them to the studio audience.

"This is Zoe and Bryce," he continues, "and Olivia and Victor."

The two couples look exactly the same.

They all turn on the deck and look toward the lake.

"This view," one says.

"Mesmerizing," another says. "I can just picture how it could be."

Could be?

"This is Taffy," Geoffrey says to his friends, pointing, "the builder we've been telling you about. He's a bit slow but just so talented." He turns to Francine. "We were hoping we might be able to sneak a peek at your place while you're still eating so we don't interrupt you."

Silence.

"Well, then," Moira says, taking a step onto the deck and motioning for her friends to follow.

I stand.

"Please stop before I stop you."

"Excuse me?" she says.

"You've never invited us to dinner," I say. "You've never said hello unless you needed something. You never even sent flowers or a sympathy card to Francine, despite living next door to her. You didn't welcome her back this summer with a hug or bottle of wine. You don't know us. You don't know how special this place is. You only see what could be, not what is."

My own words stop me cold. I look at Ollie.

"We're having a private dinner party right now," Ollie says, standing beside me. "We're enjoying a beautiful summer night with dear friends. Our desserts are getting cold."

They do not budge.

Geoffrey begins to open his mouth, but Q stands.

"Read the room, sweetheart," she says.

"How unbelievably rude," Moira says.

Becky stands. "Let me show you out," she says.

She moves toward the steps and escorts them back down the deck.

When she returns, the table bursts into applause.

"You are something else," I whisper to Ollie.

"So are you, Grandma," he says, putting his arm around me. "I know how special this place is. And I'm beginning to see not what could be but what is."

"Me, too," I whisper.

BECKY

I once put the three smartest kids from every class in charge of the county science fair one year because I wanted our school to win. I didn't just want a volcano that puffed smoke, I wanted a three-dimensional volcano the size of Vesuvius that allowed parents to walk inside and see how lava was created.

We won, but the process getting there was only slightly less intense than what we've done to create this entry for the Porch Parade.

I step off the porch of the Very Cherry General Store and drift into the parking lot to survey our work.

But what do you expect when you put an elementary-school assistant principal, the head of a theater company and an accomplished builder together on an art project? A team that could create an entire world from popsicle sticks, a can of red paint, a little cardboard and a lot of lights.

"What do you think?" Q asks.

"It's cherry good," I say.

"Ugh," she says. She whips a cherry at me, and it misses by a mile.

"I'm glad you're not entering the championship," I say. "But I am glad you're on my decorating team."

She joins me in the parking lot.

"I do have mad skills," she says.

"Yes, you do," Taffy says, tool belt around his waist.

"Back atcha," Q says. "I should hire you to work as my set director at the Muny. You are unbelievably creative."

"Thank you," he says. "We *should* talk. Geoffrey, Moira and company will be the end of me."

"How *can* you work for that insufferable couple?" Q asks.

"You do understand how life works, right?" he asks with a laugh. "The American economy? Look, I'm sure it's similar to working with a difficult actor. Sometimes, you just have to grit your teeth and focus on the end result."

"And what an end result," I say, spreading my arms.

After Francine's dinner party, Taffy, Ollie, Q and I decided—after a final glass of wine on the beach—that Mary's store should be entered for the first time in the Porch Parade.

Over the past few days, the three of us have met on the down low—over lunch on the beach, for coffee at dawn at the little café frequented only by locals, at Taffy's tiny cottage in the woods—to come up with not only a design but also a plan.

While I've helped out at the store, Q has been heading into town to loot the local Michael's, and Taffy has spent mornings surreptitiously sawing and working for us instead of for Geoffrey and Moira. Ollie has occupied Mary's time with long lunches or walks on the beach while the three of us schemed and measured.

Today, Mary and other participants had to meet with the Cherry Royale Parade committee. Ollie went along with her and offered to take her to a very long brunch afterward.

We had perused endless pictures online for inspiration, and Taffy had filled us in on what most homes and storefronts have done for previous Porch Parades.

"Balloons! Lots of red balloons," he'd said, supporting what we had seen online. "And tons of pink cherry blossoms and petals. Oh, and red geraniums. Everywhere."

The theme of the Porch Parade was, of course, cherries, with the mission statement saying *The point of decorating is to unleash your creativity and celebrate cherries and generations of fun.*

And that's when it hit us.

So Q sketched out a set, just as she would at the Muny, and Taffy and I helped her bring that vision to life.

"It looks like Disneyland," I say.

"But redder," Q says with a laugh.

We woke before dawn to bring this spectacle to life.

"Shall we?" I ask.

We walk through our creation.

Taffy has built a cherry tree featuring a cutout in the trunk through which you can stick your face and take a photo.

The limbs are dotted with oversize cherries featuring the faces of Mary, her mother and grandmother, as well as all of the people who have passed through the general store over the decades. There is a sign over the tree that reads *A Sweet Life Blooms over Generations!*

Beyond this is a series of cherry trees to greet you. Some are saplings, some are blooming, some are ripe with cherries. The life cycle of a cherry tree and its fruit is displayed by each.

Beside each tree is also a cutout of the three matriarchs with their life histories. Another plaque reads *Cherries are just like family. Over generations, with enough love, we take root and grow into something sweeter and more beautiful than you could ever dream.*

The histories culminate with the framed photos of Mary winning the Cherry Championship as a girl, and today as the store's owner handing a Michigan Treasure Cookie to a young girl.

Mary Jackson: The Champion of Good Hart
Passing Along Her History to Future Generations

"A girl can do anything a man can. You just gotta believe you can. That's the hard part."

The porch of the Very Cherry General Store is transformed into an old farm stand lined with all the bounty that Mary makes from her orchard—jams, preserves, cookies, pies, cakes—each sitting in the middle of an open cherry blossom.

"I can't believe we pulled this off," I say as we step onto the porch.

Q fills an old-fashioned crate with more cherries and sets them in the middle of a blossom.

"I feel like I'm ready for opening night," she says.

"What do you think Mary will say?" I ask Taffy who is still admiring his handiwork. "You know her better than anyone."

"She'll either be deeply touched or spittin' mad," he says. "The Cherry Festival and Championship is a touchy issue for her. Depends on how her day with Virgie goes."

"The two have a long history, I take it?" I ask.

"Longer than any cherry tree," Taffy says, "and tarter than any Montmorency."

"And filled with pits?" Q adds.

"Oh, yes," he says. "We could spend all day dissecting their relationship and making cherry puns."

Q nabs a muffin from the middle of a blossom and takes a seat on the stoop.

She pats the stoop for us to join her.

"I love you cherry much," she says to her muffin.

MARY

"She has a captive audience. We could be here until the festival's sesquicentennial."

Ollie snorts at my remark, which turns into a fit of laughter.

"Do we have a question?"

Virgie moves her glasses to the end of her nose and scans the room. Like a bat, she homes in on our sound. Her eyes train on me and Ollie, and they do not move until he has stopped laughing and the blood has drained from his face.

"Well, then, shall I return to what I was saying?"

There are some women who command authority merely by their presence. And then there are others, like Virgie, who must command a presence through a virtual mirage. Virgie is dressed as if she's attending a luncheon with foreign dignitaries and not speaking to a room filled with festival volunteers and parade participants, a majority of whom are wearing overalls, Carhartts and Farm & Fleet caps.

Virgie has seemed to have forgotten that cherries come from field and farm. She seems to forget that we are actually seated in a tent that is hotter than Detroit asphalt. Folks just want to know what to do, where to go and get back to their lives.

Virgie is channeling Nancy Reagan in a form-fitting red dress with gold buttons and is wearing as much makeup as a teenage girl working at Ulta. Her wig is as red as her dress, tucked behind her ears, tendrils swept along her cheekbones, to show off her pink diamond earrings that blind you when they hit the light.

"For those of you who are new to the festival, welcome! And for those of you returning again for our hundred and twenty-fifth, welcome back!"

Virgie extends her hands in front of her and claps like a trained porpoise.

"I want to remind you of the incredible history of the Cherry Festival and the important part it has played in our area over the last one hundred and twenty-five years. This history comes directly from our National Cherry Festival web site. For more fun facts and history, please go to cherryfestival.org. Please dim the lights! Enjoy!"

A screen behind her lights up, and images begin to flash.

"In 1910, cherry growers in the Grand Traverse area began to hold informal 'blessing of the blossoms' ceremonies each year in May, and that was followed in the 1920s with the crowning of the first-ever Cherry Queen, Gertrude Brown, the beginning of a widely celebrated local tradition that still happens every year. The next year, President Coolidge was presented a three-foot pie containing more than five thousand cherries from Hawkins Bakery in Traverse City."

Virgie pauses as many newbies in the crowd murmur and take photos. If there's one thing she knows, it's high drama.

"The 1929 festival was so successful that it was expanded to a three-day affair the next year, with President Hoover attending the opening day ceremonies," she continues. "In 1964, the festival became a full week event, and in 1975, the Cherry Royale Parade broke the all-time record attended by over 300,000 people with President Gerald Ford, a Michigan native, as Grand Marshal. And in 1987, Traverse City set a world record by baking the world's largest cherry pie that measured seventeen-feet-six inches and weighed 28,350 pounds."

Virgie pauses again.

"But this year, our quasquicentennial anniversary, will be the greatest event ever, thanks to you!"

The crowd applauds wildly.

"You will note as you head outside that your group leaders will be holding signs that designate entry or committee: Porch Parade, Cherry Royale Parade, Best Pie, or Preserves. Just go to them, and they will assist you with the specifics regarding your participation or volunteer duties. As director of the festival's celebration, thank you from the bottom of my heart."

Virgie departs the stage with a great flourish and is greeted by a horde of local women all dressed in red who flutter and giggle, all wanting to take her place in the future, as well as a group of young girls with sashes vying to sway her vote for Cherry Queen.

"Let's go find out what car I'll be riding in this year and what time I need to be there," I say. "Knowing Virgie, I'm sure she has payback in mind and has placed me in the back of a pickup with a bunch of hungry prized goats waiting to feast on my shoestrings or on a fire truck with a band of first-year drum students."

Ollie laughs. "She wouldn't do that, Grandma."

"Oh, but she would," I say.

I turn to head outside, but I'm caught behind a man walking at the speed of a sedated turtle. Virgie's hive buzzes down the aisle. She stops when she sees me.

"Hell has frozen over," she says. "Mary Jackson. Actually playing by the rules."

My mind whirs back in time to 1958. I can hear her talking about me. I take a breath.

"If I were in hell, I'm sure the devil's punishment would be forcing me speak to you every day for the rest of my life."

The hive falls silent in an instant. Virgie smiles that Cheshire grin.

"I put a lot of thought into who you should ride with this

year in the parade, and I remember how much fun you said you
had with Riley Filmore, the former Cherry Queen you rode
with on the fiftieth anniversary of your—" she clears her throat
"—championship."

Virgie looks at her cohorts, and they titter.

"It just seemed perfect that you two could reunite considering the magnitude of this year's event," Virgie says. "And do
you remember Prince Oink, Riley's prized pig? Well, his granddaughter, Princess Oink, will be riding with you, too, and I
hear she's quite the ham."

The hive is absolutely atwitter at her deviousness.

"I'll actually be driving my grandmother in the parade," Ollie
says. "So there's no need for your…thoughtfulness."

I nearly break my neck turning to gawk at my grandson.

"In fact, we have a cherry-red vintage convertible fit for a
queen…"

Ollie catches my eyes. *We do?*

His eyes say, *We will.*

I smile, ducking my head, trying not to laugh.

Ollie continues. "By the way, you forgot to mention one of
the greatest moments in the festival's history in your speech:
my grandma being the first—and only—woman to win the
Cherry Championship. There's a statue dedicated to her that
total strangers stop and admire every single summer day. And
yet those who know her and should be most inspired by her spit
in her face every single day. Figuratively speaking, of course."

Ollie leans down to face the girls in sashes.

"My grandmother has always been a queen," Ollie says. "Do
you know how she got to be one?"

The girls shake their heads.

"Simply by being herself," he says. "That's the hardest thing
in the world for a person to do: be the unique individual God
intended. And you don't need a sash, or the approval of some-

one in society, to do that. Your real crown will appear when you simply know and love who you are."

Ollie holds out his hand to me. I take it.

"C'mon, Queen," he says.

PART FOUR

"Just as cherry...blossoms all possess their own unique qualities, each person is unique. We cannot become someone else. The important thing is that we live true to ourselves and cause the great flower of our lives to blossom."

—Daisaku Ikeda

BECKY

"Remember rule number seven?" Q asks me as we peer out the window of the log cabin just like we did when we were sixteen waiting for our dates to pick us up. "No boys."

"But these are boy friends," she clarifies. "See how I paused between *boy* and *friends*?"

I smile.

This isn't a date. *Is it?*

Q watches me and answers my question telepathically with a stern shake of her head.

This is not a date.

I look out the window again.

Then, what is it?

Just two single women having dinner with two single men to discuss all aspects of the parade and maybe have a final summer send-off as our time here draws to a close?

My internal voice sounds way more convincing than when I say this aloud to Q.

"Exactly," she says, the word coming out more as a question than statement.

I feel exactly the way I did as a girl, though, when a boy I liked asked me out: giddy, dizzy, nervous, excited, flushed.

"Is it weird that I might like this guy so quickly?" I ask. "I mean, he thought I was taking advantage of his grandma at first. But now...he's just such a nice guy. I feel like we're in exactly the same place in our lives. It's like he gets me, and I get him."

"No," she says. "Oddly enough, I feel the same way about Taffy. Either we have feelings for these guys, or it's just going to be a fling. And either is kinda nice, right?"

I nod.

"A date," I say. "With a boy. A real boy. I think I'm nervous because, you know, Matt never really asked me out on dates."

"Oh, I know," Q says.

"Even in college, or after we moved in together, there were no romantic dinners, no surprise evenings where he asked me to dress up and then whisked me off for an evening of dancing underneath the stars," I say. "It was beers and burgers with his buddies after work on Friday night and then pizza at home with me every Saturday. Everything—even me—simply fit into his routine."

"Routine is necessary in life," Q says. "But you never should have allowed yourself to be valued on the same level of importance as a new vacuum for Christmas or cleaning the shower tile every other Saturday, no matter what."

"I became grout to Matt."

I continue. "Do you know, the last *real* date I remember going on was my senior prom, if you can believe that. Remember how every girl dressed in that grunge-prom look, but we wore long velvet dresses, yours in an emerald green to set off your hair and skin, mine in a midnight blue with a matching ribbon choker?"

"You went with Glenn Shores, right?" Q asks with a laugh. "The best boy name ever."

"Yes!" I say. "He played hockey at Aquinas, and he looked like he should be starring on *Full House* and had that smile that made it seem as if he knew every secret in the world."

Suddenly, I spin.

"We danced all night, and when he told me I was beautiful, I was the one who leaned in and kissed him before being separated by a nun who had a ruler she put between us to show the appropriate distance we should be apart. 'God is watching,' she warned."

Q laughs. "Nothing like a nun with a ruler."

Gravel crunches, and Taffy's truck pulls down the long drive. For a few seconds, Q and I simply fly around in circles, like bats at dusk.

We open the door and greet them.

"This place is insane," Taffy says, looking around the rental. "Did you invite Jeff Daniels to dinner?"

"It's his *friend's* summer cottage," Q says. "Aren't we reason enough to be here?"

Taffy stops. He takes Q's hands in his and says, "Of course you are. You are more than enough, and the only reason we're here."

The hurricane that is Q calms before this rugged man, and I watch them look at each as if in slow motion.

If I had to create a man who I believed could not only capture Q's attention but also her heart, I never in my wildest dreams would have created a man like, or named, Taffy.

But I think I've been so consumed in my own stagnation that I never paid close-enough attention to my friend's heart.

When Q and I go on road trips together, we play this game I invented long ago called In The Driver's Seat. As you drive, you have a choice to pick any man in any of the next three cars you pass—all sight unseen, of course, which is the fun of the game—to go on a date. If you turn those all down, you are forced to marry the fourth man on the spot. I always believed I could game the system, select the perfect man based on the car he drove. A BMW, Volvo or Mercedes was a classy man. Q always flew by the seat of her pants, picking the truck driver or the man with a trailer filled with horses.

"I've met enough wannabe artists and intellectuals in my life," she said. "Give me a real man who has a zest for life."

It was only this summer that I realized Q may have always been too busy—and hurt —in her life to slow down enough in the passing lane to actually meet the driver she selected. More-over, I'm beginning to realize, my picker has always been faulty. I admired the wrong things.

"What's that smell?" Taffy asks.

"We made a cherry chip cake," Q says. "From scratch. Just like Mary taught us. I'm waiting for it to cool so I can ice it later."

"My favorite," Ollie says. "How sweet. Literally."

"Can I lick the beaters?" Taffy asks, like a kid.

Q laughs. "Of course."

She walks by and whispers to me, "A man who wants to lick the beaters. Pinch me."

"This isn't a date," I whisper back with a wink.

"Of course not."

The two head to the kitchen, and I turn to Ollie.

"What a beautiful cabin," he says. "Such character. Reminds me of my grandma's cottage."

Ollie turns in a circle to admire the architecture.

If I had to create a man who I believed could not only capture my attention but also my heart, I never in my wildest dreams would have created a man like, or named, Ollie.

In fact, I hated everything about him just days ago.

What has changed?

Me?

Him?

A lot in a short time.

My whole career has been spent looking at a situation from the other person's perspective. After our fight in the Tunnel of Trees and our work on the Porch Parade decorations, I began to see myself through his very emotive and beautiful eyes.

Imagine how Ollie must have felt to arrive only to discover a stranger had not only befriended his grandmother but was also in her store, sharing a deeply personal connection?

Ollie wears his heart on his sleeve.

Matt did not.

That both excites and worries me.

Am I simply attracted to the opposite of Matt, or is there something in Ollie that I've been seeking my whole life?

Big questions to ask on a girls' vacation that is nearing its final sunset picture.

"Let's take happy hour to the beach before dinner," Q says.

As we walk the trail leading to the lake, Q and Taffy talk about all the stars she's worked with over the years. She drops names—Hugh Jackman, Bette Midler—as casually as items on a grocery list, and he listens in awe.

"I'm drawn to unique talent," Q says. "What a person has to say via their art. And heart. You have a lot to say with your talent, and you say it in such a humble way. You have a great admiration for true Michigan architecture, but you also are grounded, and that's most important. I've said it before, but I should kidnap you and make you my scenic designer at the Muny in St. Louis."

"How much do you pay?" Taffy asks with a laugh. "And would I get to work with you every day?"

Q turns to him. For a moment, she is just a silhouette, the heat coming from the sand obscuring details around her body, making her look as if she is melting.

And I can tell that this man is doing just that to my friend.

"I would never have expected this in my life," Ollie says, watching them.

"Me, either."

Q and Taffy walk ahead, and their voices fade.

Ollie stops on the trail.

"I used to know every trail and path through the woods and along the beach when I was a kid," he says. "I knew the best grapevines to swing off over creeks, just like Tarzan. I knew every dunes grass–covered trail to hide in so my grandma wouldn't make me do chores. I knew every spot to collect the best rocks and the exact moment to catch a big wave on the lake to bodysurf." He turns, admiring this hidden trail. "That's what Michigan is. All of these secret places and moments that hide in your heart."

As we walk, I tell him more about my bond with my grandparents and my time in Michigan as a kid. When we emerge on the beach, I say, "It's the Golden Hour."

"That's what my grandma calls this time of day," he says.

"Mine did, too." We look onto the lake. "And it is."

Q and Taffy have placed a big blanket on the beach, their shoes weighting it down in the lake breeze. Two bottles of wine sit in a ticking-striped insulated wine tote. I place the basket I'm carrying beside the wine and begin to set out some crackers, Raclette cheese and smoked whitefish dip. Taffy and Q pour themselves a glass of wine, nibble on some cheese and dip, and then excuse themselves to walk the shoreline.

"Show him that trick you do," Q says to me with a big wink as they walk away.

"Stop it," I say.

"She's a magician, Ollie," Q calls.

"Stop it!" I yell. "I will murder you, and the jury will acquit me."

She laughs.

I take a seat on the blanket. Ollie sits next to me, his hairy, bare leg brushing my skin.

"What trick?"

"I can't," I say.

"Too late," he says.

"This is humiliating."

I reach into the basket and pluck a stem off of a fresh cherry.

"What are you doing?" he asks.

A few seconds later, I poke my tongue out. The cherry stem is twisted in a perfect knot.

"She's gotten a lot of dates with that trick," Q calls from the water with a big laugh. "Men always order her a second drink after that."

"Go away!" I yell, and she finally disappears down the shore with Taffy.

"I will never live that down," I say.

"No, I'm impressed," Ollie says in a husky voice.

"My college days," I say. "Q is supposed to be a vault about those times, but she's more like an open suitcase."

"Speaking of college, I minored in philosophy and mythology," Ollie says out of the blue, staring into the horizon.

"Really?" I ask. "I never would have guessed."

"I majored in business, but I was always part dreamer, part practical, trying to please two people in my life, my dad and my grandma, neither realizing I loved both sides of me. I've always been caught somewhere in the middle." Ollie takes a sip of his wine. "And that's an awful place to be because the pressure builds from both sides until you feel like you're going to explode."

"And your mom?" I ask.

"I think she didn't want to add any additional conflict between my dad and Grandma, so she remained noncommittal. Recently, she's been intent on setting me up with women a lot like her. Someone intent on getting married and having a very nice, but predictable, life."

"How has that gone?"

"Pretty much like your breakup at recess," he says with a smile. "Most end in disaster."

"What do you want?"

Ollie doesn't answer. He looks off into the horizon. I follow his gaze, and there I see them, again coming my way, as if on a mission: the mirage of women.

"You see them again, don't you?" he asks.

I nod.

"Did you know that these visions, Fata Morgana, are named after an Arthurian sorceress named Morgan le Fay?" Ollie asks.

I look at him. "Is this your mythology major speaking?"

He smiles and nods. "People believed she conjured these fairy castles or false lands over the water to lure sailors to their deaths. But others believe she was a fairy."

"What do you mean?" I ask.

"Le Fay means *fairy* in Italian," he says. "Morgan the Fairy. I actually believe she was just a woman who saw magical things, and society couldn't understand so they had to label her in some way or another. A witch, a fairy. Men have done that our whole lives to women, haven't we?"

I nod.

"You actually yelled at me about that, remember?"

I nod again, this time with a laugh.

"Why aren't men allowed to see the magic in everyday moments?"

"You are," I say. "You just don't allow yourselves to do that. Society puts expectations on you, too." I hit his knee with mine as a wake-up gesture. "Listen, I'm Catholic, so my whole life has been filled with guilt."

Ollie laughs, and I continue.

"My entire life, I've helped educate children and encourage them to follow their dreams. I urge them to be their own unique selves in this world and to forge their own paths. And yet I've sat in an office watching these kids grow up, graduate high school and set off to do all things they've dreamed of doing. All the things I've dreamed of doing. Sometimes, they return and tell me all about their adventures in the world. I don't want to be that woman who looks up one day, like my mother, and is filled with unspoken regret."

The waves sigh.

"Can I tell you a story?" I ask.

"Of course."

"There was a little boy in my school who started coming to school in a pink dress," I say. "His parents were very accepting of how he wanted to dress but deeply worried about how he'd be treated, so we had the little boy talk to a counselor about his emotions and the fact he was getting picked on, and he said, 'I'm just being me. I just want to be happy. I just want to be my magical self.' When the counselor asked him about all the bullying he was experiencing from other kids, he said, 'I just want them to be happy, too, but I know that might take a long time.'" I take a sip of wine. "It's taken me a long time to overcome societal expectations. Your grandma and this little boy are just ahead of their time. I think we're all just out there trying to be happy and not having a clue how to do that because we've never been our authentic selves. I think we're all just trying to figure out our equivalent of a pink dress."

As if on cue, the Golden Hour turns to a magical pink.

In the distance, I see Taffy lean in and kiss Q.

"What do you see on the horizon now?" I ask Ollie.

"Pink possibility," he whispers.

MARY

Francine sticks her hand into the box to retrieve her mail, and I grab it.

She shrieks.

I stick my head into the tiny window and laugh.

"You will never stop doing that, will you?" she asks.

"Never!" I say.

I head from behind the post office with a large envelope.

"I feel like I'm singlehandedly trying to save the reputation of the United States Postal Service by trying to make it fun," I continue.

Francine, ensconced in purple, laughs. "I don't think it's working."

I place the envelope on the old counter by the cash register.

"When were you going to tell me?" I ask. "You can't keep a secret from a postal clerk."

Francine shifts on her feet and touches the envelope. The return address reads *Virgie Daniels, Tunnel of Trees Real Estate.*

"She's the only realtor around here who knows the area," Francine shrugs.

"No," I say. "Not about Virgie. About your decision to sell."

"I told you it was coming."

"I know," I say. "I just thought..."

I look up at Francine, and the store spins around her. I have to grip the counter to steady myself.

"Are you okay?" Francine asks.

"Too much coffee," I say. "I'm sorry, I know this is hard. I don't mean to be selfish."

"It is hard," she says. "But I know I'll always have a place to stay when I come visit you every summer. It's just too much for me to manage anymore, Mary, and my kids don't want it. I feel like we're giving the old girl a grand send-off this summer."

I smile. Her words seem as appropriate for her home as for me.

"I'll be the last widow on Widows' Peak," I comment.

"You will be the woman who ensures history prevails," Francine says, reaching out to take my hand. "You will always be the champion of Good Hart."

I give her hand a mighty squeeze.

"Speaking of which," she continues, "what do you think of what the kids did to your porch?"

"Kids?" I gasp. "You mean conspirators?"

"Their hearts were in the right place," she says. "And it's the best decorated porch I've seen around here in years."

I look out the general store's front window to the magical land of cherries and memories they created.

"It just means I have to see Virgie again," I sigh. "And I'd rather eat a bowl of pits. My stomach would be much less upset."

"Well, maybe she'll have to eat crow when she hands you the First Place trophy."

"Maybe."

"Need some help in the kitchen prepping lunch?" Francine asks. "I know you've been in need of some help. Everyone is still talking about that poor girl running out of here screaming, and your other workers are heading back to school soon."

The bell on the screened door jangles, and Ollie, Q and Becky enter, chatting like high-school friends.

"Were you three off planning something else behind my back?" I continue.

"We were only trying to surprise you on this big anniversary, Grandma," Ollie says. "We're not conspiring. We're celebrating. And now we're here to help."

"Don't mind your grandma. She's feeling a bit down because of this," Francine says, picking up the envelope and giving it a wave in the air. "I'm listing my cottage. With Virgie."

The trio moans a collective *Ugh*.

"I'm so sorry, Grandma. I know how hard this is."

Ollie walks over and puts his arm around me. I lean into him and put my head on his shoulder.

"I wish I could buy it," Q says. "I would keep it just as it is."

Francine opens up the envelope. Inside is a signed contract and a stack of marketing flyers.

"Here," she says, handing us some. "Just in case you win the Michigan Lottery. I'm offering it at a fair price, but real-estate prices have gone insane. That's good for my family, though."

Q takes a flyer, and Becky reads it with her.

"Wouldn't that be a dream?" she asks. "To live here." Becky looks at me. "Next to you, Mary."

"Why don't you guys get started on those cherry muffins with streusel topping, and I will help my grandma get the rest of the mail out and assist anyone who comes in, okay?"

They move into the kitchen, and Ollie and I begin to dispense the mail into the slots. As we make our way down the tiers of boxes, we eventually have to pull up stools to finish our work. We work in silence until the two mails bins are nearly empty.

"Hi, John," I say to a man picking up his mail. "Good morning, Sally!" I greet another local.

When it is quiet, I say, "In this world of constant change, people still enjoy opening their mail."

Ollie rotates on his stool.

"Change is good," I continue. "But there's something lovely about tradition, too."

"You know when you have a perception of someone that has as much to do with you as it does with them?" Ollie says out of the blue. "Because of your shared history?"

I consider his strange question. "I do, yes."

"I've had a misperception about you and this place, Grandma, and I think you've had a misperception about me, too."

I rotate on my stool to look my grandson in the eye. "Go on."

"I've only seen you in this place," Ollie says. "And you've never really seen me here as clearly as you've envisioned those women. You had this picture in your head your entire life of the way things should be, and I've felt deleted from that. And my dad has always had his own vision, but I'm realizing that's his vision, not mine. So where do I fit into all of this?"

I remain silent knowing this is a rhetorical question. He continues.

"I'm not like my father, and I'm nothing like my grandfather." He meets my eyes. "If I'm like anyone, it's you, Grandma. Your spirit lives inside me."

My eyes mist.

"I may not be a woman, but I am a part of your past." Ollie hesitates. "And your future. If you'll only let me."

"I would love nothing more."

"But your vision," he starts. "I know you've always believed the general store should be passed on to a woman. That was the family legacy for so long, even after my dad and I came along. I'm starting to think you weren't wrong, Grandma," Ollie says. "I'm starting to think that Becky *was* meant to come here. Your vision was right. I think she was the woman you saw. And I believe that seeing and believing in her set in motion Becky's arrival here in Good Hart. None of what I'm saying to you would be happening if she were not here and if you had not believed.

It took the right woman—*women*—to make me see the future more clearly."

"I don't know what to say. I've waited forever to hear you say you want to take over the store. Thank you."

We stand and hug until we smell smoke, followed by Q yelling, "Help!"

Ollie and I race into the kitchen to find smoke billowing from the oven, a tray of scorched muffins on a blackened tin, and Francine, Q and Becky waving dish towels to clear the air.

"What happened?" I ask.

"Someone turned the oven to broil," Becky says pointing at Q.

"It's an old oven," she says. "I thought I had it on convection."

"Old ovens don't have convection," I say. "You have to know an old oven like the back of your hand."

Q looks at the back of her hand.

"We've never gotten along," she says to it.

BECKY

I have not been this exhausted—or this excited and fulfilled—since my first opening day of school as an elementary teacher years ago. I spent months preparing my classroom and lesson plans. And when the kids came rushing into room 3A, I was nearly as giddy and nervous as they were.

Somewhere along the line, I lost that feeling. Maybe it was dealing with what I call the *two-percent parents*—those select few mothers or fathers who make a teacher's life a living hell by helicoptering over their children, taking over your classroom as a room parent or accosting you during carpool for giving their child an A−.

Perhaps I lost that feeling when I transitioned into administration only to deal with reduced budgets, new math, curriculum overhauls and an out-of-touch board.

Perhaps I simply need another first day of school in my life.

I have mopped vomit off my classroom tile, disinfected doorknobs and fed turtles in sinks. I have hosed hardened ice cream off the sidewalks at Ted Drewes and hand-wiped the floors after dropping too many floats I tried to juggle.

But somehow this feels different.

As I push a mop around the general store, the sunlight dip-ping into the pines, making the Tunnel of Trees glow as if they are about to take an evening stroll before dinner, I feel just like the ancient hardwoods.

Alive.

What did I do today that was so profoundly different than anything I did when I was a teen or a teacher?

I mop.

On the surface, nothing.

The floor gleams.

And yet, everything has come into crystal clear focus.

I worked with a team today, a team of friends that I like and trust.

I did a bit of everything—cooking, baking, customer service, tour guiding—much like I did as a teacher.

But mostly, I understood what it must mean to be an entrepreneur.

To do it on your own.

There were times I would stand back and simply watch Mary. She was akin to a ballerina, dancing here, pirouetting there, all with a great sense of pride.

This store is her heart and soul.

And she wanted anyone and everyone—from locals to strangers—to feel that love and pride.

And people love her. Genuinely love and respect her.

When I helped her and Ollie with the daily cash reconciliation, I was stunned at the total of the tiny store's receipts.

"I manage this store the way many financial advisers manage their clients' retirements," Mary said to us. "Many revenue streams create a river."

She explained to us the way that the store generates income, which started with her grandmother's and mother's savvy business instincts.

"The post office and general store always provide steady income and year-round customers," she explained. "Winter can be downright cold, and you need to ensure you can keep the heat and electricity running when there's two feet of snow outside. The baked goods, potpies and sandwiches sell to both locals and resorters, and then there are the gift items—T-shirts, sweatshirts, coffee mugs, tea towels, posters—that any vacationer will buy on a whim from summer through fall knowing they will likely never be back this way. And our Christmas gift baskets are a godsend."

I thought of the souvenirs I used to buy as a kid with my grandmother.

"May seem like it," Mary continued, "but no two days are ever the same, because everything—opening the door, baking the cookies, stocking the store, putting up the mail—relies completely on you. You don't show up, you don't get paid. If you want motivation in life, there it is."

"What does it feel like at the end of a day?" I asked Mary.

"A big exhalation of exhaustion and exaltation of accomplishment," she said. "Like stoking a fire that you never want to die."

I had to walk away to contain my emotions.

"You know I just staged *Mary Poppins* at the Muny," Q says, sauntering in from the kitchen and seeing me holding a mop. "If you could only sing, you would have been a star."

"I am a star," I say. "The only thing missing is my name has yet to be in lights."

"Damn straight," Q says.

The screened door squeals its springy hello, and Taffy appears. He gives Q a kiss and slides his arm around her back as if they are one, as if they have always been one.

"Is this a date?" she asks him.

"How'd you know?"

"You're not covered in sawdust and paint," she says. "Oh, and no Dickies tonight."

He laughs.

"You do look nice," Q says, looking him over slowly from head to toe.

Taffy does like nice. He's dressed in a pair of salmon-colored trousers and a white polo shirt flocked with light blue sailboats.

"I, however, need to change," Q says.

Her T-shirt is splattered in cherry juice, her jeans are covered in flour, and her hair is as large and red as Mars.

"You look…" you can see Taffy's mind whirl, trying too late to come up with the appropriate word "…okay, you're right. You probably need to change."

I laugh, and Q follows suit.

"An honest man," she says. "As hard to find as a good Othello."

"Let's go get you changed," Taffy says.

"I'll see you back at the cabin," Q says, heading toward the door. At the last minute, she turns. "We thought we'd spend every day at the beach. Who knew we'd spend our vacation recreating our Ted Drewes teenage years?… With boys!"

Her laughter trails behind her, and then she is gone.

"I'm having dinner with Francine," Mary announces, coming out with her friend.

"No more cooking today, though," Francine says. "Picking up a pizza."

"And wine on the beach," Mary adds. "Very important. See you tomorrow? I mean, if you want to come back, I'd love to have you, but I don't want to ruin the last of your vacation."

"I'd love to help you again."

The two exit, and the general store falls silent.

I stop and lean against my mop. I close my eyes.

There are certain sounds of summer that I have grown accustomed to hearing my whole life, the songs the warm earth waits all year to sing, and I realize I cannot live without them. Michigan is a virtual orchestra of my favorite tunes. The hum of cicadas, the lullaby of the tree frogs, the whisper of the breeze through dense leaves, the whip-poor-will's call, the beat of a pop song pulsing from an open car window, the gentle whoosh of the lake, which sounds like my heart when all is quiet and I'm about to fall asleep.

"Are you asleep?"

I open my eyes.

"I know it was a long day," Ollie says, watching me. "I bet you're beat."

"I'm…" just as Taffy just was, I'm searching for the right word "…content."

Light filters into the store and across Ollie's face, which breaks into a big smile. "Me, too."

My heart skips a beat.

Saved by the Bell was my obsession when I was a kid, and I had crushes on two of its characters, Zach and A.C., and posters of them lined my childhood bedroom. Most girls loved either Zach or A.C.—much like girls did with *Twilight* when they were divided into Team Edward vs. Team Jacob camps—but I was so torn in my love for both that I couldn't choose.

That, of course, faded, but I was still fascinated by how these two cute teens could grow into such handsome men, especially when so many child stars look nothing like they did as a kid.

Ollie has that look of a child star who grew into a very handsome man. That boyish quality remains—the hair, the dimples, the twinkling eyes—but like a fine wine, he's aged into something deeper, richer, more compelling.

"Want to help me put up the dishes?" Ollie asks. "Then we can go."

"Sure," I say, placing my mop into a bucket and following him into the kitchen.

Through the door of the kitchen, I see a picnic blanket set on the grass in the middle of the tiny orchard. Camp lights are strung between the trees, and the old-fashioned bulbs twinkle.

"What's going on?" I ask.

Ollie ushers me out the door. There is wine in a silver bucket, pretty plates—decorated with cherry blossoms—placed next to a picnic basket.

"Is this a date?" I blurt. "That came out wrong. I was just holding a mop, so this is a fast transition." I wait until he looks me in the eye. "It's all been a fast transition."

"I know. And I don't mean to move this fast, but—" he looks toward the fading light in the sky "—summer is ending. Your vacation is coming to an end. I don't want to miss another moment. I don't want you to be a mirage any longer."

He takes a deep breath. "I'm sorry," he says. "I'm going way too fast."

"Don't be sorry," I say. "I've waited my whole life for a man to express such emotion and care for me. What I meant to say was 'Thank you, Ollie, for this beautiful surprise. It means the world to me. '"

"And what I really want to ask," he says, grabbing me and pulling me into his strong arms, "is 'Can I finally kiss you?'"

His lips are big and soft. His kiss starts small and sweet, but it turns deep and passionate. When we finally stop, I stumble backward, directly into the bucket of wine.

"Yeah," he says, "I know I'm a good kisser. Aren't I, Becky Thatcher?"

I nod, returning for more.

"Tom Sawyer ain't got nothin' on you."

MARY

In Michigan, cherries are a way of life.

This is not a parable or a slogan on a T-shirt.

It is the way of the world.

The hard thing for us as humans is to understand—and then fully accept—that life is but a short, but beautiful, growing season.

I head into the orchard to pick the last of my Montmorency cherries. It is a glorious morning, at odds with how I've been feeling of late.

Part of me is filled with promise.

Ollie wants to be a part of the store, he and Becky had a first date, my dreams, my premonitions, all that was foretold seems to be coming to fruition.

I pick a cherry.

And you can't spell fruition *without* fruit.

But another part of me is filled with anxiety.

I've had trouble catching my breath of late. I feel dizzy—like passing out—when I exert myself.

Premonitions.

My mother and grandmother both always said when it was their time to go, they would just go.

"A promise I made with God," my mom always said.

And they did. They each fell like a sack of flour off a shelf in the general store.

Their growing season over, in a blink, in a breath.

I place the cherry into my mouth. They taste the same as they did when I was a girl.

That is the thing about growing old. Inside you still feel like a child, but your body plays tricks on you. You still want to skip into the lake and squeal. You still want to eat an ice cream cone on a hot summer day. You still want to call your best friend when something happens in your life.

You still want to live with all of that same joy despite the fact you know you are reaching...

I spit my pit across the lawn. I watch it land.

...the finish line.

What good does it do to count the days? Isn't it better just to enjoy them as they come?

I've never been a fan of doctors. Instead, I've relied on nature.

You grow up with a distrust of men and society, and that distrust makes you wary of those in power.

Instead, I come here to pick my cherries and look at the lake to make myself feel better.

I stare onto the horizon. Today, I see only hope.

And I have Becky to thank for that.

Ollie sees me now, thanks to her.

Is it possible for an eighty-year-old woman to have a friendship with a forty-year-old woman?

That would be like Becky being BFFs with a newborn.

I laugh at my analogy and continue to pluck cherries.

But there is something about having younger people in your life, be it a friend or a grandchild. They remind you of the exuberance of youth, of possibility, of the days ahead of you, not those that have passed. We must continue to look ahead even if we know the orchard is readying itself for winter.

I am looking ahead to the parade with both excitement and trepidation.

Sixty-five years.

Will people today even care about such a seemingly silly accomplishment?

Will girls and young women have any comprehension about what my record-setting win meant?

I won, and I never competed again.

Was I scared that I might lose?

I don't know the answer.

But my grandson cares. My friends care. Becky cares.

And that calms me.

My eyes scan the lake.

I realize that, like the lake, I take up a lot of space in this world, and—sometimes—I need to make room for others. Becky has taught me to open up a little space in my heart, my store, my world for others again, leave them some room to grow, some air to breathe.

The lake sparkles in the sun, shimmering into infinity.

What makes a legend?

A feat, an accomplishment, a miracle?

Or is the impact of your life on others after you're gone?

The older you get, you begin to realize that legends are born inside of you, and you are the only one who can make that legend reality. You must create a legacy of inspiration that will inspire and survive like the trees that tunnel our world here.

We all die, but our legend never fades if we take root in others' souls.

I pick and pop another cherry into my mouth. I remember another legend Ollie told me when he was in college.

"The color of the cherry's juice is akin to the blood in the human body," he said, "and the pit represents rebirth."

I kneel, and dizziness overwhelms me for a moment. I grab the ground to support myself but end up taking a hard seat. I wait for everything to clear, and then I run my fingers through the wet earth and place a pit into the ground.

"To new life," I say, covering it with a mound of dirt. I look out at the lake and then back at the general store. "To the birth of new legends."

BECKY

"Where are we going?"

"It's a surprise!"

Ollie takes my hand and leads me out of the orchard, past the general store and down a worn path through the Tunnel of Trees.

It is instantly dark, the sun squelched by the branches and foliage.

"Are you cold?" he asks.

"A little," I say. "I forget how quickly the temperature dips up here without the sun."

Ollie slips his arm around my shoulders.

It's as easy as that.

There is no interrogation—like Matt would have done—about why I didn't bring a jacket when he'd sent the hourly ten-day weather forecast to me while I was packing.

Matt wouldn't even have noticed I was cold. He would have been fifty yards ahead of me—like he always was when we were at a ball game, the grocery store, church—unaware I was even there, much less cold.

"Better?" Ollie asks.

I nod.

The warmth from his body emanates through mine, and my

heart races at the touch of his skin, the soft fur of his arms, his muscular side. You know when you are absent-mindedly sitting in your car while it idles in Park, and you accidentally hit the accelerator and the motor revs?

That is my heart.

That is my body.

That is my skin.

Finally, the path connects to the road, and we emerge from the woods. Light encompasses us now.

"My favorite time of the day," Ollie says. "The Blue Hour. Just after sunset. My grandma loves the Golden Hour, but I prefer this."

"I can see why," I say.

As a girl, I used to go into Spencer's, a gift shop in the mall specializing in novelty gifts. They sold these black-light posters that Q and I loved, which seemed to glow in an otherworldly blue. It seemed magical to me as a girl. This seems even more so to me as a woman.

The Tunnel of Trees looks as if it is moving with us as we walk, hardwoods dancing in the dazzling light of a blue disco ball. It is hauntingly beautiful.

Ollie stops.

I turn, and he is staring deeply into my eyes.

"You look beautiful in this light," he says. "Almost mythical."

I have to quell the Becky part of me from saying *Stop!* or *The only light I look good in is no light.*

But for the first time in my life, I take his compliment and let it swell inside me. I match his stare, and I see my reflection in his eyes.

And, for once, I don't judge my appearance. I see myself as he does.

I am not plain in his eyes.

I *am* beautiful.

Beautiful Becky.

"Thank you," I say.

I kiss him, deeply, and we become one, a mighty tree in the tunnel.

"Well, that was nice," he says, a big smile on his face.

He takes my hand, and we move along the road. We walk in silence, a natural ease between us. Is that what people mean when they say their relationship is *easy*? It was never easy for me. It should be easy, as natural, as beautiful as this light.

Ollie stops. "I thought we'd have dessert here," he says.

"What is this?"

"The Pit Stop," he says.

A roadside cherry stand—no bigger than a ten-by-ten square—sits back along a twist in the road. It resembles a storage shed you might place in your back yard.

But it is quintessentially northern Michigan adorable.

The shed is made of old slats of wood—warped now—but painted a crisp white with red trim. Hand-painted cherries, red fruit dangling from green stems, dot the shed. A large window is cut in the front to face the road, with shutters tied to the side that you can close at night. A large sill spans the window and holds baskets of fresh cherries, cookies, muffins and jam.

Homemade signs haphazardly dot the green in front of the Cherry Pit.

Fresh Cherries!

Fruit Jam!

Treasure Cookies!

Mornin' Muffins!

Underneath the window is a large sign—screwed into the wood—that looks like it was painted by a child that reads *The Cherry Pit!*

"I didn't notice this as we were driving," I say. "I think I was staring up at the trees."

"I built this," Ollie says, his voice soft, as if he's saying this to himself.

No. As if he's saying this to convince himself.

"Really?" I ask. "When?"

"When I was kid," he says. "I spent nearly every day of a cold, damp June out here building it with my grandma."

Ollie studies the old structure. "See the slanted roof?" he asks. I nod.

"Can't have a flat roof in Michigan, not with all the snow," Ollie says. "My grandma taught me that."

"Why did you build it?" I ask.

Ollie runs his hand slowly, lovingly across the old red sill.

"Oh, this was going to be my business," he says with a chuckle. "I told my grandma it would be a great way to expand the general store. I mean, a cute kid selling cherries at a cute stand? Who could resist?"

"Not me," I say.

"And I asked for a percentage of the profits. My grandma just loved that!"

"You were already an entrepreneur," I say.

Ollie grins. "I was, wasn't I?" He shakes his head. "Each generation of women added something of their own to the history of this store and area," Ollie says. "I wanted to do the same thing."

"Did you ever tell your grandmother that?"

"I should have earlier."

Ollie shakes his head again.

"What happens to all those dreams we have as kids?" he asks. "We thought we could be anything when we were young. An astronaut! A movie star! And then the real world intrudes, and we're told what is right and what is wrong, and we grow up but not out. I thought I was going to be a force of nature, just like my grandma. I thought I was going to be a legend in this town. Turns out there's not much distance between legend and memory." Ollie snaps his fingers. "Goes like that."

"You know," I say, "some storms are quiet, but they are still a force of nature."

"What is it about summer?" Ollie asks. "What is it about places like this that last in our memory forever? Why can't it be like this for infinity?"

Memories of my childhood and summers with my grandparents whirl in my head.

"It can," I say. "But we choose to grow up not out, as you said. It's what we're taught is right. I've done it my whole life, as a person and as a teacher."

Ollie enters through the tiny door on the side of the shed and leans through the window.

"Who paints this?" I ask.

"My grandma," Ollie says. "No big surprise. She does it all."

"Does anyone work here?" I ask.

"My grandma has a couple of high-school kids rotate on and off throughout the summer, usually on busy weekends, but she operates a little differently than most."

Ollie points.

I walk up to the shed, and it's then I notice an old, semi-rusted cashbox sitting on the sill. A note on the top reads *Honor System! Put $$$ in Box! Thank You!*

I open the cash box. It is filled with money.

"I can't believe this works," I say.

"*Trust*," Ollie says. "Simple word for such a big act."

That word hits me hard.

It is the foundation for everything—every act, every relationship—in life.

"I trust you," I say.

"I trust you, too, Becky."

Ollie leans through the window and kisses me.

I run my hands through his hair, along his face, down his shoulders, across his biceps and onto his chest.

Each part of his body feels new, exciting, different. He is a map of Michigan I wish to explore.

And this is all happening because I trust him.

I trust me for once.

"Now," Ollie asks, "what would you like for dessert?" He gestures across the sill. "We have everything. And I know the owner."

"You," I say. "I want you for dessert."

MARY

If you've ever watched the Westminster Kennel Club Dog Show on television, you understand the pomp and circumstance of the parade of dogs. The Porch Parade is filled with just as much pageantry.

I watch the big dog herself arrive in the back of a limousine—in a wig as white and puffy as the clouds—trailed by a bright red fire truck, balloons flying, horns honking, music blaring from it, Doris Day singing, "Life Is Just a Bowl of Cherries." Behind the truck, a line of cars pulls off the road. A camera crew emerges from a van, a photographer and reporter from a car, and a number of locals—businessmen and-women—from other vehicles.

Participants never know when the judges have driven by to view and score the porch designs—often at dawn or late at night—but they do know when the committee arrives to award the prizes.

Becky, Ollie and Q race from the kitchen, bewildered by the cacophony. But I already know.

"My date's here!" Q says with a laugh, sliding to a stop in front of the screened door. "They always arrive with a bang."

"Taffy's a firefighter now?" Becky asks. "I thought he was lighting your fire, not putting it out."

"Ha ha," Q says. "And why did you come home so late last night?" Q turns to look at me. "Sorry, Mary."

"I'm a grown woman," I say. "And I helped make it happen."

Ollie's boyish face flushes.

"We had a wonderful date," he says.

"And an incredible adventure," Becky adds.

Q looks at them and then at me. "What does that mean?" she asks. "Stop speaking in code."

"We speak our own language now," Becky says.

Q gags. "Stop it. Please." She looks outside. "What is this?"

"The awards for the Porch Parade," I say.

"Oh, my gosh," Becky exclaims. "We better get out there. C'mon!"

We head outside onto the decorated stoop, and people begin to applaud. I see Taffy's truck pull up and skid to a stop in the gravel. He gets out and calls, "I just heard. Did I miss it?"

I shake my head.

Virgie alights from the limo and walks up the steps to the porch before the many blossoms displaying the general store's beloved bake goods. She opens a red leather folder.

"Thank you all for joining us this morning," she reads. "As you know, the Very Cherry Awards are handed out in a variety of categories, but one of the most beloved traditions is our Porch Parade. These awards are even more special this year as we commemorate our historic anniversary. I'm truly honored that the Very Cherry General Store—a hallmark of Good Hart and our community for decades—entered the Porch Parade for the very first time."

She turns to look at me with what I can only term as a *smisgust*, a smile that hides her disgust for me. There's nothing I despise more than insincerity, a faux smile, people my grandmother used to refer to as featherbedders, those who had to build themselves up in order to make themselves look bigger and better in the eyes of society.

I blow her a kiss.

Virgie continues. "The committee was humbled that the General Store took our theme of history to heart by showcasing its legacy in its truly remarkable display. We appreciate not only the hard work that went into this but also the creativity that powered this display."

The crowd applauds.

"Best in years!" a man yells.

"Perfection!" a woman echoes.

Virgie closes her folder and looks toward the fire truck. "May I?" she asks.

A firefighter pulls out a towering trophy—shining gold in the morning light, topped by a cluster of three golden cherries—and heads through the crowd and hands it to Virgie.

I can see there is a plaque attached at the base.

Virgie reads it.

"On behalf of the National Cherry Festival, I am honored to award the Very Cherry General Store with Second Place in this year's Porch Parade!"

The crowd remains as still as a cloud on a windless day.

"Recount!" someone finally yells.

"Is this a mistake?" another calls.

Virgie turns and flashes a look of smisgust at me, before handing the trophy to me.

Taffy leans in and looks at the plaque.

"Second Place?"" he asks. "You've got to be kidding me."

"Second Place is a wonderful honor," Virgie says.

"It's Second Place," he says. "Meaning not First Place."

The crowd begins to boo.

"This is not a good look on you," Virgie says to Taffy in a hushed tone. "Nor the store." She lifts a brow toward me.

"Who won First Place, then?" Taffy asks very loudly.

"The winner will be announced shortly," Virgie says.

She heads off the porch and toward her limo.

"Who won?" Taffy yells at her.

"Who won?" the crowd begins to chant.

Virgie stops and pivots like a car model on a spinning rounder.

"Frank and Ethel Willoughby," she says. "You are all welcome to join us now for the awards ceremony at their home."

"All they did was put up a pink balloon arch," Ollie says.

"They put up most of the money for the parade," Taffy adds.

Virgie walks back to the porch and motions for me.

I move down the steps. She tilts her head next to mine and whispers, "Control your boys. You've always had difficulty with the men in your life."

I nearly fall off the step.

Taffy reaches out to steady me, and in doing so, I thrust out an arm to grab his. The trophy flies into the air and crashes onto the ground.

"Yeah!" many in the crowd yell.

"Apologize," Virgie says.

"You first," I whisper.

Virgie grabs my hand and lifts it into the air as if we are friends celebrating a victory.

"An accident!" she says to the crowd. "Friends like us can always laugh off something like this, can't we, Mary?"

I yank my hand from hers.

"Friends like us don't need enemies," I say. "We have a lifetime of unfinished business to settle. Meet me where we used to go as girls. If you can remember the time when the only thing that mattered was each other."

BECKY

Q flaps a laminated sheet in my face.

"Remember this?" she asks. "I think we've broken every rule." She trails a finger down the page.

"No boys, no work talk, no cell phones!" Q stops, her red hair a poof around her red face following a few hours on the beach despite wearing an SPF that would keep her pale skin protected standing on the sun. "And, most importantly, this was supposed to be a girls' trip." She enunciates the words again very slowly. "Girls'...trip...va...ca...tion."

I grab the list from her hand.

"We got the wine thing right," I say, taking a sip of my rosé. "And we certainly said *yes* to everything."

"I'll give you that," she says, clinking my glass. "And now we have to focus on the early rules again. Packing, playlist, snacks."

I take another sip of wine.

"You do remember we have to go home again, right?" Q asks. "That's kind of the whole point of a vacation. You forget about life for a while just so you can return to it."

I nod.

"Oh, no," Q continues. "What are you thinking? You have a weird face."

I shrug and let out a huge sigh. "What if I don't want my old life?"

Q's face transforms into that of a concerned mother. In other words, it's a bad poker face, one which is trying to remain unemotional, but the twitchy lips betray total panic.

"May we talk about this like adults?" she asks, reaching for the bottle of rosé and executing a very large pour in a glass that, ironically enough, reads *Life is better at the lake!*

I follow her onto the cozy deck nestled against the log cabin. An arc of pines and sugar maples envelop the porch, and they serve as a natural curtain to filter the summer sun. Through their green needles and leaves, the blue lake glides into infinity, stretched out as if it's taking an afternoon nap.

"Maybe that says it all," I say, nodding at her glass. "Maybe that's the answer we all seek but ignore."

Q doesn't turn, but I can see her skew an eye my direction. She takes a sip of wine. "And maybe you've had a wonderful adventure and mini fling after a terrible breakup, and that's just what the doctor ordered." She takes another sip of wine. "You just don't want it to end up the way Dr. Kevorkian ordered."

"You're being mean."

"I'm being your friend, which mean I'll always be honest with you."

Q scoots her chair a few inches closer to mine and kicks me with her foot. "I'm in this with you, too, okay?"

I nod.

She continues. "Let's just play the whole scenario out in our heads, shall we? You're not happy, right?"

"I'm happy," I say, "but I'm not happy."

I stare at the old porch floor—painted a beautiful thick barn red—and tap it with my foot. "What did this porch floor look like originally?" I ask. "It's had so many coats of paint that it's layered, lacquered, nuanced and yet still beautiful, just in a new way. I need to become like this porch floor." I stop. "Just not walked all over. Okay, this is a terrible analogy, but you understand what I'm saying."

"Clear as mud," Q says. "But, yes, I do. You want a new layer."

"Layers," I say.

"Let me play devil's advocate here for a second—and I don't intend to sound like your father and mother—but stop and think about this, and I mean really stop and think about this. Retirement, IRAs, health care, those are kind of a big deal in our world. You can't just drink rosé and eat whitefish dip and think summer will last forever." She holds her wineglass out for me to see. "That lake is going to freeze over. Winter is coming. And that's a long season in Michigan. Especially without money to pay the utilities or food to eat when you're Mary's age."

"This sounds very *Game of Thrones*," I say.

"Life is a never-ending, constant battle," she says. "I'm not joking, Becky. I mean it. This is serious stuff." Q takes a breath. "So tell me this. Do you still like your job?"

"I did," I say. "But I'm not challenged anymore. And it's not what I dream of doing. You pursued your dream."

"And I have to ask," Q says, "is Ollie just a fling, or do you feel like he's a real deal Happy Meal? It's only been a couple of weeks you've known this guy."

"What about you and Taffy? Same thing."

"I'm taking it day by day," she says. "I like him. We've talked about it. He lives here, I live in St. Louis. We both have solid careers. We both have deep roots in the areas we love. I'm not ready to uproot everything. I love my life. I've worked hard to make my dreams real."

"I haven't."

Q turns on a dime to consider what I just said. For the longest time, there is silence, save for the songbirds.

"You have your answer."

I shake my head. "It's that easy?"

"No," Q says. "It's that hard."

Q runs her hand through her hair and smiles. "I understand everything you're going through right now, you know," she says. "Everything."

Q stands, walks to the edge of the porch and leans against the log railing with her wine. "My entire life has been a huge risk, a giant question mark," she says. "Remember college? Everyone scoffing at me for majoring in theater, saying I was ruining my life, would be broke forever and would wind up working at a fast-food restaurant when I was fifty? I didn't listen to them. I listened to my heart and that voice in my head that said *You can do it. You are talented. You only get one shot at life. Don't be miserable like your parents.*"

She takes a sip of wine and gazes at the water. "I moved around my whole life, chasing whatever gig I could grab, whether it was in Des Moines or Duluth. I squatted on people's couches because I didn't have enough money for rent. I chose boyfriends who were actor-waiters just because I knew they'd bring home dinner at night. I went to audition after audition in New York where casting agents told me, 'I don't like your voice,' before I even said a line, or 'Your look is all wrong,' although I was the only naturally curly redhead in the room. It was constant rejection. And every night I would cry myself to sleep thinking I had to quit and conform to society, but then I would lie to myself and say, 'Just one more day, one more audition.'"

Q returns to her chair. "We have to give it our best shot in life, whether we're twenty, forty or eighty. Otherwise, we've wasted the opportunity and gifts we've been given. Just look at Mary. Just look at your grandma."

"Just look at you," I say.

I stand and grab her in a hug.

"I'm not crying, you're crying," she says. Then Q holds me at arm's length. "So you want to move to a tiny town and work at a general store? Talk about a punch line to a very bad vacation joke."

"I think so, yes," I say. "I'm sort of following some dreamy vision out there on the water, I realize, but I'll figure it out."

"I know you will," Q says. "I don't want you to leave me, though."

"I'll never leave you," I say and sniff. "We're best friends forever."

"And maybe I'll have a free place to stay when I go on vacation," she says.

"And when I visit St. Louis," I say.

Q walks into the middle of the porch, stands straight, then drops her arms and begins to move as if she's a marionette being manipulated on strings.

"Bye, bye, bye," she begins to sing.

"No!" I yell. "You're pulling out NSYNC on me when I'm emotional?"

"Just like we did as girls," she says. "You remember?"

"How could I forget that song and video," I say.

"Wanna join?" she asks, before yelling, "Wait!"

Q sprints inside and returns holding something behind her back.

"Forgot about these," she says.

I laugh.

Q is holding my Manolo Blahnik lurum crystal cocktail mules that she wouldn't let me throw into the shoe tree.

"Put them on! It's time to celebrate you," she says. "And to dance."

I slip into them, realizing I've been waiting for just the right moment to wear them, and it finally arrived.

"They pair so beautifully with your sweatshorts that have *Vacation Calories Don't Count* across the butt," she says with a laugh.

I position myself next to her on the porch, and we begin to sing and dance, every lyric, every move coming back to us as if we've just gotten off work at Ted Drewes and are dancing in our bedrooms to MTV.

It might sound crazy but it ain't no lie,
Baby, bye bye bye

MARY

Michigan is an iconic state.

At every twist and turn along the Tunnel of Trees, your breath is taken away. It may be the lush canopy that chokes out the light, a hardwood tree over a hundred years old or an island in the distance on the lake waving hello in a clearing.

At every stop along Lake Michigan's shoreline, a stunningly beautiful resort town with a quirky past—and at least one beloved restaurant—greets you with open arms.

But there is no place that will stop you in your tracks—and that I love more—than Legs Inn.

"Hello, old friend," I say to the restaurant as I approach. "It's been too long."

Legs Inn is a monument to nature. A sprawling structure made of local timber and stone, the Polish restaurant seems to have sprung from the ground. It was founded a hundred years ago by an immigrant who settled in tiny Cross Village and began building the inn with local Odawa craftsmen. The inside and outside of the inn is a fantasy world akin to stepping into a *Lord of the Rings* storybook tale.

I admire the restaurant. It was named Legs Inn for the hundreds of inverted white stove legs that adorn the roof line, an ode to the stove-manufacturing company that used to thrive in the area.

I smile and hold out my leg.

Virgie and I used to do this when we came here when we were young, both showing off what we considered to be our best assets while paying homage to the restaurant's history.

"To Legs and legs," we used to say.

I step inside.

"Reservations for Mary," I say. "Noon."

"This way, ma'am," a young server says.

Legs is a restaurant within a museum.

Massive lake stone fireplaces rise in the two-story building, which is filled with hand-hewn log railings and beams. And the founder crafted tables and chairs from driftwood and roots taken directly from the forest as well as wooden masterpieces including a giant bear and a totem pole honoring Michigan's wilderness.

There is nothing more northern Michigan than this place.

"Mary."

I look up.

Except perhaps Virgie.

She is ensconced in a black pantsuit—wig as dark as night— as if she is going to a funeral. Her wardrobe speaks for her, so I know her ensemble is intentional, one that matches her mood despite being in the height of the National Cherry Festival.

"Virgie."

She sits, and we scan our menus in silence. When the waiter appears and asks us if we are ready to order, we both nod and say at the exact same time, "Pork pierogis, please, with sauer-kraut and a Okocim beer."

The waiter laughs.

"You two must be twins."

He disappears, but his words linger in the air.

Virgie's rigid spine softens just a touch, and she eases back a bit in her chair.

"How are things going with the festival?" I ask.

Virgie laughs.

"Mary Jackson making small talk?" She dabs her heavily mascaraed eye with the tip of her napkin. "You must be setting me up for the kill."

"No, I'm just old," I say, looking her directly in the eye. "And tired of playing games. The only thing we've killed is what we had."

Virgie folds her napkin and lays it across her lap.

The waiter brings our beers.

She lifts it. "Cheers," she says. "To a hundred and twenty-five years of cherries and the sixty-fifth anniversary of your championship."

She is playing nice today.

"And to your leadership," I add.

We take big draws of our Polish beers.

"Tradition," she says. "It should always continue."

"But friendship?" I ask.

She doesn't answer.

"I didn't mean to break the trophy," I say. "I didn't even know they decorated the store and entered it in the Porch Parade."

Virgie takes another sip of her beer.

"And I'm sorry if I embarrassed you," I say.

She lifts an eyebrow as if she's trying to make it meet the height of the soaring fireplace.

"And now Mary Jackson is apologizing? This *is* a historic anniversary."

And now she's not playing so nice anymore.

I push my big, wooden chair back and stand.

"Forget it," I say. "This was a terrible mistake."

"Stop!" Virgie says. "Sit."

I do not.

"Please."

I take a seat.

"You should have won First Place," she says with a sigh and wave of her hand. "The committee actually awarded you more votes, but since the chair has the final say, I did it to hurt you."

"Why?"

"Because you've hurt me," she says. "What's the old phrase? *Hurt people hurt people.*"

"I think you've got your story backward," I say. "*You* turned your back on me. *You* cast me out when I needed you. *You* chose money over friendship. Tradition should always continue? Please. Don't be a hypocrite."

Virgie places her hands on the table, firmly, as if she's grounding herself just like the roots that made it.

"*You* have always had friends," she says, her voice trembling. "You didn't need *me* anymore."

"I *needed* you," I tell her, "more than anyone. But let's be honest here. I no longer fit into your life. I embarrassed you. I embarrassed your husband. I married a bad man. My mom and grandma did the same. I was raising a child alone. Our lives were shrouded in mystery. We saw visions. We were widows running a country business when women didn't do that. I was a reminder of everything you were that you no longer wanted to be."

"Did it ever occur to you that you were simply stronger than me?" Without warning, Virgie bursts into tears. For a second, I am so stunned at her vulnerability that I can't move a muscle. Finally, I reach out my hand, and she takes it.

"No," I say. "It never did."

"You've always been so strong, Mary," Virgie says, gripping my hand, tighter and tighter. "And women have always admired that strength. Do you know what it's like to go through life knowing people hate you? Liking you only because they know you will do something for them, like the girls in school, or because you have money?"

Virgie gathers herself.

"I never loved Phillip," she continues.

"I know."

"But I never had the strength to leave him, either," she says. "Do you know how much I wanted a family? Do you know how much I wanted what you had? I lived alone in a big house with a husband who treated me as if I were a piece of pretty furniture. He'd dust me off when he wanted to put me on display, and then back in the house I went. That's why I became a realtor. To escape. To make my own money." Virgie takes a sip of beer. "Phillip left the majority of his trust to various charities, but most of it went to his brothers. I got very little. Do you know why I have the money I do? Because I worked for it. Kept it separate from his. You know whose example I followed to get there? Yours."

My heart rises in my throat.

"Then, why did you throw me out when I needed you?"

"Because your husband would never have left. You would have learned it was okay to keep going back. You would have learned to bury all the pain and the hate most of your life like I did." Virgie stares at me for the longest time. "Because you would have gone home after a few days of me looking after you. Soon enough you'd be back at my door, this time with a black eye. But you'd always have gone back to him. And he would have killed you, Mary, and your son. I tried to stoke the rage in you and make you face the demon in order to give you the chance to do it first." She stops. "And you did, just like I knew you would."

My mug of beer shakes in my hand, foam spilling over the sides.

"An eye for an eye, Mary," Virgie continues.

"How...?" I start.

"I was your best friend." Virgie scans the restaurant and waves a polite hello to a man across the way. "A best friend knows everything. A rich, connected best friend knows even more."

My jaw drops.

"You made this town a better place. You did what you had

to do to survive in this world," Virgie continues, "just like I had to do, just like your grandma had to do to get that store."

I have trouble catching my breath.

"Your mother told me a long time ago," she says. "Wanted to keep me on your good side in case you needed my help in the future." Virgie smiles. "You didn't need it, though. You never needed anyone but yourself."

"Not anymore," I say.

"Ollie's back," she says. "And that girl who's been coming around—"

"Becky," I say.

"Yes. They really seem to have breathed new life into you and the store."

"They have," I say. "I was alone a long time, too, just like you."

"But you had Francine and Myrtle, Taffy, too, and your family."

"I did," I say. "And the store saved me." I make sure Virgie is looking at me when I say, "Tradition does matter."

"Do you know, out of everything in this year's festival—the parties, parades, pies, floats, celebrations—the one thing most people are excited about?" Virgie asks.

I shake my head.

"You!"

The waiter brings our lunches.

"If a cherry festival can survive all the ups and downs of life for a hundred and twenty-five years, then surely we can, too," Virgie continues.

"We certainly have had our share of pits," I say.

"That's what made Cherry Mary famous."

She lifts her glass, and we clink and drink and then polish off our Polish dumplings.

When we head outside to say our goodbyes, I stop.

"Remember?" I ask.

"How could I forget?"

"Want me to take your picture?" a tourist asks on her way to the restaurant. Virgie hands the woman her cell phone. "Friends should never let a moment like this pass."

We put our arms around one another.

Virgie extends her leg, and I do the same.

"Say *cheese*," the woman calls in a singsong voice.

"To Legs and legs," we say instead.

BECKY

Any place—or person—as old as the Very Cherry General Store is always filled with a lot of history and a touch of mystery.

Dawn is just beginning to brighten the sky when I pull into the parking lot. I offered to open the store for Mary this morning despite my waning vacation days and Q's yells from her bedroom to shut up as I stomped around the cabin to make coffee while it was still dark.

What storms has the store—and Mary—endured over their lives? How did each get from then to now with such beauty, grace and resilience?

Mary has shared some of her history with me—and even a bit of her mystery—but so many of our elders who have endured the pain and loss of life and war tend to share little of how they got from point A to point B in their lives.

I have always been fascinated with those people and structures who have had long lives. I used to wander the campuses at Saint Louis University and Washington University in St. Louis and just sit in the old buildings whose floors creaked and walls whispered. My home in St. Louis is an old, shingled bungalow built in the early 1900s as a summer cottage for those who lived in the city but wanted open air, green space and quiet from the city hubbub. My office in the elementary school used to be housed in the original part of the building. It was tiny but had an arching window that overlooked the old church. I could watch the children play at recess. Everyone but me rejoiced when we moved into a new wing that was as sterile as a hospital room.

I suddenly think of my grandma.

Knowing that my mother would not respect her final wishes, my grandma entrusted me—quite literally in her trust—to oversee her funeral.

"Make it a party!" Memaw told me.

And I did.

There was music and dancing, a slideshow and my grandma's favorite foods, and everyone shared their happiest memories of her.

Memaw had written on a whiteboard a few days before she died *No crying! No tears! Only laughter!*

My mother was horrified.

"This is not dignified at all," she said, pulling me outside of the celebration. "This is worse than I ever could have imagined."

"Grandma wanted a celebration to a life well-lived," I said. "And we should celebrate her."

I unlock the old front door and go inside, and the screened door bangs shut, the bell tinkling. I turn on the lights. I used to love being the first one to work, the first to turn on the lights, the first to start a new day.

I need that feeling again.

I inhale.

Do you know the smell of an old house? One that is so familiar that it instantly comforts your soul? One that, when you enter and inhale, you know you are home? That is the feeling I have here.

I continue to turn on the lights, questions—despite the wine-induced optimism of my conversation with Q—popping up over my head as quickly as the bulbs.

Am I simply running from life? Matt? Work? My mom and dad?

Did this girls' trip simply conjure up a lot of emotions that I needed to address?

Am I trying to recreate my grandma in Mary?

Are my visions—like Mary's—those of a lonely woman searching for answers she will never find?

Is Ollie—a man I initially didn't like—the man of my dreams or just a summer fling?

And yet, in the quiet of this quaint general store cum post office situated in the Tunnel of Trees—seemingly far from the real world—I feel as if I'm not only able to hear the important questions of my life but also to answer them.

I head into the kitchen. On the butcher-block island is a note from Mary. I smile. It is similar to the pick-me-up notes I secretly placed in students' backpacks when I was a teacher. I smile.

Good Morning, Becky!
Welcome to your official first day opening the Very Cherry General Store! Following is a list of baked goods you need to have prepared and in the oven by 7:00 a.m. so you can have them fresh and ready when the store opens at 8:00. There will be a rush of locals and vacationers for the coffee cakes and muffins when the store opens, so you need to put up the mail before the post office "officially" opens at 9:30 (you'll never hear the end of it if the mail isn't ready for the locals who start their days here!) and immediately start prepping the potpies and slicing the veggies for sandwiches as the lunch rush will start about 11:00 as people head to the beach.

I stop, no longer smiling. My head is spinning. I continue reading.

Ollie and I will be in midmorning to help with whatever needs finished.

"Whatever needs finished?" I mumble, my voice surprising me in solitude. "Everything will need to be finished!"

Here is the list of what needs prepared. You'll find the recipes are already set out on the counter. Have fun, and good luck!

* *Cherry Pie Crumb Bars*
* *White Chocolate Cherry Muffins*
* *Cherry Muffins with Streusel Topping (use Grandma's recipe, not Mom's!)*
* *Cherry Cola Cake*
* *Summer Buzz Fruit Salad*
* *Cherry Chicken Lettuce Wraps*

Prep:
* *Veggie & Chicken Potpies (crusts in freezer; unthaw)*
* *Slice tomato, onion (put in ice water to remove bite!), radish & pull lettuce leaves*

HAVE FUN! XOXO, MARY

"Have fun?" I yell. "This will take all day!"

I begin to buzz around the kitchen—which is something I haven't done in ages—pitting cherries, jangling measuring spoons, standing over a mixer pouring in ingredients, filling muffin tins. I stack the oven with the muffins, then fill it again with bars and a cake, place the muffins in the pretty cake domes, return to slice onions—wondering whether it's them or the stress making me cry—and rush out to turn the store sign to We're Open! exactly at eight just before the first customer arrives. There is a steady rush until nine, when I suddenly gasp, "Oh, no! The mail!" at a woman buying a loaf of sourdough and Michigan maple syrup to make French toast for her guests. She leaves in a hurry, and I shove mail into slots in between racing over to assist customers.

I am nearly done when I hear man's voice, stern and as rumbling as a train, ask, "Mary? Where's my mail?"

I peer out from behind the boxes.

"Good morning! I'm Becky. I'm helping Mary today."

"I don't care what your name is. I just want my mail. On time. Every day. As usual."

I flash him my biggest smile.

"I completely understand, Mr....? May I ask your name?"

"If you lived here, you would know it," he says. "Not fond of interlopers."

"I'm so sorry," I say. "I'm falling in love with this area and hope not to be an interloper one day."

"Chuck Harrier," he says. "Harrier Orchards. Been around these parts as long as Cherry Mary."

I extend my hand. He refuses to shake it.

"She's amazing, isn't she?"

"She gets my mail out on time," he says. "That's pretty amazing, isn't it?"

"Just one moment."

I step behind the boxes and retrieve Mr. Harrier's mail.

"Here you go," I say.

"Bill, bill, bill," he says, leafing through it. "Death and taxes. The story of life."

I go to the counter and remove the dome from a cake stand. I pick up the tongs and place a muffin on a general store napkin.

"Cherry muffins always make life a little better. My treat."

He exhales a mighty "Harrumph!" but takes the muffin and exits without another word.

I hear applause and turn to find Mary and Ollie standing behind the counter.

"Well done!" Mary says.

"Amazing," Ollie adds. "Although, I take it you are paying for the muffin."

He winks, coming around the counter to give me a kiss.

"It's the two-percent rule," I say.

"The what?" Mary asks. Ollie plucks muffins from a stand and hands one to his grandma while taking a big bite of his own.

"Two-percent rule. It's the way I've always described working in education. Ninety-eight percent of the parents, students, faculty and administration you work with are incredible. But there are about two percent of them who make your life a living hell, and unfortunately, those are the ones you focus on and require too much of your time. I remind myself it's not me who's made them miserable, and it's not a hard life, either. We all have difficult lives. It's just they don't want to be happy because they've gotten attention their whole lives—be it at eight or eighty—by being unhappy."

Mary claps again.

"I don't want to be unhappy anymore. I want to be a part of this," I say and gesture with my arms, "somehow, if you will just allow me to go completely insane for a little while and uproot my life from St. Louis to the Tunnel of Trees."

Mary drops her muffin. Crumbs fall from Ollie's mouth.

"Um, that's not the reaction I really expected," I say. "I've already talked to Q about this, and..."

I stop when I see Mary crying. She rushes over and grabs me so hard I nearly fall off my feet. Ollie joins in, and we rock for a few seconds.

"Are you sure?" I ask.

"Yes!" Mary says.

"Are you?" I ask Ollie.

"I am," he says. "I promise we'll figure it all out."

"Together," Mary adds.

The bell jingles.

"I think I missed something," Q says when she sees us in our tearful huddle. "Should I leave? Is this a moment?"

We open our arms, and Q walks over and joins the group hug.

"I feel like we just won a Tony Award," Q whispers. "Or *Family Feud*."

Our laughter is broken by the sound of a horn honking non-stop.

"What in the world?" Mary says.

We all rush to the screened door. A red convertible is circling in the parking lot. The top is down, music is blaring, and a man and woman are waving.

"Mom?" I yell, racing outside. "Dad?"

The car comes to a stop when they see me.

"Becky!" my mom waves.

"Hi, honey!" my dad calls.

I stand there, blinking like an idiot, unable to say a word.

My dad parks the car, and they step out, embracing me with big hugs and kisses.

Finally, I utter, "What have you done with my parents?"

They both laugh as if laughter has just been invented.

"No, really. What *are* you doing here?" I ask.

"We wanted to surprise you," my dad says.

"Surprise? I think I need to be hospitalized. This is like *Invasion of the Body Thatchers*."

My mom turns to take in the general store in all its decorated glory. A smile breaks across her face. Then she shuts her eyes, and I can see a tear trail down her cheek. She opens her eyes and turns to me. "I was home the other night doing some laundry when your father yelled for a beer. I walked into the kitchen, and there on the refrigerator were the postcards you'd sent me. They were just like the ones my mom and dad sent me when they took you as a girl on vacation to northern Michigan."

I smile. "That's why I sent them."

"I got your dad's beer, walked into the living room—across

the same carpet I've had my entire adult life—and the photo of your grandparents on that roller-coaster was staring at me. Did you know that, even as a girl, I never rode a roller-coaster because I was too afraid of what might happen? I was too afraid to have fun because of the risk."

My mother's chin quivers ever so slightly. "I turned off the pregame and yanked your father out of his recliner, and we walked to the MetroLink line, rode downtown, bought nosebleed tickets to the Cardinals game, sat in the bleachers, had a beer too many and the time of our lives. When we got home I was getting ready for bed, but I realized your father hadn't come in yet. I found him in the garage sitting in this convertible, holding that letter my father had given him so long ago."

My father says, "Your grampa was right. Sometimes, you have to put the top down and just enjoy the ride."

"We came here to see you and all that you've discovered, but we also came here to find us again," my mom says.

"Did you know that baseball is one of the few sports that doesn't have a clock on it?" my dad says. "It's just like life. We can do anything we want, make all kinds of mistakes even until the bottom of the ninth, and still win the game. It's never too late."

"I realized it's finally better to take that risk because, believe me, it's worse if you never do," my mom says, in a hoarse whisper.

I hug my mother.

"I'm not changing my carpet," my mom says to me.

I hold her at arm's length, searching her face. "I don't understand."

"I'm putting in hardwood floors," she says with a big smile.

"You guys!" I call. "Come meet my mom and dad!"

Ollie and Q fly down the porch, followed by Mary, everyone exchanging introductions.

"It's so nice to finally meet you in person," Mary says to

my mother. She opens her arms. My mother actually hugs her warmly, openly. "And it's nice to meet you, Mr. Thatcher."

"Where are you staying?" I ask my mom and dad.

"Don't worry," my mom says. "We're not going to intrude on you and Q."

Q wipes her brow dramatically.

"Mary's friend, Francine, graciously invited us to stay with her," my mom continues.

"Wait! What?" I ask, then turn to Mary. "You knew about this?"

"We started chatting after Francine's dinner party," Mary says. "Just two moms talking."

"And keeping a secret," my mom says.

She winks at Mary, and Q begins to hum the theme from *The Twilight Zone*.

As we're all standing and chatting in the parking lot, Taffy's truck pulls in.

"Wow!" he says, walking over. "Beautiful car! Whose brilliant idea was it for Mary to ride in the parade in style?"

"Dad," I say, "I have a big favor to ask."

MARY

There's nothing like a parade.

You instantly become a kid again.

Today, I am a little girl again. I see myself in the children scrambling toward the street, releasing the tight grip of their parents and grandparents to retrieve the candy necklaces and bubblegum I am tossing to paradegoers.

I sway to the music of the marching bands, the booming bass of the trombones, the call of the clarinet, the way the drums echo off the lake.

Oh, and the floats!

How many weeks and how much energy and creativity did it take to turn a simple foundation of steel and chicken wire into an orchard of blooming cherry trees or a queen's float in which she is riding high above the world atop a cherry stem?

It is a picture-perfect day for the Cherry Royale Parade, the temperature in the upper seventies, low humidity and a light lake breeze.

The downtown streets of Traverse City are packed with spectators of all ages, and I'm overwhelmed at how much the festival has expanded over the years. People are dressed in red, eating cherries and dancing to the music from the bands marching in the parade.

I have been placed—surprisingly, and for the first time in my life—near the front of the parade. I am not riding shotgun in a pickup with a prized pig, nor am I following a team of flatulent horses. I am riding in style in Becky's parents' red convertible just behind Virgie and the honorary parade marshal, actor Jeff Daniels—a Michigan native and resident—who I saw Q whispering to conspiratorially before the parade started.

I wonder, did she work to get him to be the surprise marshal to kick off parade to impress Virgie and secure my place of honor?

Or has Virgie changed after our heartfelt discussion?

There was a flood of publicity about me the last few days, talking about the big anniversary of the parade, the championship and my win.

Yes, this truly is a year of celebration.

I spy a little girl eating a piece of cherry pie. Her face is covered in red, and she is smushing the pie all over her cheek as if that is where her taste buds are located. I wave at her, feeling not much different than I did sixty-five years ago when I won the championship.

I am still a girl at heart.

We should remain children at heart.

"Go, Mary!"

I glance to my left, and three teenagers are jumping and yelling.

"Look!" yell Ollie and Becky, who flank me in the back of the convertible.

I follow their points.

It's then I see people are holding fans with cutouts of my face on them. They feature the photo of me as a girl, cheeks puffed, and read—in big letters—*I'm a Fan of Cherry Mary!*

Q reaches over in the front seat and honks the convertible's horn, and Taffy, who is driving, laughs.

Becky's parents wanted to experience the parade for the first time as spectators.

"I can't drive with a beer, can I?" Darryl had asked. "I'm out."

We come to a stop.

I turn and scan the parade behind me. The lawn-chair drill team—a perennial crowd favorite comprised of men and women of all ages—clicks and claps their lawn chairs as precisely as the military, albeit if the men and women in uniform were engaged only in relaxation. The crowd laughs and cheers.

I look farther down the parade route. It extends for over a mile—bands, dance troupes, pom-pom squads, fire trucks and cherry-decorated floats seemingly going on for infinity.

I hear another group of young girls yell, "Mary! Mary! Over here!"

I look, and they hold up a sign that reads *You Go, Girl!*

My eyes turn misty.

The convertible takes off again.

However, it is when I see Francine, standing with Becky's parents, holding a sign that reads *That's My Best Friend!* featuring a photo of me and her drinking cherry margaritas that I begin to cry.

"You okay, Grandma?" Ollie asks.

How do you explain to a young man who has his whole life ahead of him that you can see the end of the parade route?

How do you put into words all the emotions of growing up supposedly less than in society and now see a world that is diverse and accepting, where women are championing and leading, where girls can be anything they dreamed?

"I'm great," I say.

"This is your day," Ollie says. "Your moment."

"You've always led your own parade, haven't you, Mary?" Becky asks. "And the beautiful thing is—no matter how much time and effort it required, no matter if you cared or believed anyone would ever listen to you or follow—you marched to the beat of your own drum."

Becky points.

A girl—twelve or thirteen, perhaps—runs into the street and toward the float.

"I'm entering the contest today because of you!" she yells. "Girls can do anything!"

I grab a candy necklace and toss it to her. She catches it and slips it around her neck.

"Eventually," Becky says, "an entire band forms. It may take a lifetime, but it does."

"Thank you," I say.

"So many of us are just waiting for that special someone to toss the mantle our way so we can carry it into the future," Becky continues.

She puts her head on my shoulder, and I slip a candy necklace over her head.

BECKY

"Don't be nervous," Mary says.

"Easy for you to say."

A giant crowd has gathered at Cherry Republic to watch this year's competition but mostly to honor and celebrate Mary. A throng of people—rows ten deep run the entire length of the sandy pit—is packed around the arena.

"This sort of feels like the Olympics," I continue, "if the athletes spit cherry pits."

"Actually," Ollie says, "it sort of feels like the Kentucky Derby, and when I step up to the starting line, everyone will know I'm the long-shot horse wearing blinders they should bet against."

Mary and I laugh.

"Just remember what I taught you," Mary says. "Focused. Fearless."

Mary lasers in on a flag flapping in the breeze, sticks a finger in her mouth and then holds it in the air.

"The wind is out of the south, meaning it's going to blow against you," Mary says. "And it's a swirling wind, so remember that if you don't time it right and that wind catches your pit, it will knock it out-of-bounds and you'll be disqualified."

She continues. "Just be calm. Wait for the wind to die, even if you have to stand there a full minute. Don't let anyone distract you."

"Thanks, Grandma," Ollie says.

"Hey, Ollie!" a young man calls. "Are you taking it home today?"

Ollie laughs and goes to greet his friend. "I'll be right back."

When he leaves, Mary grabs my arm.

"My grandson doesn't have a shot in hell to win," she says, "but you do. Not only to win but to break my record. Every moment of our lives, every vision, every decision has led to this moment today. Are you ready?"

"No."

"Are you ready?" she repeats.

"I am!" I say.

"Go get 'em, girl!" Mary says, pulling me in for a hug. "You show them Becky Thatcher isn't just a fictional character in an old novel. She's alive and well and taking the world by storm today."

Mary saunters off, and I hear the announcer's voice boom.

"Welcome, ladies and gentlemen, to the hundred and twenty-fifth anniversary of the Cherry Pit Spitting Championship of Leelanau and Emmet County, Michigan!"

The crowd claps.

The announcer continues in his deep baritone.

"I'm Bobby Bass, grandson of northern Michigan's famed Baritone Bob, a fixture on the local radio for over sixty years, and the man who called the now-famous Cherry Championship of 1958. It's an honor to be here today."

He continues.

"One hundred and twenty-five years ago, the Cherry Pit Spitting Championship began, and the record was set that very year of 1898 by "Too Tall" Fred Jones, who spit a pit ninety-one feet, four-inches, a record that stood for sixty years until it was broken by our very own "Cherry Mary" Jackson in 1958, who, at the age of fifteen, spat a stone a *Guinness* record-breaking distance of ninety-three feet, six-and-a-half inches."

The crowd claps.

"Mary not only shattered that record, but she also shattered stereotypes," the announcer says, as the crowd grows quiet. "Not only does that record still stand to this day, but Mary does as well, as our postmistress and beloved owner of the Very Cherry General Store. Today, we celebrate the sixty-fifth anniversary of Mary's historic win and her legacy to the area and this contest, all of which is highlighted by the fact that a record number of girls and women have entered today's contest. Mary, will you come to the arena and greet your adoring fans?"

I watch Mary wend her way through the crowd, men and women greeting her, young girls holding out their arms for a hug. When she reaches the arena, she stops and steadies herself on a stump. She stares out at the crowd for a moment as if she is lost, but then moves toward the wooden sign with her face on it. She rubs her carved puffed cheeks and then whispers something to her youthful face as if telling it a secret before giving her youthful face a big kiss. Suddenly, she stands and waves, arm in the air triumphantly. The crowd explodes.

"Thank you, Cherry Mary!" Bobby Bass booms. "Now, let the competition begin! Pit-spitters, take your marks!"

There are over fifty entrants today, and Ollie and I are the final two scheduled due to the fact we were the last to enter the contest.

One by one, competitors—aged from eight to eighty—approach the Pit Spitting Arena and stand before the long lane of sand, Mary's face staring at them from the other end. Each competitor employs a slightly different method. Some arch their backs like ostriches, while others cock their heads all the way back as if they're on a spring. Some expand their cheeks like chipmunks hauling a winter's load of acorns, and others invert their cheeks as if trying to appear thinner. Some roll the pit around in their mouths seemingly forever or want to get the pit in the air as quickly as possible.

None, however, give much thought to the wind.

Time after time, as a pit flies into the air, the wind will catch it and then cruelly deflect it back to the ground or out-of-bounds like an angry volleyball player.

When it is finally time for Ollie and me to go, the longest distance any pit has flown is just over seventy feet.

"Becky Thatcher!" Bobby Bass says.

Some in the crowd titter at my name. I glance around, unnerved, but Mary catches my eye and mouths *Focus*.

I turn to Ollie who is waiting behind me.

"I can't do this," I whisper. "She's counting on me."

"I know it's hard," Ollie says in a hushed tone. "But we're doing it to honor her."

I smile and nod.

Suddenly, I hear Q yell, "Yes, Queen!"

The crowd laughs. I glance over at my friend, and my mom— standing alongside her with my father—blows me a kiss.

My heart drops.

"Becky Thatcher?" Bobby Bass calls again.

I walk to the line, and a little girl in a red gingham jumper holds a basket of fresh cherries before me. I act as if I'm searching for the perfect cherry, then choose one and pop it into my mouth and stand at the edge of the pit.

The crowd falls silent. I wait for the wind to subside, puff my cheeks and...

...the cherry pit dribbles out of my mouth and drops into the sand with a sad plop.

The crowd releases a collective *Oh, no!*

I don't want to look at Mary, but I catch her eye. Her face is sagging, she is shaking her head, eyes wide in disbelief. My mother and Q are looking at one another.

What happened? Mary mouths.

I avert my eyes, lower my head and walk past Ollie.

"Let's give her a hand for trying," Bobby Bass says. "Last up is Ollie Jackson, Cherry Mary's grandson! Let's see if the gift runs in the family!"

Ollie marches to the front of the pit, picks a cherry, readies himself and spits it, oh, maybe six feet.

I see Mary throw her arms into the air, utterly flabbergasted.

"Nice try, Ollie," Bobby Bass calls. The crowd begins to shift on their feet, awaiting the announcement of the winner. "Wait! It looks like we have one more entry. It's in a sealed envelope that was given to the committee just before the deadline."

The sound of an envelope being opened echoes across Cherry Republic.

"Mary Jackson?" Bobby Bass says, her name coming out as a question. "Is this right? *The* Cherry Mary? Attempting to break her own record?"

The crowd goes wild and begins to chant her name.

"Cher-ry Ma-ry! Cher-ry Ma-ry! Cher-ry Ma-ry!"

I barely have time to turn when Mary is standing beside me and Ollie, her face as red as the shirt featuring her face.

"What did you two do?" she says, trying to remain calm.

She searches our faces.

"It was both our idea," I say.

"We wanted you to honor you, Grandma."

"We wanted your record to stand forever," I say.

"You were supposed to break my record, Becky," Mary says. "It was destiny."

"No," I say. "*This* is destiny. Every moment has led to *this*."

Her face is etched in confusion.

"Sixty-five years ago, you stood here as a girl and did something no one believed you could do and few wanted you to accomplish," I say. "Today, you stand here as a woman who can show the world you are still as fierce and set an example for a new generation of women."

I point across the arena to Mary's face.

"You aren't the same girl you were then," I continue. "You're even more amazing. Show 'em, Cherry Mary. One last time."

Mary looks at Ollie.

"My grandma may have taught me to forge a signature just as well your grandma did," Ollie says.

Mary shakes her head. "But I haven't practiced. I'm not ready."

"Oh, please. You're always ready, Grandma," Ollie says.

Mary smiles and nods her head with conviction.

"Would you do me the honor, Becky, of picking my weapon of choice?"

I smile at the girl in the jumper, reach into the basket and pull a perfect cherry. I hand it to Mary.

The crowd cheers as Cherry Mary takes her mark.

MARY

Red.

The color of the world is red.

The summer-afternoon sun blazes in the sky, and it reflects off the Cherry Republic signage bathing everything in red. I scan the crowd, all dressed in shades of red. The faces of children are covered in all things cherry: pie, ice cream, juice. The cheeks and shoulders of adults are sunburned.

And in my hand is a perfect cherry.

Sixty-five years ago, I stood in a different place and time.

I never returned, until now.

It was a different place and time.

A man laughs drunkenly somewhere on the street, and my heart sinks. I have a flashback of my father coming for me. And then I see a hand waving. I squint in the sun. My heart leaps.

"Jonah!" I call.

The crowd turns.

"I love you, Mom," he calls. "Sorry I'm late."

Ollie and Becky catch my eye. It's as if they knew every second mattered today.

My son is here. My grandson is here.

They are not like their father, nor the men who preceded them.

They are simply as beautiful, flawed and fragile as their mother.

Family.

I, too, am a different person in a different time.

I am Mary.

But I am more.

Though the world has changed, the tools that allow us to change it, the things that make us so different but also unite us—mind, soul, heart—have not.

Those simple things will never change.

It simply requires us to utilize them in the best way we can in the time we're given.

I see Virgie. She is wigless, her short, spare silver hair shimmering along with her unadorned soul. She gives me a mighty thumbs-up. Francine blows me a kiss. Taffy shoots me a wink.

I stare at the cherry and pop it into my mouth.

No, this game, like life, really hasn't changed.

We must make our mark with the tools we are given.

I approach the line. I swirl the pit in my mouth. I shut my eyes.

I am a girl again eating sunflower seeds on the boat with my grandma.

I am standing in the middle of the Tunnel of Trees, spitting stones into the wind, while a storm brews over the lake.

I am standing here, the world believing I could not win.

I am running for my life, blind and scared, and then standing up against life's cruelty.

In the blink of an eye, I am here again.

What separates a girl from an old woman?

Nothing but a bad back and aching knees, if we can simply continue to believe that life can be anything we desire and if we just give our dreams a chance to soar on the wind.

I open my eyes, wait for the wind to diminish, puff my cheeks and blow.

The pit arcs into the sky. For a moment, I lose it in the sun, like an outfielder might a baseball, but then I catch it soaring higher into the red sky.

The crowd gasps, a collective inhale. In my periphery, their heads turn as one.

I see a judge take a step back from the end of the arena. And then another.

The judge marks it with his foot.

Silence.

The measurement.

A piece of paper is handed to a young man who sprints to the announcer.

"One hundred feet, one-and-a-half inches!" Bobby Bass yells. "Cherry Mary has shattered her own record!"

The crowd explodes.

I see Jonah, Ollie, Becky, Q, Francine, Taffy and Virgie racing toward me, arms raised, screaming in joy.

"Cher-ry Ma-ry! Cher-ry Ma-ry!" the crowd chants.

A girl can do anything a man can, I hear myself say as a girl. *You just gotta believe you can. That's the hard part.*

As I fall, I realize the world has now turned pink.

I hit the ground hard, but my eyes remain open, staring heavenward.

The sun is hitting the clouds, and the sky looks as if it's filled with cherry blossoms.

"Someone call 9-1-1!" Jonah yells.

My friends and family are standing over me.

My grandma once told me God had to be a woman in order to have created a world so beautiful, and I can't help but believe her because this is a wondrous way to welcome me to heaven: a spring orchard of pink surrounded by those I love.

I can feel myself being lifted onto a stretcher, but I am flying now.

I am soaring over the arena, flying down the Tunnel of Trees, waving to the general store and heading toward the lake.

I land on the water, floating above it. I am not walking toward the land, however: I am moving toward the horizon.

I look to my right and left.

I am surrounded by the three women I've seen my whole life.

I am shocked.

They are not my mom or my grandma or my forever friends.

They are all me.

I finally realize that the women I've seen my entire life on the horizon were all versions of myself: child, young mother, grandmother. Now, the fourth version—me, today—has joined them for the final walk.

We link hands.

In my head, I hear the voice of the old woman at Devil's Elbow from so long ago.

Just know there will be another woman who will join you out of the blue. It may take a lifetime. Be patient. Choose to believe no matter how long it takes. You will know. It will all make sense one day, these four women. Decide whether what you believe in your heart is true or not. Decide whether what you see on the horizon is real or simply a mirage.

I finally believed.

In myself, in my family, in my friends, in my heart that what I had—from the Cherry Championship to the general store— was not earned by cheating or deceit, but simply by love, hard work, kindness and believing in myself.

And when that happens, it's okay that your journey here— like that of a cherry pit—has also reached its glorious, long, beautiful conclusion.

When that happens, you become a legend.

I hear another voice.

Becky's.

"Don't leave me," she whispers, voice hoarse, tears hitting my face. "I still need you!"

Suddenly, I open my eyes and see myself reflected in hers.

"The fourth woman," I whisper.

"Tell me," she says.

"She's you. It's us."

I close my eyes, and I am walking on the lake again, with a purpose, away from shore, directly toward the pink horizon.

This time, I am all alone, but the world is filled with bright light.

A voice in the light says, "Your last breath was a doozy, Mary."

I turn.

The women are again walking toward the shore, their hands extended to Becky.

EPILOGUE

"So we grew together, like to a double cherry, seeming parted; but yet a union in partition, two lovely berries moulded on one stem."

—William Shakespeare

BECKY

Summer 2024

We are seated in Adirondacks on the beach.

"Mary was right," my father says. "Cherries are the secret to a long life."

He takes a sip of a cherry margarita.

"I think she always meant to say that tequila was," Francine says.

Virgie laughs. "So true, Francine."

Everyone lifts their glasses in silent tribute.

All of my—and Mary's—family and friends have gathered on the beach.

The lake is changing from its sparkling swimsuit into a navy cover-up. The Golden Hour is fading into the Blue Hour.

Each hour has taken on a new importance and beauty.

We are gathered in a semicircle of Adirondacks, our feet in the sand, our eyes on one another, celebrating one more sunset together. Everyone is wearing T-shirts with Mary's face emblazoned on them, her record-setting spit in bold letters. *Cherry Mary Forever!*

Mary's death has changed us all in so many ways, inspiring some to slow down, while speeding up changes in the lives of others.

Jonah and his wife are visiting more.

He is working with Ollie to preserve and expand the Very Cherry General Store. With Mary's cult status growing every month, Ollie and I set up an online shop for the store that is hard to keep stocked. The world, it seems, wants a piece of Mary's heart along with T-shirts, mugs and all things cherry with her face on them.

Q and Taffy have pledged not only to continue a long-distance relationship but also to begin the construction and creation of the Tunnel of Trees Theater—a small performing-arts center on the lot behind the store, in conjunction with Jeff Daniels—to nurture the arts and celebrate the history of the area. They want it to be not only their next sunset together but also their legacy.

My parents have purchased Francine's cottage —leaving it as is and with a great assist from Virgie, who took no commission on the deal—and are visiting every few weeks. They invite Francine to stay whenever they're in town.

"Sorry we're late!"

We all look up. Geoffrey and Moira appear in caftans.

"We brought another pitcher of margaritas," she says. "Don't know if it will live up to hers, but we tried."

"Have a seat," I say.

They came to the funeral, made amends and have scaled back on future plans for their cottage. Forgiveness is always a start.

They make the rounds, refilling glasses. When they come to me, Moira holds out a separate pitcher.

"Just fresh cherry juice," she says. "For you."

I hold out my glass.

"Oh," I say, rubbing my stomach.

"Kicking again?" Ollie asks.

I nod.

"I can't believe I'm finally going to be a grandmother!" my mom says.

Ollie and I married in the spring, on the orchard behind the store, just as the cherry trees were blossoming. We now live in Mary's cottage next door to my parents.

I am having a girl.

The legacy continues, Mary. A miracle for me at forty-one.

The world changes, every second, every day, but we must remember moments like this. Life really all boils down to the simplest of things: family, friends, a beautiful sunset, a good drink…each other.

But, mostly, believing in yourself and what's on the horizon.

The sun settles lower in the sky. The lake turns deep blue. In the distance, a song plays on the beach. The breeze carries a familiar lyric.

Everybody dies famous in a small town.

My eyes catch Ollie's, and he shakes his head and then emits a big knowing, happy laugh.

The music carries out and over the water.

I see the women on the lake.

When I look now, I see the family I always dreamed and wanted: my grandma, my mother, Mary, my daughter.

I finally understand that there is no age limit on growth and self-discovery. We see our lives and ourselves in different chapters, different versions, through different perspectives as we age. We are a prism of ourselves. But we cannot clearly see our future until we clearly see ourselves. I am glad I became a wanderer— a *flâneur*—because it led me to the place I should be. You cannot wonder if you do not wander.

I smile at the women.

What is it you see when you look at the horizon? What is it you dream when it is just you and the water?

You don't have to visualize a Fata Morgana because there will always be a golden arrow glowing on the water at sunset pointing directly at you and only you. You can race down the shore to run away from it, but the golden arrow follows. You may not return to the water's edge for decades, but it is still there.

It is your future.

Calling.

Suddenly, the four women merge into one. She is coming directly toward me.

I glance at my family and friends, laughing, looking onto the water. They do not see what I see.

The woman is close now, very close, hand extended.

And I can see her face clearly.

It is me *and* Mary.

United.

The woman is no longer a mirage. She is the final version of myself. The one I am and can still become, thanks to the woman who taught me how to do that.

"Cheers!" I say to my friends and family.

"Cheers, Mary!" I whisper to myself.

I lift my glass to the horizon.

★ ★ ★ ★ ★

ACKNOWLEDGMENTS

First, thank you, my dear readers! You are truly the cherry on top of my literary sundae, and I can never thank you enough for loving and supporting my work and allowing me to do what I love most in this world. You fill my life with sweetness.

HUGE, heartfelt thanks to the following who make what I do not only possible but joyous:

My agent, Wendy Sherman;

My editor, Susan Swinwood;

My publicity team: Kathleen Carter, Heather Connor and Leah Morse;

My marketing manager, Diane Lavoie;

The indie booksellers across the U.S., the heart and soul of my—and our—world;

To Gary;

To Michigan;

To summer;

To YOU!

A LETTER FROM THE AUTHOR

My grandmothers were my best friends growing up. I never considered them to be old: I thought of them as I did my friends from school. We played board games, we read books, we baked together, we floated in inner tubes down the creek holding hands, we danced to *Lawrence Welk*, we laughed watching *Happy Days*.

To this day, I've always had friends who were much older than me. In fact, some of my dearest friends today are in their eighties. I also have friends much younger than me and am a godparent to teenagers. Like all good friends, we not only support each other through the good and bad, but we also push each other to dream big and be our best selves. We lend each other individual strengths to make the other whole and stronger. We fill in those missing gaps in our souls. We all keep each other young.

This novel celebrates intergenerational friendships and why it's important in life—and in society—to look at people not simply at face value but within their hearts. It celebrates the fact that there is no age limit on friendship, new adventures, taking risks and becoming the person you always dreamed of being. It's also a celebration of women, especially those who have had to overcome incredible obstacles and hardships—and often bad men—in their lives to protect their families and come into their own. Much like my grandmas, the women in this book use ingenuity, hard work, faith, a love of the land and a love for one another to soldier on with grace, determination, resilience and open hearts.

As all my novels do, *Famous in a Small Town* celebrates the beauty and wonder of Michigan and its bounty. It takes place in the storybook (and very real) town of Good Hart, Michigan, along the storybook (and very real) Tunnel of Trees. This is a breathtaking stretch of road in which the trees grow so dense they canopy the road for miles, choking out the sunlight and offering stunning views at every twist and turn.

I also used the very real, very quaint and very historic Good Hart General Store as the foundation to create the Very Cherry General Store. There is no place I love to visit more in the summer or fall than this historic general store (look it up!). Much of the store's history is real, but I made up the rest, from Cherry Mary to her mother and grandmother and their entire lives. I hope it honors this great gift of a store. Cherry Republic is also very real, and it is the Michigan motherland for all things cherries (again, look it up and order away!). Michigan readers and Cherry Republic lovers will notice that I did take liberty with some of their locations, moving them around a bit to make sure my setting and the distances traveled were more realistic. For the sake of fiction, forgive me. There is nothing I love more than filling my belly with all things cherry and chocolate from Cherry Republic.

If you are from Michigan, you begin to understand—in a very short time and especially in summer—that cherries are life. From a stop at a roadside stand to the very real Cherry Festival in Traverse City every year, this fruit is the cherry on top of Michigan. I love all things cherry, and it was a joy to bring them to life—history, recipes, lore—in this novel.

This book started long ago on a summer-vacation day in

northern Michigan. I went to Cherry Republic, gorged on all things chocolate and cherry, and then—after a glass of wine—tried to spit a cherry pit as far as I could. I laughed so hard I cried. One of my friends said later that afternoon, as the sun was setting over the bay, "Now, *this* was a quintessential Michigan summer day."

I began to take notes that very moment, and those early tendrils led to this novel.

That's also a big part—and heart—of this book: taking time to wander through a summer day, getting lost, acting like a kid, having fun, laughing with friends, having one too many scoops of ice cream, chocolate-covered cherries or glasses of wine. When you wander, you begin to *wonder*, in the true sense of that word, at all that surrounds you that we take for granted in our too-busy lives. Wander. Wonder. So close.

So wander and wonder away...and I will see you in November with my next Christmas novel, *The Wishing Bridge*, a holiday gift if there ever was one, set in the magical Michigan Bavarian Christmas town of Frankenmuth.

As you read *Famous in a Small Town*, I just want to leave you with this: be the legend you were meant to be.

XOXO,
Viola

ON A PERSONAL NOTE...

It's an honor to learn that I had some influence in the making of this celebrated book. I love how well Viola captured Michigan's cherry industry, our small town of Glen Arbor and our place in the greater world. For a simpleton like me, who feels selling more than one fruit would be too complicated, I can't imagine how a whole novel could be written about such a humble life and peaceful place.

I started Cherry Republic as a way to make a living in a region with more beaches and wilderness hiking than jobs. This business became the perfect venue to express my love for the lakes, woods, and orchards of the north. And it especially became that venue for the love I have for the people up here. With one exceptionally special person above all, of course; my mother.

Very much like the heroine in this book, my Mom was a champion. Diving and swimming were her specialties and although I rarely saw her in the water doing her magic, she exuded the success and confidence of a champion in every domestic move she made. And there wasn't a day that she didn't share that belief and confidence and trust she had in herself with others. I was fortunate to be in close proximity.

I lost this great lady in January 2023, but I feel her legacy lives in these pages. Because these pages are about family and the values and shared experience that ties us all together. This book is about the value of the super matriarch– that outstanding woman who is so strong that they not only knit a family together, but a community as well.

I can testify that Viola did her homework as these pages capture the essence of our great land so poetically. But it is the writing on family that makes this story sing. These intertwined northerners, living deeply in each family member's lives captures my family and so many families I grew up with.

Bob Sutherland
President of Cherry Republic

CHERRY CHIP CAKE WITH CHERRY VANILLA BUTTERCREAM

This is my favorite cake in the world! My Grandma Shipman made it for me on every special occasion – birthdays, straight-A report cards, holidays – and pretty much any time I would ask for it. She would always cut two slices of cake, pour a cup of coffee for herself, a glass of milk for me, and we'd sit at the Formica table in her kitchen, and she'd ask me about all my hopes and dreams. The cake is light and moist, the icing luscious and pink as a spring tulip, and it is the perfect dessert to make when it's cherry season (or when you're reading *Famous in a Small Town*). I hope you love it as much as I do!

INGREDIENTS

Cake

1 10-ounce jar (about 30 cherries) maraschino cherries
10-15 large cherries, pitted and finely chopped
½ cup unsalted butter, at room temperature
1 ½ cups granulated sugar
4 large egg whites

1 teaspoon vanilla extract
¼ teaspoon almond extract
2 cups cake flour
2 teaspoons baking powder
½ teaspoon baking soda
½ teaspoon salt
1 ⅓ cup buttermilk
4 tablespoons maraschino cherry juice or pitted cherry juice

Cherry Vanilla Buttercream Frosting
¼ teaspoon vanilla
¾ cup salted butter, room temperature
3 ½ cups powdered sugar
¼ cup heavy whipping cream
4 tablespoons maraschino cherry juice (for color)

Directions

Cake:
Preheat oven to 350 degrees F. Butter and flour two 8-inch round cake pans and line the bottoms with parchment paper.

Drain the maraschino cherries, reserving the juice. In a food processor or with a sharp knife, finely chop the cherries. Set aside.

In the bowl of a stand mixer fitted with a paddle attachment, or in a large bowl with a hand-held mixer, beat the butter and sugar at high speed until light and fluffy (about 5 minutes).

Scrape down the bowl and add the egg whites one at a time, mixing after each. Add the vanilla and almond extracts and mix until combined.

In a separate bowl, combine the cake flour, baking powder, baking soda and salt. In a smaller bowl, combine the buttermilk and maraschino cherry juice.

Add the flour mixture to the mixer in 3 stages, alternating with the buttermilk mixture. Mix after each addition and scrape down the bowl as necessary. Stir in the chopped cherries.

Divide the batter evenly between the cake pans and bake until a toothpick inserted into the center comes out with a few moist crumbs, about 30-35 minutes. Let cool in the pans for 10 minutes, then transfer to a wire rack to cool completely.

Frosting:
In the bowl of a stand mixer, beat the butter for about one minute at medium speed. Add the powdered sugar, and mix at low speed until the sugar is completely incorporated. Add the whipping cream and cherry juice. Increase the speed to medium and beat for 1-2 minutes, or until light and fluffy.

To assemble the cake:
Place one cake layer on a plate or cake stand. Cover with 1/2 cup of the buttercream frosting. Place the second cake layer on top of the first and cover top and sides with remaining buttercream. If desired, ring the top of cake with pitted, fresh cherries or maraschino cherries (or both).

Let sit at room temperature for a few minutes before serving.

QUESTIONS FOR DISCUSSION

1. This novel explores the hardships women often have to overcome in a male-dominated world not only to survive but to succeed. What challenges have you and the women in your life had to endure? How did that change you? How are you still trying to overcome obstacles in life/society?

2. Another major theme in the novel centers on believing in yourself. How have you doubted yourself in your life? Why? Have you ever let fear stop you from pursuing your dreams? What dreams do you wish to fulfill? What dreams have come true?

3. Living along Lake Michigan, I have often looked to the horizon—and like the characters in the novel—seen a Fata Morgana, or a mirage, that looked incredibly real. I've also experienced what my mother and grandmother once called *God winks*. Have you ever experienced such a vision? Did it frighten or embolden you?

4. This novel centers on an intergenerational friendship between two women at forty and eighty. It was inspired by my real-life friendships with my grandmothers. Do you have a

best friend who is significantly younger or older than you (be it a BFF or relative)? Talk about the beauty, and challenges, of that relationship.

5. I have always loved cherries (which serve as the foundation of the story and a beautiful analogy to life in this novel). My grandma used to make me a Cherry Chip Cake when I was a kid. When I moved to Michigan, my love of cherries was renewed. What is your favorite fruit, and what are some of your favorite recipes that incorporate them?

6. Setting is always as big a character in my novels as much as my characters themselves. When I first visited the Tunnel of Trees in northern Michigan, I was stunned and transported by its natural beauty. What place have you visited in your life whose stunning setting has stayed with you forever?

7. I grew up going to general stores, where I could buy penny candy from the counter, an ice-cold soda right out of the icebox or a Popsicle straight out of the freezer. Did you have a general store where you grew up? What memories do you have? What do you miss most about it?

8. This novel is an ode to my grandmothers, strong, hard-working women who were often knocked down by life but soldiered on—like Mary—with faith, grace and resilience. Are you, or were you, close to your grandmothers? What memories do you have of your grandmas?

9. Becky becomes a *flâneur* in life, something we are socialized not to do. Have you ever simply taken a day to wander your hometown? What did you discover? In addition, have you ever stopped walking the path before you and created a new one to follow? What was that like? How did that change you? (I quit my full-time job to write and wandered

to the shore of Lake Michigan on a whim, a journey that has changed my life.)

10. This novel is filled with lore and legend, from Devil's Elbow to the history of cherries. Do you believe in such legends? What local lore surrounds you?

11. Have you ever, on a whim, done something that scared you but, ultimately, changed you, whether it was taking an art class or running a 5K? Discuss that experience and how it changed you.

12. This novel celebrates all things summer. What are some of your favorite summer traditions? Vacations? Memories? Sounds, foods and smells?